Avenging Angela and
Other Uncanny Encounters

Avenging Angela

and Other Uncanny Encounters

Jonathan Thomas

Hippocampus Press

New York

Published by Hippocampus Press
P.O. Box 641, New York, NY 10156.
www.hippocampuspress.com

Cover art by George Cotronis.
Cover design by Daniel V. Sauer, dansauerdesign.com.
Hippocampus Press logo designed by Anastasia Damianakos.

First Edition
1 3 5 7 9 8 6 4 2

ISBN 978-1-61498-341-5 (paperback)
ISBN 978-1-61498-351-4 (ebook)

Contents

The Shaman's Smile

In the cozy Neolithic village known millennia later as Skara Brae, on the largest of the Orkney islands off Scotland, every house but one locked from the inside. The populace of fourscore or so was clannishly proud of its flagstone roundhouses, packed in earth and midden up to the rooflines, snug in winter, mostly weatherproof. Making the tight cluster of houses tighter was a network of corridors from door to door, under a ceiling of slabs that furthered the impression of residing in burrows. Privacy was a rare commodity people safeguarded by drilling holes into their slate doorjambs to receive the ends of a timber pole, to bar inward-swinging stone doors from the inside.

As for the house that locked from without, nobody lived there, but it was inhabited. It was the village's oldest house, had been repaired rather than demolished and rebuilt from scratch in great-great-grandsires' days. Nobody dared loiter by it, and some said it was responsible for the village-wide resort to securer quarters.

That was moot; everything grandmothers taught of happenings before their own births belonged in the same fog of myth and faith as the creation of the world. Imponderables such as creation, though, were of no import to Rel, the new shaman who'd withstood a grueling apprenticeship till the decease of the old. The lore that mattered was of practical value in fulfilling ambition, that secret vice in a place of smothering communal virtues. Ambition was expressible only from the unique vantage of the house that locked from the outside.

The lore about that house was unique because ongoing experience bore it out. Spinster sisters Ils and Els were buried in a flagstone-lined cavity under the flagstone floor, to the right of the

7

hearth with their feet to its symbolic warmth. Right up until their dotage at an uncommonly ripe age, they'd been beloved for their soft-spoken counsel amid repeated crises of black ergot in the flour, interfamily feuds, hurricane deluge. But finally they both succumbed, scant days apart, to the blood-puking sickness.

At first their residue had, like everyone's then and into Rel's day, lain in a cairn under a blanket of turf, in the cemetery meadow between village and bay. Nobody could have predicted, or believed, that encroaching ocean would someday nibble away the entire meadow. Nor could they have predicted how death would corrupt the venerable maidens, in soul more hideously than body, as if self-less lives had degraded into wolfish hereafters. In the old-fangled language of grandmothers, the sisters "did not rest quiet, but re-born from earth's womb, learned to walk again by moonlight."

Thus did the recitation fare from matriarch's mouth to daughter's ear in every house: patently an "old wives' tale" someone hardheaded as Rel would have ridiculed, had he not from earliest childhood been subjected to its reality; and as an adult, self-preservation had depended on taming the revenant maidens by nimbly dispensing magical accessories. To describe them as "not resting quiet" partook of drollest understatement, for when they initially broke out of the cairn, one full moon after their inter-ment, they bludgeoned sheep and cattle to death with clubs of driftwood, as if exacting spiteful fees for the good they'd freely done in life.

The stricken folk mistook the scatter of soil and cobbles around a rent in the cairn for a wandering maniac's further wick-edness, and effected repairs. The next full moon disabused them, though, for by then the undead sisters had burrowed back out to steal among the houses, breaching unbarred doors to mangle and dismember three households before their fetid muscles weakened with fatigue. One child escaped by cowering in a latrine drain, and blamed the "dead ladies" for the mayhem; people were quick to believe her, as the cairn had been defaced once more.

Storytellers from other islands had forewarned villagers that special people might spurn the grave, albeit with changes of heart, as well as flesh, for the worse. Unfinished dealings, unresolved grievances, might have driven them; had the sisters never truly been the paragons of grace they'd seemed? Not important! They'd proven their aptitude for tunneling through thickset cobbles, and cremation, said the other-islanders, would spread plague with the smoke and ashes.

Hence the sisters were exhumed by daylight, when death re-imposed its petrifying grip on them, and reburied under the floor of their old house. Nobody had cared to claim premises so recently tainted by misfortune, revenants or no revenants, whereas the sisters might abide more content in homier environs. Yes or no, they couldn't get past a slab barred from the outside, and whenever they tried, the noise of slamming and mauling at rock would alert the folk, wouldn't it?

The grandmothers never did explain how Ils and Els had come to be released at sunset of each winter solstice, to seize the pitiable sacrifice of a hobbled black calf on the pavement out their door. On that pivotal occasion, the figures otherwise of dread and disgust were revered as incarnations of holy ancestors represented elsewhere by skulls and shinbones retrieved from barrows and paraded around.

Nobody ever balked, at least aloud, at the contradiction between the monsters of grandmothers' saga and the honorees of annual worship. Were those teachings about the past plain falsehoods, taken at face value out of lazy habit? Rel didn't care. Ils and Els were solely of importance as tools by which to monumentalize himself.

After rehearsing their exploitation for years, he exulted in his looming glory, tempered strictly by the possibility age would smite him before he'd realized his designs. Baffling, frankly, that neither the old shaman nor any before him had fathomed how a little extra herbal smoke, acrid oil, and glinting powder would render the sisters as tractable anytime as at midwinter. And unleashing them in summer's dog days would maximize the element of surprise. With exquisite discretion he'd slunk into their house, testing midnight necromancy without anyone the wiser, after mastering incantations to becalm the sisters briefly before unbarring their door.

On his deathbed the old shaman had wheezed that nobody should be as eager as Rel for the spiritual obligations in store. The self-righteous prig probably hadn't suspected a fraction of Rel's scheming (and would have died many birthdays ago, had he not been too canny for Rel to hex him with impunity), and might well be ranting helpless at him from the afterworld. But feeble ghostly dander couldn't deter Rel from the unassailable position where he'd tender the folk a choice: obey him or cope with the sisters run amok. What's more, kill him and they'd have no one to exorcise Ils and Els.

In other portions of the island, and on other islands, priesthoods had decreed arrangements of slabs twice a man's height into circles wide enough to contain the village; or the best-respected families consigned forebears to grand cairns under grand mounds, to dwarf anything in the cemetery meadow, and containing loftier chambers than the living ever enjoyed. Rel coveted a ring of towering boulders plus a towering barrow, in tribute to his brilliance at sorcery and extortion, testaments to his name that would endure for generations innumerable in this world and the next.

To die and let his soul bask in the awe accruing to him from both earth and heaven was preferable to torturous, unnaturally prolonged senescence or a resurrection like the sisters' in rotting, murderous carcasses. They hardly attracted admiration and wonderment, yearly adulation aside. Such would be Rel's eminence beyond the grave that he'd laugh off posthumous confrontations with prissy ex-mentor, and if the gods didn't like what he was doing, they could always stop him. Hah! They'd done nothing against the sisters, and what was there to like about them?

To lead effectively, he foremost had to prove his ruthlessness, flout deep-rooted bonds of allegiance, pestle and remold village existence to suit him. His aunt and father's brother, conveniently, dwelt nearest the sisters and were too infirm to pry slabs from cliffsides, dig boundary ditches with antler picks, dump baskets of dirt to raise embankments. In a word, they were disposable, save in one capacity, ideally served by the thanksgiving procession he newly led.

The people grew no barley, instead bartering for it around the island with their workshop's flint implements and leatherware. Still, tradition dictated they repay gods of fecundity with a door-to-door collection of charred, hammerstone-sized cakes to crumble upon an altar-stone in the meadow. The roving celebrants in Rel's wake were already tipsy from sharing the pail of barley ferment. Rel had just received the cakes from his decrepit relations, who began shuffling along and were as mystified as the rest when Rel's chanting became harsh gibberish, and he impetuously unbarred and threw open the revenants' door.

Out burst Ils and Els like eels from a sunken currach, and Rel's jabbing finger singled out their prey. He commanded the undead with olden phrases not unlike those in the grandmothers' hand-me-down sagas. Dropping the urn of cakes indifferently as if it contained manure, he buttressed his will over the sisters by sprinkling oil from a sponge and pouches of red and yellow pigment onto death-eaten, blackened flesh as they lurched by. The sisters, though mute as eels, mimicked snarls.

Amid the overall stupefaction, with fists like knobby maces, the sisters felled Rel's palsied kinfolk and pounced like mainland bears. The victims were disemboweled well before the butchery lost momentum. Memories since childhood portrayed aunt and uncle as dullards, contemptibly passive, agape at any exercise of imagination, shrugging at his keenness to become shaman. Good riddance to them! They'd never looked more interesting than now, bright blood, bile, half-digested breakfast mottling a mishmash of body parts and organs. But enough: his shouts suspended the carnage, compelled the sisters up and backward, to rest their skinless spines against their doorjambs while Rel harangued the dumbfounded people.

"A new dawn is breaking for us. To you is meted out the happy destiny of joining me in rearing works at which our progeny will marvel, and your shaman's name will glorify you, while any dwell on this island. The gods confide to me we must reshape our ways of pleasing them. First off, we will char no more barley cakes or perform other outworn observances. Instead, in renewing our piety we will shame and astound those who reign over the circles of stones and burial hillocks eastward." He indulged a dramatic flourish yonder, but eyes in ashen faces continued downcast.

"And according to holy dispensation, blood ties no longer bind me, nor lifelong bonds of familiarity. This I and my helpmeets have shown you. How kindly should the gods regard you unless you swear fealty to your shaman and devote yourselves to our renown?" Despair weighted the shoulders of the more farsighted at this thinly veiled ultimatum. The rest quaked in imbecile shock at the squashed eyeballs, gnawed forearms, shredded bellies at their feet, or at the pigment-bespattered killers.

Grandiose though Rel's dreams were, in one respect they entailed a simplicity that prior monuments didn't. While circular stoneworks and tumulus entrances were variously oriented toward solstice sunups, sundowns, and moonrises, the sole orientation of concern to Rel was toward himself. But beyond that, the complications, the sheer scope involved, were daunting.

Selecting the construction site was no brain-teaser, for the plain on the village's landward side marked home territory nearest the priestly district, and the path therefrom into the village would pass Rel's taunting, awesome triumphs. Nor could he ever want for building materials, with the ocean every winter exposing and detaching more layers of slabs in coves indenting the cemetery meadow.

Yet who'd have reckoned how epic the undertaking would be, how much manpower was required just to shift one sizable rock from the beach onto the turf and drag it countless paces on greasy timber rollers? Most vexing was the need for people in two places at once: imperative for every able body to toil morning to night, but fishing, flint-knapping, fuel-gathering, a hundred other activities had to go on lest everyone starve or freeze. He'd dedicated all his ingenuity to dominating the sisters, and then his people, and none to how he'd proceed afterward.

Perhaps, he deliberated, instead of demanding two separate monuments, he should erect the barrow at the center of his ring of stones. That would spare him years of clearing a second acreage and exploit more frugally the muscles of women and children, pecking away with antlers at the stupendous ditch to enclose his sacred precincts. Alternately, up and down the coast were farmsteads of those who valued independence, elbow room, over village togetherness. Let their imprudence be corrected! Surely sweating in his service and not their own was the nobler cause.

Rel led four raiding parties in as many weeks, and each success bolstered his insolence. His spear-wielding apprentices were mostly decorative; watchdogs outside flimsy gates fled on scenting the revenants' stench, and bidding the sisters slaughter every household's frailest member earned him the prompt submission of more durable survivors.

But what long-term benefit came of another fifty hands? Their efforts were not perceptibly hastening the completion of his prodigal works. In the meantime he had twenty-five more mouths to feed, and when the cold ruled out sleeping rough, twenty-five more people to squeeze into cramped housing. And the dilemma persisted of producing food and barter objects, necessary evils, when he hadn't the menials as it was to finish the work in his lifetime.

He'd already captured every living soul within feasible range of night raids. Living souls, yes, but then inspiration jolted him. He'd summoned Ils and Els from their hearthside graves to obey him. Why not a swarm of the deceased from the cemetery meadow, whoever hadn't moldered unto falling apart? Lack of food and shelter wouldn't trouble them, nor disease and exhaustion. His mortal servitors he'd still push to the utmost, certainly, except for the injured and the weakest who could deal with flint, leather, provender. And whoso died of overwork, all the better. Rel would resurrect them as more resilient thralls.

His apprentices wore airs of greater sagacity than Rel deemed justifiable, and never evinced apt gratitude for exemption from hard labor. They weren't clever enough to grasp he was dividing his lessons between them because teaching either one too much was practically begging for usurpation. Yet they were the cleverest villagers, discounting him, and better to have them on his side.

They did relish lording it over everyone just as Rel did, when each wasn't vying to establish his own occult superiority. Subtle Rel encouraged backbiting rivalry to keep them more firmly under his thumb, prevent their ganging up on him. He was reasonably positive each kept to his jealous self the results of trials-and-errors toward revivifying the salvageable dead. And obviously he didn't tempt fate by directing necromancy toward his defunct mentor.

Rel posted Ils, Els, and one apprentice at the village's palisade entrance to ensure everybody's confinement after dark. The other apprentice handled the unpleasantness of breaching a cairn and extracting its contents, and then Rel impatiently refined the amounts of vapors, powders, oils, syllables to make a corpse twitch, flail, follow movement with purulent eyes. When no doubt remained he could restore a cadaver's shadow vitality from one sunrise to the next, he went to the meadow alone: he wasn't about to let either self-aggrandizing helper peek at the optimal procedure.

Hence from day to day the haggard folk were ever more aghast to behold one, then several, then a throng of the festering undead gouging at outer ditch or towing rock shoulder-to-shoulder with them. And worse, these were sometimes grandsires, wives, friends, and kinsmen lately committed to barrows. Rel was unflinching about unburying aunts, cousins, nephews; he was playing for immortal fame, stakes too lofty to quibble over mere familial ties.

If two biddable revenants had softened village resistance, the recruitment of a few dozen more blunted the thorniest dispositions into despair. Shuffling, listless, lackwit as the undead were in carrying out Rel's commands, no one dared challenge their effectiveness as executioners. By way of meager consolation, the oily, powder-dappled thralls never rested, toiling through the darkness, such that mortal drudges woke each morning to a little less hardship overall than when they went to bed.

Rel bristled, in fact, at the less impressive attainments of the living compared with the dead. He was, indeed, well pleased to overwork men to death. A day after their demise, minus the interim of funeral rites or interment, they were back amid friends and family, sowing profounder distress and revulsion than did worm-eaten forebears.

Some among the more decayed did come apart while toiling: arms detached, pelvises split, lolling heads like frostbitten apples snapped off brittle stems of necks. Vexing, absolutely, and what could Rel do beyond finessing spells to strengthen withered cartilage and sinews? These enhancements he tested by fish-oil lamplight, lining revenants up as he would anyway for nightly treatment, without which they'd revert to inert meat before morning.

He always commenced with that paradoxical injunction, "I call upon you to exist!" The impossibility of calling upon anything that didn't exist was an irrelevant nicety; the wording was efficacious. That was paramount, and as for Ils and Els, the essential double-knot tying his designs together, he now marched them into their home after nightfall to save them wear and tear till dawn. Why waste them as sentries when a flock of the undead and a ruthless apprentice were on hand to intimidate any villagers contemplating nocturnal flight?

This ploy relegated his foremen to separate day and night shifts, with scant opportunity to conspire. Not that either didn't have it in him to court disaster on his own. They and Rel had separately overheard, and shrugged off, grumblings on the eve of the first abolished festival, at the full moon after the swallows had vacated their mud-and-spittle nests. Feasting had always accompanied the pre-winter slaughter of surplus livestock. Under the shorthanded new regime, though, animals went permanently astray, fewer were butchered, ham-handed artisanship in the workshop barely brought subsistence quantities of barley, onions, hazelnuts. Pointless, really, to ban feasting, with no bounty to feast on.

Yet one man, out of defiant piety or cracking under stress, must have filched and nigh drained a precious bucket of barley ferment. In the thick of night he reeled out of the gate no longer guarded by the sisters and staggered around the cemetery meadow. He bellowed about escape, uprising, the blasphemy of forsaking festivals: inflammatory indeed, except that stiff winds cast his words harmlessly out to sea.

Still, the apprentice, haranguing the undead to inch a massive slab forward, smirked at prospects of nipping a drunken bad influence in the bud. And why consult with Rel now or inform him later? Why water down the fun? He was doing nothing the shaman wouldn't. Selecting the revenant on whom his glance randomly alit, the apprentice waved him away from tugging on fibrous rope and set him on the transgressor.

The carousing fool rejoiced and welcomed his brother, but just before that brother leapt, memory of his death must have resurfaced, or else telltale stink and ulcerous corruption struck the roisterer speechless. To make of him a more unforgettable example, the apprentice had his windpipe uprooted, backbone pulverized, and legs sundered at the knees on the altar-stone that should tonight have received a calf's ribs, a horn's worth of libation.

Some villagers did catch snatches of the atrocity and huddled more miserably about their hearths. Behind stoutly barred door, Rel snored through the incident, and come morning his path to the earthworks avoided the altar-stone; nor would the carnage, as his lackey surmised, have stirred pity or especial curiosity. A waste of breath, they'd have agreed, to bother justifying their treatment of inferiors. Unwavering control trumped all. Why split hairs between casualties of overwork and the culling of troublemakers? Both were sacrifices to visionary grandeur. If Rel detected a rottener breeze than usual off the meadow, he'd never have guessed it signified a line had been crossed.

The cemetery had been in deplorable shape since the previous full moon at least. The potholes and miniature cave-ins marring tumuli, plus the rubble and dustheaps like a floodtide of loveless disorder, left it hard to keep straight who was and wasn't buried anymore. Some corpses were in the grossest sense unburied, mingling piecemeal with the debris wherever the rigors of exhumation and portage had disintegrated them. Rel had no further truck with the meadow upon its depletion of tractable bodies, was equally unmindful of its spoliation and the altar-stone's.

Instead, he clambered atop one of the three recumbent slabs for the slightly longer view, disdaining arthritic pangs in his knee, and was of two minds as he inspected the site. How slowly everything was coming along, he fumed; no stones were upright yet, and only yesterday was the soil entirely stripped from within his barrow's circular kerb. On the other hand, stakes of gorse defined the future outline of the surrounding ditch and guided delvers to inflict an everlasting scar in the earth, currently a crescent almost deep enough to swallow them, though it had to go much deeper, the embankment of discarded dirt and rocks much higher.

A low ridge to his left overlooked a wider vista, but he'd stationed Ils and Els up there and declined to tarry too near their funk. One faced the worksite eastward, and the other the quarrying westward: a shout, a wave at either of them would dispatch pacification toward any unrest. They also functioned as a vivid reminder to the people of his power, and fanned his heart's dim sparks of gratitude, for they were the virtual mothers of his immortality.

On that score, he sheltered their insensate husks under a canopy of whalebone poles and white cowhides. More pragmatically, excessive sun, even on these shorter days, might mummify the sisters into leathery inflexibility or liquefy their innards within the cooking-pouches of their abscessed skins. Did they, beneath their spellbound stillness and underlying rabid frenzy, have the vestigial faculties to harbor appreciation? They fixed slimy eyeballs on

Rel more avidly than anywhere else, but parsing the wherefore of that would get him nowhere, would only squander his patience. Moreover, he'd never managed to tell them apart, between the anonymity of rot and the sparkly powders and slick unguents masking them.

When the sliver of sun above ocean horizon described the same arc as the trench underway, he beckoned the sisters off the ridgetop. Let his warm-blooded servitors eke out more shoveling, more hammerstrokes pending soupier darkness and the night apprentice's arrival. He would dismiss the living and goad the unflagging undead till his own morning bedtime. Presumably his daytime counterpart was on the beach, lashing those snails of a workforce forward. Rel really should spy on his arrogant foremen, satisfy himself they weren't in cahoots. For now, though, he briskly herded the sisters into their house and their pit by the hearth.

What did they do at night, he wondered, after his sorcery wore off? Did they lie dormant, spent after standing dawn-to-dusk, or rage silently at their confines, careening off the walls? He snorted at his foolish musings as wisdom nagged him to decamp, or risk scrambling desperately to subdue the sisters with spellcraft. They were, ominously, venting little spasms like dreamers due to wake, clenching fists, kicking pebbles, crinkling itchy noses. Rel's smug gaze lingered on them another instant, cocksure as he was of how long he could live dangerously before magic ebbed clean away.

He curtly turned, his eyes popped with shock; he almost dropped the lamp but rallied to shine it at the door, which had stealthily swung shut and wouldn't budge. His hand shot into the leather bag strung over his shoulder. The stoppered pots of powders and oils, even his sponge and pigment-stained blowpipes, were gone! How could such thievery have violated his person, except by magic? Through his alarm penetrated rustlings from the graves. He should have started spying on his treacherous attendants weeks ago! How to wrest control from them at this ill-starred juncture?

"I will blight you where you stand! No door can block my curse!" For whatever cold comfort was in it, one raspy cackle, not two, taunted him. "Idiot!" he railed. "I alone know the enchantment in full to rouse and deploy the dead! They are soon useless clay without me! I alone can curb the folk from throwing down their ropes and tools and gutting you like pigs!"

Again the raspy cackling affronted him. "Nobody can kill me. And soon your pitiful revenants will be useless clay again. But think no worse of your apprentices. They did tell me where to seek you, as if that were any riddle, and more that I demanded of them, though not of their free will. Nor will they speak further. They lied shamelessly in pleading they were less blameworthy than you."

Rel would not debase himself beseeching mercy, for he recognized, despite the muffling sandstone between them, the froggy timbre of the late shaman, gurglier with decay.

All the same, Rel stupidly objected, "I never resurrected you!"

"Nobody had to. I had the foresight not to teach you everything. Goodbye."

Rel's pithy exchange with his ex-mentor had briefly distracted him from the sisters, whose glare upon him hadn't faltered. Even as Rel gawked in unexpected amazement that no more was forthcoming from him to whom he'd been closest in the world, the sisters stalked up behind him with their lipless grimaces and eyes aglow like luminous fungi on deadwood. The lamp flew from his grip as Ils and Els sank claws into his respective flanks, raked him away from the door. From outside filtered baleful, manipulative chanting like an influx of wasps.

The people next morning were skeptical at first of their improved lots. Rel and his foremen swaggered neither among the dwellings nor on the beach, nor at the digging site. Gone without a trace! Folk were dazed but more elated than any likely ever had been or would be again to tiptoe about a scattered host of quiescent, reeking cadavers. These went back into barrows that, once restored, were thereafter breached, and ultimately destroyed, only by the encroaching sea. For the nonce, the thankful were under no shaman's spiritual thumb, and prayed to whichever gods they credited for their salvation; the true liberator never showed himself, though his distinctive droning that night had infringed on people's dreams.

The village resumed its wonted rounds, and the kidnapped farmers reoccupied their homesteads, surrounding them with wicker fences in more embittered distrust of outsiders. From eastward on the ness, where the priesthood had too many aspirants to ordain, the villagers inveigled Rel's successor. On him, of course, devolved the onus of overseeing their rites. Stifling his distaste, he led the sturdiest grandfathers in tethering a black calf in front of the sisters' house at midwinter dusk. Solemnizing sordid local practices was a fair price, wasn't it, for a status he might never achieve on the ness?

The people's breath stuck in its collective throat, expressing customary squeamishness and trepidation, as the timber pole scraped free of its boreholes and poked the groaning door-slab open. No ravenous undead sprang out. The shaman had torchbearers precede him into the house; everybody braced for a bedlam of ambush and carnage.

Instead, they finally located Rel and were equally bewildered and offended. Ils and Els were placid in their cavity, crowding Rel's supine body between them. He was mauled and bloated in every extremity, naked from the waist down. The sisters were on their sides, each draping a rawhide arm across him—tenderly, it seemed, or amorously.

None pitied Rel his macabre fate, least of all his successor; he was reviled the more because the sisters, though grisly and malicious, were embodiments of sacred ancestry. Rel's insertion here smacked of impropriety, desecration, perversion. Taking advantage of the sisters' quietude, the shaman had Rel lugged out by his swollen blue feet and the house resealed.

Rel himself had said the old rites were outmoded, and the village heeded him insofar as no one ever re-entered that house.

Flint axes chopped his obscene carcass into quarters, to be immolated on the north, south, east, and west limits of village territory. Consensus had it, and correctly, that forebodings about airborne ashes breeding plague were ill-founded.

The slabs and earthworks henceforth lay untouched, to subside into the soil, for grass to overgrow. A crescent scar, however, lingered in a field to the east, for generations after anyone could remember how it had gotten there, or why it was called the Shaman's Smile.

The Once and Future Waite

As it was in '33, so it is in '83, up in Cell 44 for starters, Meg observed ruefully. And our Gothic gingerbread façade has gone decades longer without a facelift, fooling more than one carload of tourists into mistaking the sanitarium for a grand Victorian resort. Well, as "image problems" went, it was unique. Less droll, and much deeper-rooted than quaint brownstone trim, was the Board's Victorian attitude, but that was a tangent for later.

Cell 44 was the more pressing issue. She wrinkled her nose and shoved her hands into labcoat pockets as if that would spare them contagion. The wreckage of furniture was gone, the holes in the wall replastered, the fecal smears bleached out, but oh, to open the dormer skylight way up in steeply slanted ceiling, create a draft, dispel the ambience that transcended mere lingering funk.

The cell's third patient in as many weeks had spiraled into worse condition than at commitment, suddenly prone to delusions, hallucinations, self-harm, uncannily like his counterparts of fifty years ago. Meg knew what she'd do if she ran the zoo: reseal the cell, stop chucking good money after bad. We were talking single occupancy, one measly bed, and apropos patient outcomes and repair costs, miles past the point of diminishing returns. Better to call it quits, write off the costs of remodeling, updating, swapping out a radiator for baseboard heating.

Unfortunately, it wasn't her zoo. Should have been, but wasn't, so the future of Cell 44 wasn't up to her. The director was the gutless yes-man of new owners, corporate bozos who'd relieved the state of a "money pit" that sank further into the red the more overcrowded it got. And privatization's cure for fiscal ills? Cram in more beds! Hence Cell 44 was 8 × 10 feet the institute didn't have before, the overriding priority in the bean-counters' "big picture."

Most irksomely, Meg had been tapped to diagnose 44's un-wholesomeness and fix it, whereas to anyone who could see beyond short-term windfalls, room for one more, or a dozen more, hadn't a snowball's chance of compensating for federal cuts that forced state governments, already strapped, to foot the care for their psychiatric populations. Fucking Reaganomics!

And lest we forget, the patients, bless 'em, what about their quality of life? If indignation had to stand in for compassion, and that was the best Meg could offer, it still counted as patient advocacy, absolutely. The poor souls bunking in 44 had jabbered of harassment by horseflies and yellowjackets that suspiciously vanished whenever staff rushed in. Yet insects had been legion, via the vents or a loose sill around the skylight, on first accessing the room, warranting same-day service from the exterminators.

Mold in those same vents, or fumes from a leaky flue, may have been responsible for crawly figments, and for their conflation into the night-terror described as Rasputin or Svengali or Ayatollah Khomeini, who'd "rejected" the inmates and threatened murder because their brains were "wrong" somehow. At that juncture, middle management ceased shillyshallying and wrangled each inmate space in one of the wards.

Then Meg was lolling in the doorway, with an impression blank-slate minutes had elapsed. She'd zoned out like a senile geezer, might have toppled backward if the doorjamb hadn't stopped her: mold or fumes acting up on cue, as it were. Something noxious was happening in here all right.

The director, whom Meg hated dignifying with so much as a personal name, couldn't even let her authority stand on this pathetic islet of autonomy. The cell's air tested negative for spores, carbon monoxide, sundry psychoactive agents, and since 44's influence boiled down to "one of those things" beyond current powers of analysis, she intrepidly argued that official policy was misguided, that reclaiming meager square footage might soon become the institute's own quagmire à la Vietnam.

But no, the director, practically flaunting New Agey tendencies he must have muzzled during his recruitment, exhorted her to delve past the strictly scientific, into anecdotal accounts of 44 and its occupants, into causations more "intangible or oneiric," whatever that meant. She did note that the newspaper on his desk was folded over to the page with the daily horoscope.

Meg chafed at squandering energy on a fool's errand, but did prefer the paper chase, immersion in research, to interacting with oft-incurable patients. From that angle, she'd be saddled with one fool's errand or another. Still, simply because she lacked the saintliness of Mother Teresa, was she automatically Lucretia Borgia? How could she help what her forte was?

The director's iffy allegiance to rationalism made it decidedly more galling for the Board to pass her over and hire him "off the street" despite her decade climbing the managerial ladder. Sexism had to be a factor—how onerous in her enlightened field, in these postfeminist '80s! And for bureaucrats bent on pinching pennies, they'd stupidly missed a trick: though discussing salaries was taboo, everyone knew women earned less; promoting her should have been an economic no-brainer. She'd have bowed gladly to the chauvinistic double standard for the prestige of a directorate.

But seeing as her involvement with 44 might drag on indefinitely, what a godsend she could at least be shut of it physically. On numerous occasions he'd sent her to establish "everything was okay" in the cell, without defining "okay." She always spaced out across the threshold, to the extent most recently of an out-of-body experience, snapping out of nothingness to gape at kaleidoscopic mayhem, till a will to focus reduced a hundredfold overlapping honeycomb views to a singular vantage from the skylight down onto 44 and the top of her own twitching head.

Shock zapped her back into herself; for want of objective findings she didn't bother reporting to him, nor did he, out of forgetfulness maybe, follow up with her. Soon afterward she wondered if she'd looked as disheveled exiting the cell as he did when their paths crossed several doors down from 44, his breathing labored, pupils dilated, sweat trickling from blond pompadour. Was his own research into the 8 × 10 mystery taking its toll, or was he nursing a fern-bar hangover? In any event, served the damn arriviste right.

Meg's first stop on her furlough from hands-on therapy was the basement's "records annex," a parade of green steel filing cabinets probably too close to the steamy boiler room. Down among the dead men, that was about the size of it, combing the oubliette of a more primitive science's treatment failures. Case histories of 44's last three guests for fifty years substantiated urban legends of a "cursed" asylum cell, as durable locally as the rhyme about Lizzie Borden's "forty whacks." Yesteryear's alienists had concocted a deplorably glib excuse to mothball 44; otherwise, yellowing typescripts accorded ominously with modern circumstances.

From mid-March through April 1933, three consecutive neurasthenics, upper-crust scions who could afford "rest cures" in private quarters, wound up caterwauling deliriously about horseflies and hornets that plunged into their hair, biting and stinging to the death. The patients improved upon relocation, and their doctors never termed the attackers imaginary. Rather, the cell underwent repeated fumigations, back when pest control equaled a spray-pump of Flit.

Official speculation blamed a vagary of the heating system for warm pockets between the joists where vermin spawned or thawed out of season. The same clinicians attributed the escalations from neurosis to mania to those literal gadflies, conceded this front in the war against nature, and walled off the victors. Rasputin and Svengali scored nary a mention, surprisingly.

Further digging revealed a month's vacancy in 44 preceding the neurasthenic trio. And before then? The damp air stuck in her throat and her stomach knotted at an intake of revelation she felt ill-equipped to digest. Since late 1932, 44 had contained another blueblood, Edward Derby, whose brains had been blown out on Groundhog Day 1933. Yes, right in the cell. By a fellow patrician and so-called pal.

Suddenly she had to quash her own lurking irrationality, reject the premise 44 was haunted or accursed. Shades of *Amityville Horror,* and shopworn ones at that, between assaultive flies and a brutal murder! She reproached herself for adolescent jitters at such B-movie hokum, only to wax emotional again, incensed at the director. No doubt the damn charlatan was exploiting her to confirm, to build upon, his suspicions of 44's occult infestation.

His misuse of her time, of a strapped facility's resources, might already qualify as grounds for dismissal, but let's give him some more rope, make it open-and-shut he was paying her to play ghostbuster. She initiated a detailed log of her excursions in company vehicle plus associated expenses. If anything, the fun of entrapping the boss made her a more enthusiastic delver, and the lurid spectacle of 44 did exert an undeniable fascination.

The notes on Derby read more like a riddle. His killer, Daniel Upton, was also the prime mover pushing for his committal. Professional consensus had deemed Derby a danger to himself and others, a catatonic depressive prone to violent episodes. Insofar as his ravings were decipherable, he'd suffered delusions his wife was out to enslave or destroy him. After a straitjacketed fortnight, his symptoms went into abrupt remission, and no less baffling, it was on the eve of his release that Upton, his devoted friend and sole visitor, gained after-hours admittance to his cell and murdered him.

Based on these *dramatis personae,* Meg toyed with rivalry over Derby's wife as Upton's motivation. But how did that jibe with the hospital's inability to contact her, the "popular rumor" that the wife, Asenath, had deserted Derby in October and was incommunicado in New York or California? Wherever she was, she clearly wasn't around to "enslave or destroy" him.

Regrettably, case notes didn't provide the background of relationships, the context of crimes, minus which 44 would remain a frustrating puzzle. Assuming Derby and Upton came of newsworthy dynasties, she logged in the hours and mileage for an afternoon at the *Arkham Advertiser,* requesting access at the front desk to the newspaper's morgue. The receptionist, a feathered and frosted '70s holdover, squinched at Meg's workplace ID but still addressed her as "Ms. Kilduff."

"It's 'Doctor,'" Meg patiently corrected, and yes, she did know how to operate a microfiche reader, she'd been to college. The receptionist recommended somewhat tartly that she keep her coat on. The morgue was in a backroom festooned with cobwebs. The radiators were cold, though the windows shook with December gusts. The staff left her on her own: the honor system, or the apathy of world-weary hacks?

The more she unearthed, the more her confusion mounted. Derby's homicide was duly bruited, but not as front-page headlines, which were split between Hitler flouting the Treaty of Versailles and carnage at another asylum, outside Cleveland, where nine inmates, rescued from a burning structure, sprinted back inside to self-immolation. Whether cronyism, solicitude, or incompetence consigned hometown drama to page 5, Meg transcribed plenty to whet the director's appetite for weirdness:

Item, Daniel Upton freely professed pulling the trigger, but refused to sign a confession, and was himself slated for psychiatric assessment, because he insisted he'd shot someone else, Derby having died a day earlier.

Item, dental records confirmed that viscously corrupt human remains, shoveled from Upton's vestibule on the morning of the shooting, belonged to Derby's wife Asenath, née Waite. This bombshell was unceremoniously tacked on, connected only by proximity to the foregoing text.

Item, police discovered the semblance of a disturbed grave in the cellar at Derby's address, with traces of decomposed human tissue within and around it. Derby's former servants were being sought for questioning.

Meg clucked at this textbook classism. Was Derby's pedigree so rarefied as to suspend him above the law? Why wasn't he a "person of interest," deceased or not, who'd wound up in 44 by dint of guilt or angst over slaying and cellaring the wife, assuming those graveside traces were hers? How her liquefying residue had traveled to Upton's doorstep was beyond Meg, especially as Derby had been *hors de combat* that evening, but did that justify the kneejerk association of some poor laid-off domestics with a capital crime?

All water under the bridge now, she shrugged, and irrelevant, what with ample scuttlebutt to sell the director on Derby as the tragic specter in the cell, whether positing a love triangle or not behind madness and double murder. During Meg's departure through the lobby, the receptionist piped up, "Any luck, Ms. Kilduff?"

Without pausing, Meg half turned and riposted, "That's *Doctor* Kilduff." Why was her title so difficult to swallow, most lamentably among women, who ought to applaud the loudest at gender-barrier breakthroughs in male-overrun careers? That is, unless the receptionist was feigning cretinism out of petty jealousy . . .

When Meg had typed up her findings, tendered them along with an oral summation, and joshed, "From what I've gathered then, you'd have to pin Cell 44's unpleasantness on Edward Derby's ghost," the director, to her chagrin, didn't act a bit amused. He drummed his fingertips in series on the desk, his expression dour, disappointed, coyly patronizing. Was he about to upbraid her for unseemly frivolity? Or assert the reality of this *Amityville* bushwa from his bully pulpit?

Oh, for a hidden tape recorder as he prattled, "Derby? He fancied himself among the smart set. No, Doctor, you've neglected to account for the apparition likened by three witnesses to Svengali, someone entirely dissimilar to Derby." Meg hunted in vain for any telltale body language to signal he was joshing her back. On the contrary, he enjoined her to trawl deeper into basement and municipal archives. And a positivity in his manner conveyed that he more than suspected occult activity in 44, that he was principally eager for her to duplicate his own findings.

A quaver broke into his equipoise, though, a crack in his executive façade. Without budging, he appeared to shrink away, to cringe from remembered distress, reprising that same routed as-

pect he'd worn after exiting 44. He stood up a tad unsteadily, as if
unused to his own weight, a gesture plainly announcing the interview was over, but wherein she also decoded a vibe of supplica-
tion, a mortified plea to prove he wasn't crazy. Too bad she was
itching to prove the opposite, and in tandem she'd gratify, maybe
even exorcise, her own gauche curiosity about 44's penny-dreadful
saga.

She harbored misgivings toward becoming one more chapter
of that saga herself in the wake of Christmas Eve party. The
"Events Committee" had banished patients from the solarium for
the duration, not that anyone gravitated there after dark, where
chill airstreams whistled through rattling windows on the sunni-
est afternoons. Before waltzing in, she checked her makeup in the
employees' Ladies Room, and sure, she looked fine, but why the
hell was the onus on her to "look fine" when male colleagues seldom did? There was that double standard again, and what choice
but to fish or cut bait?

She always felt extra grubby after braving the humid squalor
down in the "records annex," fretting over fly-away curls and run-
ny eyeshadow, for all that the mirror showed nothing amiss. She'd
heeded the director's request to pore over files pre- and postdat-
ing 1933, and had dredged up developments startling enough that
she plowed past the roomful of cocktail klatches to brief him,
scorning etiquette against shoptalk on a purely social occasion, and
on a Friday yet.

First off, there was a striking absence of material. Though police had, according to the *Advertiser*, remanded Daniel Upton to
the sanitarium for evaluation after shooting his "best friend" and
then claiming him an impostor, no dossier on Upton came to
light, neither where it should have been nor wherever Meg sec-
ond-guessed it had been misfiled. Had Arkham's old-boy network
expunged the family disgrace of paperwork regarding madhouse
internment, or had it altogether circumvented the formality of an
evaluation and criminal prosecution? Unbelievable but not surprising!

More momentous were those siftings from the 1920s in which she gleaned the surname "Waite," doubtless kin to Asenath Derby "née Waite," a denizen of 44, naturally, and in for psychosis, delusion, and "dementia praecox," no less. Curiouser and curiouser, he was labeled "late of Innsmouth," someplace unfamiliar though Meg grew up a townie and swore she knew every jerkwater statewide, till some trivia bobbed to the surface of her memory: yeah, Innsmouth was that hamlet smashed to flotsam by the Hurricane of '38, MIA like Atlantis.

As for this "Ephraim Waite," of age vaguely "over 65," Meg was agog to learn he'd died of heart failure after several days under restraint, ranting nonstop how he was really Asenath, how his "own father Ephraim" was going to kill him. Here was a mind-boggle an order of magnitude beyond one overbred Brahmin blasting another.

Meg struggled to marshal the facts. An elderly father dies raving he's his own daughter. A few years pass, and the father's son-in-law, who if Dad's rants were to be humored hadn't really married Asenath because she was dead already in the guise of Ephraim, is murdered by his "best friend" on the grounds he, in turn, was "someone else." Meanwhile Asenath, or at least her physical portions, had fetched up, execrably decomposed, on Upton's doorstep.

And what of that "someone else" whom Upton snuffed? The "Rasputin" or "Ayatollah" tormenting latter-day patients was, by default, a match for Ephraim, also ensconced in 44. Was he the culprit the director had cajoled her to track down, whose postmortem influence the director wanted her to validate, independent of his inspired hunches or Ouija-board sessions?

If so, his high-strung, aversive behavior in the context of 44 insinuated he despaired as much as hoped that she'd fulfill his expectations. Bringing up Ephraim might well do a number on him, undermine his beleaguered faith in rational causality, render his leadership eminently impeachable should he act upon what he patently deemed wrong with 44. Therefore Meg was dying to collar him at the party, hit him with information to widen the cracks in his veneer of stability, inaugurate the glorious process of ousting him.

But in the seconds she expended crossing the solarium, the director, as if on to her nefarious designs, ladled two cupfuls of eggnog, set his back against the wall by the nearest doorway, and pressed a cup upon her as she approached and opened her mouth. She hated eggnog. Her finger hooked reluctantly around the cup's glass handle as if around the ring of a grenade, and her meticulously phrased come-on misfired, her tongue tripping clumsily over upstart substitutions.

"Doctor, doctor," he chided, with unsober lapses in modulation, "let's not be workaholics. Nothing's so urgent you can't save it till after the long weekend." Had what she'd said even registered? His eyes roved hither and yon as if surveying *terra incognita*. She hadn't begun to regroup when he lunged at her quick as instinct and grabbed her free hand in his, gingerly yet tenacious. "Relax, let your hair down, don't be too anxious to dredge up the past." He slurped some eggnog with a gusto that begged the question of how much he'd already had.

Did people change when they drank or become more bluntly who they were? From Meg's position the issue was academic, as she more crucially debated whether he was evolving into a father-figure or a letch. Or both? Either way, his was now a greyer, more overbearing presence, in contrast to the mealy-mouthed yuppie.

Suddenly psychoanalytic musings were over, as he dumbfounded her with a curt but impactful kiss, the tip of his tongue sketching lightning-strokes across her upper and lower lips. And before she could jerk away, he'd flicked his tongue as rapidly around the inner rim of her ear. The hell of it was, his transgression smacked of clinical efficiency, as if it were exploratory and not amorous, to identify the taste of her lipstick, her earwax.

Then lo and behold, personal space lay between them, and he'd unhanded her. She'd been unaware of breaking free, but her cup was half-empty and a white splotch at her feet further insulted the downtrodden blue carpet. Her skin crawled with the cold eggnog that had sloshed over her fingers, adding drop by drop to the obscene spatter.

She was still dumbfounded when the director raised his cup with a flourish, as if acclaiming a greater power than them both, toward the mistletoe dangling from the doorway lintel behind them. And just like that she should excuse the inexcusable, on the strength of some démodé Yule custom? A toxic little twig taped to the molding granted carte blanche? Would that sexual harassment was a crime!

Yet if it were, rallying witnesses would have been a thorough bust. The party carried on oblivious to his liberties. At least nobody acted the wiser. The in-house microclimate of austerity conferred a free pass; rank-and-file whistleblowers were shoo-ins for downsizing. She retrained her sights on where the boss had been, but he'd repaired to the punchbowl, sparing them both the effort of pretending nothing had happened. She ditched her cup behind a tabletop poinsettia and unsullied her knuckles with a candy-striped paper napkin. Deliberately or not, the smarmy SOB had sidestepped her opening salvo.

Her purported "holiday weekend" was a stint in limbo, tinder-dry Xmas turkey with the folks, bachelorette quarters by her lonesome. No biggie, she didn't need a man underfoot to feel complete, he'd only pose a distraction, an impediment to her career trajectory. She'd have preferred clocking in Monday, furthering her agenda, instead of stewing at home over how the boss had violated her, how dealing with his phantasmal hobbyhorse was in effect marginalizing her. The longer she was absent from her therapeutic rounds, her supervisory role, the better his case for touting her redundancy, how everyone got along splendidly without her.

Maybe that wasn't his premeditated endgame, but to presume the lightbulb of opportunism wouldn't brighten above his head was totally naive. Beneath his bonhomie, he couldn't have liked her any more than she liked him. To get the goods on him first was only

prudent. What's more, his physical advances were also in themselves a bid to marginalize her, weren't they, to devalue her creden-
tials and talents, reduce her to an object of exploitation. It wasn't
even like he desired her. There was manifestly no "chemistry" between them.

True to cynical prediction, Meg uncovered neither police nor
courthouse records referring to Derby's murder after Upton's ar-
rest, or to Asenath's presumptive murder at all. The longer she
tilled that fallow soil, though, the more damning a waste of funds
she'd rack up to convince the Board of directorial incompetence.
Which wasn't to say her pulse didn't quicken at learning an Edward
Derby Upton had posted bail for Daniel Upton, that surname's final
official mention for the decade. The surety bond listed Edward
Derby Upton as son, clearly an adult son, if just by a year or two.

And so it was. Edward Derby and Daniel Upton really must
have been best pals, for Upton to name offspring after him. That
offspring's DOB would have been 1912 or earlier, putting his Dad's
DOB circa 1890 at the likely latest; Meg didn't bother chasing
down a death certificate for Daniel, who'd be in his nineties anyway. But his son? She may have hooked a live one here, a mere
septuagenarian who might be around to shed some clarity on this
sordid mess.

Praying the apple had rolled no great distance from the tree,
she consulted property tax rolls in City Hall. God's unparalleled,
or perhaps ironic, level of cooperation floored her. Edward Derby
Upton had paid his first-quarter bill for 1982, then sold posh Sal-
tonstall Street digs, with a forwarding address at the Pickman
Wing, Arkham Sanitarium. Her buoyant "aha moment" instantly
deflated. On the face of it he couldn't have been more accessible,
had escaped her attention only because the Pickman Wing maintained its own semi-autonomous files and bureaucracy.

Unfortunately, it did so because it specialized exclusively in
long-term geriatric and dementia care, in essence a nursing home
within an asylum. He resided a minute from her office, but very
possibly nonverbal light-years away. For the Pickman to cultivate

a separate identity, to foster the pretense nobody was consigning dotty Grandpa to the nuthouse, made good business sense. To that end, different entrances served "nursing home" and "nuthouse," but the two were otherwise peas in one brick-and-brownstone pod, aside from the Pickman's profusion of wheelchairs and arrhythmic pings of monitors and infusion pumps.

At first glance, Edward Derby Upton looked okay. Meg would have been taken aback, given his relatively tender age, had he been hooked up to machinery. The nurses' station yielded a basic history of commitment by his lawyer, pursuant to instructions in a living will. Edward was unmarried, no in-state relatives, no visitors, period. His chart described rapidly progressive Alzheimer's. Nightstand and dresser were devoid of keepsakes, books, photos, the slightest personal touch. The weak sheen of winter daylight from the window lent the furnishings their closest approximation to particularity.

Edward's façade of normalcy, his ruddy complexion, Waspy Izod apparel, dignified posture in his Scotchgarded armchair, filled Meg with malaise when she realized he was beaming through her, not at her. Leaning in, she also realized his underwear needed changing. She toughed it out, though, gently persisting that afternoon and twice more that week at chipping past his opacity—in part, she owned bleakly, because his remove from her, his unresponsiveness, promoted the awful feeling that she wasn't there either.

She sure as hell didn't go to the director for advice, or even fess up about the younger Upton's existence. No guarantees the boss wasn't a step ahead of her, of course. Nor was it incumbent on the nurses to keep tabs on his unscheduled comings and goings. Meanwhile, she'd gotten nowhere fishing for Upton's lucidity with the bait of his name, former address, a tally of kinfolk, front-page news from his youth. When a swing revival band, replete with crooner, commenced blatting in the refectory opposite Upton's door, Meg was tempted to cry uncle: swing was about as irksome to her as intractable catalepsy.

She couldn't picture amplified hokum, or chamber music for that matter, exerting a salutary effect in her more volatile wards, and what arrant spendthrift had rubber-stamped this extravagance? She was further skeptical about the unvetted good of "music therapy" among the frail and vegetative, and aghast at the crooner's poor taste in mauling "Thanks for the Memory" in front of dementia patients.

But loath as she was to embrace anecdotal evidence, how not to marvel, even if it were coincidence, at droopy eyelids popping open like window shades, palsied lips trembling to break the seal on long-hoarded answers? "Dad never rested too easy about killing him." Huh? Here was a glaring non sequitur in relation to the humdrum memories she'd tried evoking, but damned if it wasn't a gold strike, and she gratefully ran with it.

"Who? Edward Derby? Your dad killed him?"

Upton's focus drifted as if in confusion at whether she meant him or his namesake. Then he huffed, "No, no. Ephraim. Would a bullet in the head finish him? That fool Derby kept on ticking in his wife's remains after he split her skull himself. And it was Ephraim put him in Asenath's corpse and took over Derby's body in the booby hatch, where Dad put Derby."

Meg squelched a graceless urge to ask where Upton thought he was, if not in that selfsame "booby hatch." Branding him a "two-faced Yankee" was off the mark, said more about her prejudices than about him. But he was the study subject here, and to hear him tell it, round-robin metempsychosis had bedeviled his dad's social circle. Well, as group hysterias went, it was original enough, unless it were wholly Upton's unhinged invention. "So you're telling me Ephraim possessed his son-in-law's body after the son-in-law had murdered Ephraim's daughter Asenath? And then your dad killed Ephraim, inside Derby's body?"

"Or did he?" Upton retorted, rather archly for a senile codger.

"Who else could Ephraim possess? Your dad?"

"Hah! Dad swore they'd never get him within a mile of the booby hatch again, and it cost him dear to swing that. Didn't begrudge a penny of it either, not as events panned out. It was quite the public secret how the lunatics left Derby's old cell a damn sight worse than they went in. The whitecoats got sick of it, blocked it up, should've done sooner. They wouldn't own up that Ephraim was still around, though the schoolgirls had a jump-rope ditty to that effect."

"Did anybody in the cell claim to see Ephraim?"

"Nope, but he was somebody who'd haunt a house, a great one for whammies and hoodoo. Nobody'd look him in the eye when he came to town. He was supposed to have died in the asylum ages before, but people fancied that was just his body, and his spirit lived on in his daughter." Meg had nodded politely through plenty of elaborate delusions, but this one's convolutions were giving her a headache.

"Wait a second," she enjoined, hard-pressed to retain her footing in the slipstream of blather. "We're talking about personalities jumping from body to body. But where was Ephraim's personality when the cell was empty? Why didn't he stick with any of the inmates when they left the cell?"

"Because he was never in any of them. Dad blew his brains out. A soul would need a while to pull itself together after that. But Ephraim had no shortage of temporary shelters, back before your modern sanitation. The punier the brain, the better. Ephraim was the type to go bite a person on the scalp if he couldn't get in his head otherwise, and that was why Dad hated bugs and such, had a flyswatter on him always and mousetraps on the floor, as if vermin could hop a bus from the asylum clean over to our place."

He chuckled at Dad's silliness, though nothing shy of vermin riding the bus had heretofore struck him as too fantastical. And now he was gawking at her. Dammit, she must have dropped her professional guard. Luckily, he mistook her bemusement for stodgy wits. "Don't get it, do you? The little girls understood. 'Ephraim didn't want to die, He went into a fly, The fly got eaten by a spider, So he went inside her, She got eaten by a rat, So he went inside of that . . .' That's what they used to sing, eh?"

Meg essayed a brittle smile. She appreciated his clever ploy of recruiting Depression-era kids to validate his gibberish, but it only helped persuade her he belonged in her wing of the institute, not that poaching Pickman "clients" was on her to-do list. If anything, she was more uncomfortable with an Upton intense instead of comatose, and how would this manic phase play out? She'd already elicited details galore to jot down while they were fresh, to collate with the story so far, to fuel the director's budding irrationality.

Speaking of whom, it behooved her to ascertain, while Upton was in so expansive a mood, "Edward, has anyone else stopped by to ask about your dad and Cell 44?"

A cogent, searching expression gave way to alarming blowup. "I'm not here!" Vocal exertion picked him up off his seat and plunked him down again. "He comes back, mark me AWOL! He's a wall, Kilroy's behind him, never went away, shit-eating nose flopping over the top! Kilroy was here, man the pumps! Quick anyone, the Flit!" Upton shuddered crown-to-toe, eyes darting fitfully, fists beating a paradiddle on his chair's wooden arms. "He comes buzzing around, here's some food for thought!"

Meg gagged and sprinted to the nurses' station, barely pausing to announce, "Edward Upton's had an accident. He needs an immediate change of clothing. He may be unruly." A classic Ratched of a brickhouse nurse raised wire-thin eyebrows that projected, *Who the hell are you?* "I'm your deputy managing officer," Meg grated. "I'm Dr. Kilduff." Her parting glower intimated the plebs had better snap to it or else, while the dining-hall crooner warbled, "You must remember this . . ." Jesus Christ, what was wrong with that Kmart Sinatra? Or did she have him to thank, however ill-advised his repertoire, for defrosting Upton?

She typed up Edward's remarks from behind locked office door, as if merely recording them implied belief in them, impugning her own *mens sana*. Worse, she couldn't just transcribe mechanically, no, compulsive riffing on Upton's drivel ensued, inducing her to repeat, I'm going through the motions of buying into nonsense, that's all, strictly for the sake of argument. She wouldn't, for example, commit to typescript her surmise that a human personality could scarcely hope to interface with arthropod brains for fifty years, for thousands of evanescent generations, with nothing rubbing off on it.

And Upton's wild aversion to "Kilroy"—did that derive entirely from turbid flashbacks to wartime experiences, or could she read into it a chat with the director gone awry? If so, Upton might also have treated him, before their tête-à-tête imploded, to his folderol about Ephraim cheating death by taking refuge in vermin. In which case, would the director be dippy enough to apply that folderol to the problem of 44? It was something for Meg to look forward to. Or if he was unacquainted with "Kilroy," fine, she'd have the pleasure of catching him up.

She traipsed into his office as smug and self-possessed as proverbial Greeks bearing gifts, though not without trepidation. It was almost mid-January, and she hadn't been alone with him since his Yuletide hijinks under the mistletoe. At the threshold she noticed he'd cranked the thermostat; she couldn't be this hot under the collar in the span of seconds from her own emotional state. It was steamy greenhouse heat, conducive only to orchids and the insects nibbling them.

The director had his back to her, and when she cleared her throat and clacked her hard heels across the parquet, he about-faced from the nor'easter out the window, wide-eyed as if he hadn't a clue what snow was. "Well, they were forecasting upwards of a foot overnight," she greeted him.

He muttered, "They . . ." He seemed perplexed at who "they" were, disoriented, untethered from the present. Fits and starts of recognition blinked into his vision, and finding her already seated in the chair toward which he waved, he spouted, "Please make yourself at home. What have you got?"

She adhered to the custom of winging an oral summation while he, at his desk, skimmed from page to page. In brief, yes, he'd been right, a patient other than Edward Derby was the prime candidate for haunting 44. Ephraim Waite, a crackpot infamous for meting out the hairy eyeball and worse witchery, had also died there, and in yet another incredible coincidence, would have become Edward Derby's father-in-law a few years later. The director's brow wrinkled, probably at the paragraph about straitjacketed Ephraim raving he was his own daughter.

Meg had, she reminded him, tried imparting all this at the staff party, but just as well she hadn't, because today a fascinating, albeit ridiculous, new rationale for the tribulations in 44 had emerged. A syllable wedged in her throat when the director's eyes met hers with a flinty, piercing appraisal. In a flash it was over and he reverted to clinical dispassion; her sangfroid recovered and she forged on, though she'd never resolve whether her oblique allusion to his tipsy behavior, or her unprofessionalism in labeling Ephraim a "crackpot," had annoyed him.

At any rate, Ephraim wasn't exactly haunting the cell, as she'd prematurely espoused, so much as transplanting himself in the myriad critters infesting it, sustaining his consciousness for decades till reopening the cell last month brought human brains to infiltrate. These violations, unsuccessful to date, translated among the victims as harassment by Rasputin or the Ayatollah. How formidable Ephraim must have been to inspire that range of comparisons! And none other than Daniel Upton's only son, right under our noses in the Pickman, had concocted this most abstruse, outlandish explanation for a cell's poor health-and-safety profile.

The director's swivel chair squealed and twisted some degrees, he slid an inch to one side on its cushion as if nudged, and his studied reserve sharpened into hawkish interest. Optimistic Meg strove for an air of neutrality while yearning for hairline cracks in his composure, for a tic of credulity toward Edward Upton's hogwash. That hogwash was perturbing him all right, but in a scarily uncharted direction.

He smacked her papers down on his desk and snatched his fingertips away as if expecting they would stick. With a steely, domineering attitude quite unlike him, and diction the more chilling for its quiescence, he demanded, "Why was I not informed?" More disconcerting yet, his sightline had lowered toward the emptiness between them, fostering a notion he wasn't addressing her. And in more daunting proof the cracks were spreading, his eyes goggled unblinking and he succumbed to herky-jerky spasms, switching his head left-right-left with a vigor liable to sprain his neck. She had a firm but arbitrary inkling the two conditions were linked, the spasms somehow contriving to restore, or recalibrate, his vision.

The spasms persisted till a string of spittle spewed past the dam of his clenched teeth, to zigzag across the desk and her topmost sheet. She winced as his head wrenched to a jarring halt, and went cold at the same leer he'd fixed on her at the party. It partook of nothing amorous but was no less carnal, and unnerving, for that. She felt unsafe as she never had among the garden-variety maniacs. In the fewest words, she felt like food. Her feet were fidgety with the stirrings of fight-or-flight response. Damn her smartass resolution to knock him off his high horse!

If he began heaving from his chair, would it be to gesture her out or pounce? Meg was on hair-trigger alert, tensing to take to her heels, and fuck it if that made her seem the crazy one. "Will you excuse me?" he murmured at torturous length, a sheath of whisper around an iron imperative. "I have much to pore over, Doctor. Thank you." She nodded warily and hustled out, not quite bolting, declining to dwell on his borderline sardonic enunciation of "Doctor."

She retreated to her office, not far enough down the hall, and resisted a batty impulse to barricade herself in. For one thing, she'd be signing out within the hour, and in view of the snow pelting diagonally through the cones of light from the Victorian lampposts along the drive, absconding sooner sounded wise. The two-lane blacktop into town might already amount to a slip-'n'-slide enlivened by dead-man's curves, and the rusty old truss bridge over the Miskatonic had been slick with pre-snowfall rime this morning.

She just couldn't disengage, though, from bureaucratic futzing with weekly treatment reports, staff performance reviews, the tedium she'd ordinarily dash into a blizzard to avoid. Nebulous forebodings about the boss held her deskbound, needled her into reviewing their fraught discussion, deconstructing his strangeness. His alienation from the world outside, his mood swings into a starker personality, his fleeting but trenchant interrogation of an impalpable third party, the psychic upheaval underlying his frothing convulsions, these were helter-skelter signposts to an overlapping pair of propositions: Ephraim had invaded the director's head, or more realistically, the director thought he had.

She could readily credit the power of autosuggestion to possess him. He'd been receptive to a supernatural basis for the cell's toxicity from the get-go, and once the option of naming that basis "Ephraim" became available, the director seemed unable to breeze into 44 without absorbing more and more of him. And the independence of that persona had evolved to the extent that "Ephraim" wasn't automatically privy to whatever the director knew. Edward Upton, for example, apparently hadn't been on "Ephraim's" radar until Meg had inserted him there.

Her forebodings redoubled at grasping how she may have blundered terribly, how she may have painted a bull's-eye on Edward Upton's chest. Meg couldn't rule out an Old Testament attitude toward "sins of the fathers" between the director's ears, whoever was in there. That must have been why her better nature hadn't let her clock out. She'd be indirectly, a.k.a. morally, responsible for the deadly vengeance "Ephraim" might wreak on the son of the man who'd slain him.

Out of habit she'd kicked off her pumps under the desk, no use on her own turf for that further inch of stature, that extra stab at prettifying herself for the banal menfolk. Her arches always smoldered and ached by four o'clock. Urgency launched her up and out in her nylon-stocking feet to the Pickman; who the hell could run in those heels?

Shortcuts through derelict service tunnels and up equally

grungy stairwells brought her, winded and sweaty, to the nurses' station, where she vowed heads would roll. The day shift had jumped the gun at prospects of whiteout conditions, while the night shift, battling those conditions, had yet to materialize. Nobody was in sight beyond a scatter of patients drooping inert in wheelchairs or soaking up blue glow in the TV lounge. What a conducive interlude for a murder!

The blips and pings of monitors and palliative equipment made her feel like a pinball as she careened down the hall into the room where Upton wasn't, where the absence of anything personal had become his absence, period, nothing to show he'd ever been there, unless those were his gobs of blood on which she skidded. No blood, no indicators of violence had caught her eye outside the room, not that she ever doubted the director was cunning and careful.

Those qualities were on further display in his office, where no souvenirs of mayhem met her frantic survey. Not till she turned to go did she discover the smeary footprints she'd tracked from Upton's room; they flustered her as if guilt at exposing him were taking graphic form.

She could conceive of only one more destination in the whole sanitarium. And the air in 44, at first haggard gasp, was easier to breathe, less burdensome, as if an oppressive element had departed. Moreover, she didn't have to throw the light-switch on her way in. Via the skylight an ashen glow suffused the cell, a protrusion of the white overcast, not so much converting night to day as exchanging mundane reality for its darkroom negative. No gore spattered walls and floor, and maybe anxiety induced her to imagine the air growing thick and stifling again as footfalls clomped brashly down the corridor.

She pressed her spine against the wall beside the door, her best impromptu measure to "play it safe," and a heartbeat later the director snuffled in, bent so low he verged on toppling over, knuckles almost sweeping the floor, smudging the bloody trail he ogled with bulging eyes, his nostrils flaring. Blood encircled his lips like clown makeup. Was he on her scent or Upton's?

She had no inclination to find out. The instant his momentum carried him past her into the cell, a pace or two from where her red footprints U-turned toward the threshold, she sidled out and slammed the door, and hurray, the key was in the lock. Her respiration had yet to quiet down when caterwauling from the cell fazed her all over again. "Don't put me in here with him! Open that door! I'm your superior!" she deciphered amid more garbled uproar. Ah, but even had she been more sympathetically disposed, 44 was the sole single-occupant vacancy tonight.

Breathing exercises gradually allowed her to regain the wherewithal to look around. A gaggle of nurses and orderlies had assembled in response to the director's ruckus, or maybe to her footprints, and was giving her wide berth, waiting on her to open her mouth, as if to ensure she wasn't the one who needed confinement. At least she had a rank-and-file who wouldn't desert the snowed-in ship, unlike those shirkers in the Pickman.

She kept it simple, loud and clear to cut through the hysterics. The director has suffered a breakdown. He has likely murdered someone. You, you, and you, call the police, call an ambulance, don't let anyone into 44 who isn't armed, he's extremely dangerous. The rest of you, search for the body of an Edward Upton, include the Pickman Wing, inform anyone who answers the phone over there that he's missing. And all the while the ear-splitting protests raved on, very disruptive to linear cognition, "He'll cast me out! He'll force me into one of them! He'll make me like he is!"

Messengers soon reported back with body language entreating her not to shoot them please. The roads were bad, the bridge impassable due to a ten-car pileup, long story short, no cops, no medics, we're on our own till morning. Meg wryly considered the drivers might have been Pickman commuters fecklessly outbound or valiantly inbound, perchance colliding head-on. Her verbal reaction was a model of philosophic reserve: don't beat yourselves up, we can muddle through for a lousy twelve hours, can't we?

Internally she was basking in the schadenfreude. She'd proved the director unfit for duty, what a glaring understatement, never mind her active role in rendering him unfit. Here was simply the outcome of subscribing to half-baked New Age thinking, daily horoscope, ghosts, the twaddle that softened him up, made him a sitting duck for cruel-world stressors. On perceiving she'd been tuning out his hysterics, becoming desensitized, she told the flinchy doormen she'd be in her office. She could sack out on the futon and trust that anyone who sniffed out Upton's corpse was competent to locate her too.

The dazzling sunshine of a post-nor'easter freeze poured between the slats of her venetian blinds and jarred her awake. She was irrationally nonplussed not to hear the director's screams, and even at a stone's throw from 44, she strained her ears to no avail. Nothing disrupted the snores of the night watch, who'd been conscientious enough to plunk his ass squarely in front of the door.

She shook his shoulder, he shuddered and listened and asked, somewhat obtusely on first impression, "Is he still in there?"

"Let's see, shall we?" she urged, already admitting to herself, Yeah, it is uncannily peaceful in there. She had him open up, then waved him aside, preferring to be first to take stock, despite lurking danger, of her campaign's success. True, she couldn't have done it without the snow as collaborator, which thank God was still delaying the arrival of any managerial peers, with whom she was unaccountably reluctant to share this triumph. Meanwhile, she'd become, by default, the acting director!

She tromped in, but before her brain could process visual input, the smell slammed her in the solar plexus, nearly backhanded her out the door. Shit, puke, and death, in descending order, made her tear ducts overflow, dizzied her with nausea, impelled her with brute desperation to focus.

The director had come up with an all-consuming alternative to screaming. He was on hands and knees, naked, clothes in soggy shreds littering the floor, his face in a hillock of his own shit, slurping it up, its contours obscured by the vomit topping it. And in the mucoid vomit were mouthfuls of raw mushy meat, some with milky skin and limb hair still attached, along with several slimy, partly defleshed fingers. If last night's search party had stumbled across other morsels, would it have realized they were Upton's piecemeal remains?

A strangulated squawk impinged on her from behind. The big, manly slab of an orderly had peeked over her shoulder and wasn't bracing up especially well. "Keep it together!" she barked without taking her eyes off the director, who hadn't yet acknowledged his observers. "It's your job to deal with what's in front of you, is it not?" If he managed to answer, she was deaf to it, intent on a little experiment. "Ephraim?" she accosted the director, though aware she might only establish that the director thought he was Ephraim.

But she'd won his attention. His head swiveled toward her, in the fashion of a mantis or wasp; otherwise he didn't budge a muscle. Okay, now what to say? Before anything occurred to her, an impatient buzzing sprang from his throat and he resumed breakfast. Barring a defunct warlock in genuine control, the director really had bought into the implications of Ephraim abiding in a thousandfold generations of vermin, and she had to curb a self-satisfied smirk on mulling the silver lining to this miasma.

The directorship was good as hers, via the one route open to her, and as her mind's eyes lifted toward that busted glass ceiling, her actual eyes hove toward a horsefly on the wall, so incongruous with the snowscape outside, the Arctic draft leaking in from the skylight. The horsefly was inert as if in shock at hatching in this hostile season, or at reflecting, perhaps, it hadn't been a horsefly yesterday?

What a mad supposition, but why leave anything about her elevation to chance, risk defeat bursting from the jaws of victory? The fly might take wing anytime. Meanwhile, the orderly was exerting no more of a presence than the fly, doubtless praying she'd send him for in-house reinforcements or phone the cops, anything to be elsewhere. Fine. She issued her first command as acting director. "Get me a flyswatter, please. Or a rolled-up magazine will do. What are you waiting for?"

He skedaddled, and before smiling more brazenly at the wreckage of her ex-boss, she made a mental note to give her insubordinate drudge a severe dressing down. How dare he look at her sidelong as if she was the crazy one?

Widow's Walk

Once, suicidal thoughts had been inconceivable, and with any luck would be again someday. That more halcyon era pre-dated Skyler, ended a year ago when he crashed the honeymoon rental limo before the last guests had exited the reception. This twist of fate's knife was especially devastating because he'd often driven much tipsier without incident. From the portico of the banquet hall she'd heard the kaboom a block away, seen the spiraling column of smoke.

These self-destructive ideations, more frequent lately, were nothing to share with friends and family, always harping on her chronic depression, what to do about it. At home Candace was a captive audience for unsolicited pep talks. Hence she opted for unpaid leave from the drudgery from which marriage should have reprieved her, empowered her to trade the rat-race for stay-at-home motherhood. To process grief, depression, self-destructiveness in peace, she'd sought the solitude of English countryside, the lavishly hyped Great Stones Way.

Hers was the perfect mental state to contemplate grandiose monuments to mortality, reminders of time's enormity, though she couldn't even get her head around the few millennia these monoliths and tombs had endured. Too bad Day 1's mileage had been utterly unconducive to sober reflection, particularly on this first anniversary of Skyler's demise. The balmy June Sunday had brought out swarms of dog-walkers, trailbikers, motorcycle clubbers, equestrians in silly black velveteen helmets. That maudlin oldie "You'll Never Walk Alone," which she hadn't heard since the reception, was stuck in her head like an ironic taunt.

The bumper crop of holidaymakers bred worse frustration in

terms of lodging. To book this junket on impulse had felt therapeutic, as had her nonchalance about ironing out logistic details
on arrival. The trickiness of train, bus, pedestrian connections to
the trail (especially after a jetlagged night of noisy London) had
injected a crass dose of reality into that nonchalance. And for all
her schlepping, the first "monument" on her route, a hill fort, was
merely a steep slog up a causeway across a succession of gullies
and ridges to an empty field. Not a rock in sight! Her sole consolation was momentary solitude, as nobody exploiting wheels or
hooves was duplicating her fool's errand.

But the coup-de-grâce for her nonchalance struck toward
evening: pesky fellow hikers had beaten her to all the accommo-
dations she figured were hers for the asking. She trudged a mile
off-trail into East Kennet to be turned away, as she was by every
innkeeper on the miles of mazy rustic lanes to West Kennet. With
mounting shrillness she pleaded, "What am I supposed to do?"
They defaulted to their standard helpless shrug. Infuriating!

She'd no inkling where she was anymore relative to the trail,
was on the road to Beckhampton by dint of signage extolling it as
the nearest destination. She hated how traffic hurtled by even as
she faded toward invisibility in the gathering dusk. None of her
suicidal daydreams had involved getting smushed by reckless idiot motorists. She wanted off this nerve-wracking route, was
miffed at trekking sweaty hours for nary a "Great Stone," had to
admit her hunt for hotels on an empty stomach had made her
loopy.

Maybe she'd feel more clearheaded if she took stock. To her
left was a lush green hill erupting pimple-like from damp lowland,
starkly conical as if artificial, but that was doubtless the loopiness
talking. Who would build a hill? To her right she espied a subtle
projection along the summit of some upland, like a recumbent
behemoth in silhouette. She almost missed the parking spots indenting the verge, the signpost for a West Kennet Long Barrow.
She couldn't say how a scenic detour to eyeball at least one stone
monument today solved anything, but she followed the flinty

track because, well, that's what she was here for, right?

That track to the summit was longer, more vertical, more tiresome than she'd anticipated. When the ground leveled off, there was the barrow near the edge of a plateau overlooking the conical hill, which was hands-down the major feature amid pasture and plowed acreage to the purplish horizon. Untidily screening the boulder-framed entrance was an uneven row of oblong slabs, some rounded, some snaggly, some looming above her head, overall as if the hilltop was flaunting a wicked underbite. An informational placard ten feet away wasn't worth the eyestrain and exertion just this minute.

Railroad ties embedded in gravelly soil curved up to the barrow's roof, where nothing more epic was revealed than the same vista from a slightly higher elevation. But the grassed-over scale of this elongated burial mound became evident, with yardage enough for opposing goalposts; unfortunately, the behemoth's outlines strongly suggested an immense slug or larva. Again, not what she'd come for!

At least she had her solitude. She ducked between jumbo, mismatched incisors and under the doorway's capstone. Last-ditch chance to gawk at prehistoric splendor before writing off today as a total loss! She'd have preferred a towering, sunlit site to a glorified rabbit-hole, but tiptoed in budding wonderment despite the hampering gloom. More slabs like those out front and cobbles ponderous as tractor wheels interlocked via dawn-age knowhow into a claustrophobic passageway that enlarged into a chamber, like a uterus. Amazing she had even a diffuse glow by which to navigate, and only on heading back did she observe four side-chambers along the passageway.

She blundered into a muddy puddle, found herself musing how the central passage, too constricted anyway, would never do, that the cell on her right was most suitable, dry as talc. Only then did she grasp why she'd forsaken the road to Beckhampton, where the rooming shortage would doubtless have preceded her. Yes, she'd meant all along to unroll her disposable poncho on the chalky floor, curl up under a coat for a blanket, plump her back-pack for a pillow, camp rough in this exclusive dormitory. She was starving, but given her résumé of death wishes, could withstand the suicidal baby step of skipping supper.

Exhaustion functioned as an unbeatable sedative, numbing her to pebbles beneath the poncho, qualms about trespassing on sacred ground, this crypt's downright spookiness. How could it still be holy or haunted after disuse for millennia? A moot issue, since she really wasn't worried; she'd unwound sufficiently from her barrage of hassles to consider the irony that her foremost emotion was loneliness, now that she'd finally won her heart's de-sire of solitude.

How she wanted Skyler back: at present, because that would have spared her this regrettable trip. Funny, in the past year she'd contemplated self-harm more often than she had him, and what was that about? Like many another brainteaser, the effort of de-liberating pushed her beyond the border of slumberland.

Her eyes snapped open to the same submarine murk in which they'd closed. Had she slept a wink? She must have, because the alarm was going. She sat up, bucking vertigo, pawing at the nightstand before she recognized her surroundings, and the past twenty-four hours sluiced in upon her. Bedside clock morphed in-to an agitation of sleigh bells, moseying by her cell, en route to the terminal chamber.

She was too baffled to be afraid, crawled on hands and knees to the threshold of her boudoir to gape at the backs of a bunch of white-robed figures fanning out to span the uterine chamber. They were shaking square racks with rows of bells in them from side to side; she had fleeting glimpses of these, agleam in the fee-ble shaft of a skylight she must have missed before. The better-lit visitants within the shaft were much the ghostlier for it. The jin-gling abruptly segued into a drone with irregular barking empha-ses. It was gobbledygook, but its bass and baritone registers did convey the chorus was of guys.

Their ankle-length robes and droopy habits suggested they

were crossdressing as nuns. Or far scarier, were they some Brit variant of Klansmen? No, the vibe was distinctly religious. She spaced out rummaging through her foggy scrapyard of Discovery Channel factoids to ID the man-dresses as Druid. But Druids hung out in woods and not tombs, right? Brandishing mistletoe and sickles? In this square-peg context, they were even more like figments.

She was carelessly poking her head beyond the threshold for a better view when a flutter in peripheral vision impelled her to retract like a tortoise into her cell. One more white-robed dude padded by in sandals, bearing a platter under a silver dome, manifestly in too much haste to see her in the gloom. The chanting ceased once he joined his colleagues. With an awkward clang the lid was off, the liturgy resumed, the scent of ham and eggs bedeviled her. She had to grit her teeth as hunger gnashed at her abdomen.

What kind of Druids went in for ceremonial ham and eggs? Quiet now! A less disciplined person might lose it and wind up in the middle of a hostile crowd, scarfing a breakfast that absolutely wasn't hers. They weren't touching the food either, and their singsong faltered out of unison as they salaamed, groveled, clawed the dirt according to individual taste. Candace winced at the schmutz they were grinding into their white garb.

They betrayed no reaction when the sallow glow streaming down among them switched off for a solid three-count, as if a big dog had come sniffing around and lumbered off, or a big hawk had hovered overhead till an updraft nudged it aside. But they weren't oblivious, for after the light reappeared they desisted as one in their droning and abasement, to arise without brushing themselves off. Candace yearned for Skyler's hand to hold, a diversion from the SOS pangs in her belly and her bladder.

The "Druids" were filing out, squalid with brown splotches on white fabric. Candace pressed against the alcove wall, holding her breath, picturing herself invisible to help make it so. The bells rang out again, with jarring volume as they passed the cell door. She closed her eyes and grimaced, and most excruciating, the Boston Pops doing "Sleigh Bells" was glued to the turntable of her mind. Even as the jingling receded, she compulsively mouthed, "Come on, it's lovely weather for a sleigh ride together with you . . ."

Each bell-rack, she gathered, was squelched the instant its player was outside. Only in the eventual quiet could she shake away the cobwebs and out-of-season tune and grasp that the poncho had been a literal red flag, an unmissable telltale. Had fixation on their goofy ritual blinded the procession to her?

Not an overriding concern while she really had to go. She bolted out despite legs riddled with pins and needles, dropped her trousers with the barrow between her and the highway below. How lucky to be alone in the landscape, though that begged the question of whether the bell-ringers, who'd withdrawn at supernatural speed, had been ghosts. From the barrow's green roof, she detected no vehicles parked along or cruising the road. By predawn pallor she did finally apprehend that the passageway up to the square Plexiglas skylight had been half the length of the grassy "behemoth." Good for a recreational shiver to speculate she'd spent the night with a slew of skeletons immured beyond the rear chamber.

The breakfast aroma had diffused throughout the interior. No-brainer instinct set her beeline course to the neatly arranged, heaping plate on the tomb floor. Ordinarily she'd have balked at eating off ground dusty with the dead. But a platter separated foodstuffs from the soil, and the Druidic bout of groveling hadn't peppered the meal with any pollution detectable by skylight. Sacrificial fare included no utensils, but zero scruples went into reconceiving fried eggs and hunks of ham as finger-food. She had Wet-Naps in her backpack; had anyone ever used them under crazier conditions?

What a break, meanwhile, that the barrow's alleged occult presence was partial to a greasy-spoon menu versus, say, a mangled rabbit. Energized by the grace of protein-loading, she sought from the hilltop in vain for any tipoff to the Great Stones Way. A wrinkle in the terrain must have obscured it, along with her unwitting waitstaff. Nor was the low wattage from the crescent of sunrise good for parsing far-off details. She trundled gamely down the hillside path, deaf to anxiety this early, content as she'd been yet in England. So what if a glad stomach deserved full credit for that?

Retracing her steps away from Beckhampton was inarguably commonsensical. The trail had to be back whence she came, for all yesterday's meanderings. And her close encounter with the neo-pagans had worked to her benefit: unnerving or not, they'd proved harmless, and even belied received wisdom about the Brits' incompetence as cooks. More to the point, they represented the madcap England she'd hoped would distract her from suicidal brooding, the country where otherwise ordinary chaps chased a wheel of cheddar down a near-vertical incline, or donned antlers and danced in a circle.

These customs had stubbornly outlasted memories of their rationales and happened at most once a year, to recap her basic-cable learning. Therefore no encore from the white-robed troupe would be forthcoming; what a coup to catch their annual performance! This nation amounted to a treasure trove of local eccentricities, a much quainter proposition than the USA of her experience, a more potent tonic for her chronic blues than prehistoric rockpiles. But how unlike that whimsical England was her roadside path, inches from cars rocketing by, seemingly turbocharged by morning sunshine.

And now what? About the least roadworthy jalopy she'd ever seen, a European compact (sadly, she couldn't tell a Citroën from a Volvo) was braking after passing her, easing into its lane's inadequate verge. To quaint England, speedster England, would she have to add the England of tourist kidnappers, of sexual assault? Should she optimize her meager head-start to put the fake-looking hill between them, pray this predator was too lazy to give chase? Uh-oh. While she'd waffled, the chugging rustbucket had reversed to idle directly across the road, as the likewise dumpy driver yoohooed, "Great Stones Way? Care for a lift?"

Getting strangled in a dented-up clunker figured in her suicidal urges no more than dying under a clunker's wheels. But she heard herself chirp, "Okay!" She glanced both ways before throwing caution to the wind and sprinting around to the passenger door. She had no clue where the Great Stones Way was, whereas he apparently did. Plus, a vagrant impulse to learn why he'd associated it with her was trumping everyday caginess. An astute "cold read," or did her interest in Britain's antiquities carry somehow to simpatico souls?

"How do you know I want the Great Stones Way?" Candace probed, as the rattletrap merged shakily with traffic. She smiled at him out of politeness and turned away for the same reason from the curly bristles spewing from his ear, his nostrils, the skin tag bisecting an eyebrow, the complexion of mutton, the flattish profile as if a sheer white stocking enveloped his head.

"Oh, I've noticed you about," he hedged. "In small villages you notice new people."

She vented an exhilarated gasp. Out her window, paralleling the road, was a series of paired monoliths in a field, playing virtual peekaboo with her through gaps in scruffy foliage. The vehicle was on the outskirts of a settlement with further upright slabs among the sheep in pastures, among thatched and slate-roofed houses. Here was exactly what she'd traveled for, and please, she gushed with childlike excitement, can't we stop?

The driver frowned disapprovingly. "I'm afraid that would be out of order. You have more to witness first. You do want something to look forward to, in this as in other respects? You wouldn't just take Christmas and jam it into Halloween like some Eton mess!"

She felt more self-consciously juvenile at her ignorance over whatever an "Eton mess" was, apparently common English knowledge. In any case, if he'd observed her on her quest for lodgings, she couldn't say the same of him; he'd have made an impression. She strained her neck, resisted the shoulder strap, to wistfully survey the receding hamlet amid the monoliths. Motion on the backseat diverted her to a silver bowl that became, on second look, her breakfast platter's lid, lolling on its axis with each bend in the road.

His eyes darted toward her, then to the serpentine asphalt again. He gallantly leapt into the breach of her speechlessness and remarked, "Till today, the summer god never literally touched what we offered, let alone cleaned his plate." To beleaguered Candace, wisdom dictated continued silence, sustaining a poker face. "Oh, we spotted you as we entered, while you were still a sleeping beauty. And since you didn't barge in and spoil our occasion, why not live and let live, pretend you'd fooled us?"

Uh-oh, where was this all going? Since his co-worshippers had pretended she wasn't there, he mightn't be above pretending blind chance had fostered this tête-à-tête, not that he'd actually said it had. "Don't worry, nobody begrudges you the pleasure of assuaging your hunger." His delivery partook of a stagey flow, as if he were answering the question she should logically, or graciously, have posed next. "Once we unhand the oblation, it belongs to the god. He would have to frame any objection to pilferage, and why would he when it's otherwise a feast for mice and beetles?"

Did he seriously expect her to pick up this conversational thread? She hoped her good-faith effort was at least in the right ballpark: "So I get the idea you people are Druids."

In faded madras shirt and chinos, he hardly looked the role. He glanced grunting down his own shirtfront as if it underscored her error. "Oh no, our rites and regalia are quite divergent!" Beneath his mock indignation, bad blood was truly bubbling, wasn't it? Great! She prided herself on a talent for defusing situations. England, however, in its etiquette, its social norms, was a foreign country of uncharted pitfalls. She was still casting about for some innocuous change of subject when he snatched up the onerous thread.

"Of course you haven't been schooled in the niceties that distinguish our brotherhood. But the day's young. Before it's over, you'll have ample cause to sing our praises." The crooked-toothed smile he flashed at her must have been meant as solicitous; it trig-

gered a chain reaction of misgivings: dammit, she was here to escape over-solicitous types, not bumble into a coven's worth of
them. Nor had he allayed her prior angst about abduction, in fact
had bolstered it with his ominous subtext. Cult indoctrination
passed for the optimal endgame, versus human trafficking, organ
harvesting.

Meanwhile, rural byway had become the equivalent of an in-
terstate, slicing through a dreary quilt of unkempt grass and
stunted woods whose US counterpart subsisted between any major cities on Route 95. Candace fairly jabbered at him for reassur-
ance, "Excuse me? Is this how you get to the Great Stones Way?
It's looking less and less like it."

"Ah, that's England for you, soon as you take an exit off the
motorway, the scenery can do a complete one-eighty." He pursed
his anemic lips, without leveling his gaze upon her. "Of the two of
us, who do you reckon would be the more familiar with the area?"

Not a straightforward yes, though a tactful approach to calling
him on it eluded her. She covered a yawn and mouthed, Caffeine!
At home she'd never have been up this long without it. No wonder her cognition was impaired. "Are there, like, Starbucks on the
highways here? I'm jonesing for some coffee."

"What, a god's breakfast didn't satisfy you?" He essayed another fleeting smile. "I'm joking. We have to stop for petrol, you
can grab a cup then unless you require something posh."

She stifled the sentiment that miles of middle ground separated gas-station coffee from "something posh." How much was this
"free ride" costing in mental hardship? Skyler never had a problem
putting his foot down to quash impositions real or imagined. But
while she was ruminating, they'd swapped out the highway for a
side road through pastoral environs not incompatible with her
trail, then on to a crappy retail zone where he pulled off in front of
the green-and-white monolith of a BP sign.

He manned the pump; she trotted into the minimart across
the apron. She poured a Styrofoam cup to the brim from the self-
serve pot, bent to slurp a taste of scalding but blessed java before

gingerly toting the cup to the counter. She debated warning the moonfaced, sleepy-eyed kid at the register of her potential "stranger danger," yet could muster nothing more germane than, "Please, where is the Great Stones Way from here?"

He watched her fumble with the mystifying Brit coinage as if she were the first Yank he'd ever seen buy coffee. "Sorry, never heard of it. Maybe over in Marlborough?" Her confusion was curiously absorbing to him.

"Pump number three, and this as well, thanks." "Stranger danger" had bellied up to the counter, plunked down his own coffee, was peeling layers from a wad of notes (as opposed to a traceable credit-card transaction). Had he overheard her exchange with the clerk? If so, he wasn't letting on as they both picked up their cups at once and he tapped his against hers, proclaiming "Cheers!" The impact sloshed a blistering wavelet onto her thumb. Ow! He seemed oblivious to her wincing distress, and maybe he was. The clerk acted oblivious too. Was British reserve a cipher for cloddish inattention?

Candace warily buckled up in the clunker parked out front. Her possible abductor remained the best bet for reaccessing the trail, was currently indictable for defective social skills, nothing worse. She could simply unbuckle and scram, but the prospect of extricating herself from this grungy nowheresville was overwhelming. On a brighter note, CCTV was theoretically standard in shops even in nowheresville. What semi-intelligent felon would commit the rookie gaffe of interacting with his victim on camera?

More troubling right now, though, was his relapse into heathenish malarkey. "Druids, bah! Shouldn't blame the layman for mixing us up, but really! They don't do anything vis-à-vis real-world results, do they?" He groped for his coffee in the cupholder, guzzled, grew increasingly hyper. "They just swan about marking the seasons, imparting nothing a calendar wouldn't without the fuss. Our erstwhile affiliation with them, till our discontent bonded us, is embarrassing. Those prissy codgers are jealous of us, quite rightly so. Ergo they accuse us of spiritual perversion, of disgracing their Old Religion. Poseurs!"

As if she needed to be jumpier, she kept picturing, unused as she was to left-side driving, head-on collisions split seconds away at every normal maneuver. That and her chauffeur's mounting ferment after each swallow of coffee were about to make her scream when he apologized, "But how remiss of me! Nattering on like a prima donna, and you yet to put a word in. Few backpackers journey five thousand miles who aren't seeking an alternative to their unfulfilling life. Am I wrong?"

"No." And her well-honed diatribe about the day gig leapt obediently to mind. "I'm underpaid at a terribly disorganized nonprofit, understaffed, run by amateurs. Rotten at delegating. Sometimes I'm an administrator with secretarial chores, sometimes I'm a secretary who makes executive decisions. Either way I'm overworked and underappreciated."

"Oh, no doubt. But aren't you being a bit glib? Your discontent goes much deeper, or you wouldn't be so uncomfortable in your own body."

The personal nature of this remark should have offended her. She hadn't wholly unburdened herself since Skyler, though, had she? What harm in unpacking at the request of someone she'd never see again? She gazed out the window to boost her composure, was inordinately pleased at the terrain's reversion to I-95 intercity barrens. God help her, it was looking nice and rural after their pit stop on crap row.

"Well, yesterday was kind of a sad anniversary for me." She'd have gone on, but to her astonishment was choking up, blinking hard to staunch the waterworks.

"You've suffered the loss of a loved one." His cadences were expertly sympathetic, like an undertaker's, and she was too blindsided by vulnerability to consider he had anything beyond her best interests at heart. "The circumstances of that loss are difficult for you. No worries, I needn't pry."

The countryside was pretty again, though it felt contrarily more ominous as the clunker parked on pebbly ground beside one-lane tarmac along the base of a wooded ridge. She was leery of "stranger danger" once more, alone amid the songbirds, but afraid to come off as an idiot by refusing to exit the car with him. He'd already commenced scaling a steep path with indentations for footholds, like an earthen ladder. He was, after all, supposed to drop her off in the middle of nowhere. She swung her door wide, pointed uphill from the passenger seat, and called out, "Great Stones Way?" He swiveled about, nodded encouragingly.

She stuck her cup into the passenger-side cupholder, dragged her backpack from between her feet, and tromped several yards before remembering to slam the jalopy door. Scooting up within a clothesline's length of him, she'd have grinned uncharitably at how wheezy he was, except she was likewise winded seconds later. At the crest, she spun round to admire a vista like that from the barrow, albeit compromised by spindly trees whose black trunks tilted each at its own angle.

However, taking the long view opened up the mental space to accommodate fresh concerns about her guide. Innate empathy, he'd implied, had informed him she'd "suffered loss," or had that been another astute "cold read" of a woman sporting a gold band but vacationing solo? He cleared his throat and elongated his arm like a traffic cop when she looked his way. "Your path, Candace." How the hell had he learned her name? Why didn't she know his?

His outstretched hand directed her vision past the trees and onto the trail, and she might have bid him thanks and a galloping farewell had she not recognized a hunk of topography half a mile ahead. Her mouth hung open in confusion till she rallied to stammer, "Isn't that the Iron Age thing?" Did he not comprehend he'd consigned her to slog ten-plus disappointing miles all over again?

"Yes, Barbury Castle!" he affirmed. "Keen eye you have!"

"I've seen it!" she wailed, additionally upset that the coffee wasn't making her more eloquent.

"Oh, it's nowhere for us. A spiritual warzone! Hardly conducive to your happiness."

Okay, he had that right. "I have to get back to where I was when you picked me up. I don't want to repeat, like, a whole day out here." Whining was unseemly, but the patience to humor him was fast eroding.

"Yes, yes, of course," he burbled. "Wouldn't you rather be cleansed of affliction first, though? The place to do that is literally seconds away. No one's going to touch you! On our honor! No harm will come from us."

Us? How had he become we? And how farcical that her college-grad brain couldn't hash out whether skedaddling or further humoring him was smarter. "I'm still really unclear what you mean by curing my affliction or whatever," she stalled.

"What would cure it in your estimation?" His tone had the affected ring of posing a purely rhetorical question. "Don't you want him back?"

"Maybe you misread me earlier. That would take a lot more than a love potion."

"Hence you're so uncomfortable in your body. Bereavement weighs heavy. But leave it to thaumaturgy, I guarantee relief."

No, don't laugh, whatever you do! Challenging delusions was foolhardy, right? On that principle alone, she was neck-deep in her commitment to humoring him. "In for a penny, in for a pound"—wasn't that an English expression? Not that she didn't pine for Skyler, nothing else accounted for one full year of depression and deathwishes, though separating him from the freedom to exit the labor pool, from homebody wifehood, was impossible. Did that make her a bad person? Honestly, she couldn't certify his face would have persisted as vividly had his photo not graced the nightstand. That was only natural; time was on the hook for that.

Let the loonies have a go, why not? She was well versed as anybody on the drawbacks of wishing on a monkey's paw, but realistically her safety might hinge on sitting through some mumbo-jumbo and then agreeably buying their excuses when nothing happened. "Fine, I'm game, but you have to drop me off wherever I say afterward."

"Yes, wherever!" Who was humoring whom?

Yet she was surprised, despite consenting to this deal, to find herself following "stranger danger" down one of the Great Stone Way's manifold sidetracks into the vegetation. "I'll wager you're somewhat peckish," he tossed over his shoulder, "considering breakfast was ages ago."

What did that have to do with anything? She hoped her shrug came off as amenable. Theirs was one of several tracks that converged upon a glade within the black trees, at whose center was a heart-shaped bed of irises, and beside whose encircling path was a folding card table, flanked by two plastic lawn chairs, encumbered by a picnic feast (and a glade, she tactfully omitted to mention—didn't that reek of "prissy" Druids?). Flamboyant purple irises didn't jibe with heathenish style, judging by her drab escort; they must have borrowed, not planted, this setting. No matter! The whiff of manipulation revived her mistrust, galled her. "Really, what is the story here?"

"We'd be rude to have you wait for the rest of us on an empty stomach!" His abashment over her dig at his rectitude sounded sincere enough. "I'll partake as well, if you don't mind." All right, so he probably wasn't out to poison her.

The trail and any Good Samaritans were out of visual range. Down the rabbit-hole beyond reprieve for now! Hers was the unenviable lot of guest at a virtual Mad Hatter's teatime. But if she were reprising the role of the beloved Alice, surely sexual assault or suchlike criminality wasn't in the offing. Her host casually littered the grass with glass lids and silver domes from covered dishes of cold cuts, fusilli salad, slaw, whole-wheat and sourdough loaves, a decent Rioja, a thermos of coffee (said the masking-tape label). "Are we supposed to eat all this by ourselves?"

He studied her as if on guard for double meanings. "Offering too much instead of too little seemed more chivalrous. It will be we two for a while. My colleagues have work and other commitments, eh?"

Was he telling her or trying on a fib for credibility? Meanwhile, the white plastic chair sinking a half-inch under her weight, the plastic goblet of red with which he toasted her, the paper plate he loaded with comestibles all acquired a surreal air in this idyllic glade. More wine before noon? Why not? Received wisdom grimaced at the risk of a mickey, if not poison, but rationality sided against excess caution: dining companion was tucking in with gusto, was scarcely the type to go halfsies in a suicide pact.

An automatic nod or "umph" held up her end of the palaver about locally sourced cheese and whatnot, as she idly wondered who'd sown irises in the wilderness and why. After an unclocked spell she eyeballed him, anxious he'd be glaring at her for tuning him out. When had he clammed up? Remarkably, he couldn't keep his puffy eyelids apart, his chin descending torpidly toward the laminated tablecloth. Aha! Here was prime opportunity to tilt free of the sinking chair, hoist her backpack, and steal off, blithely forsaking a bushel of mysteries about anemic, heathen Mad Hatter. Or Madras Hatter? Hey, that was a good one!

The chair, or else her ass, was too leaden to budge, however, and the effort dizzied her. The day's stressors were finally exacting their toll. She closed her eyes to get her bearings, and no pressing cause dissuaded her from dozing, just for a euphoric sec or two.

She woke in the dark, disoriented, a state she'd begun to accept as her new post-shuteye normal. Gawking hither and yon confirmed she was still in the glade, sitting opposite the Mad Hatter, and he blinking away slumber too. A change in their environs even noteworthier than nightfall was the mob of nunlike silhouettes around them, and he now clothed as one of them. Had his fellow nuns redressed him in his sleep?

He perked up and lurched to his feet, knocking his flimsy chair backward, and beholding his bulk in action, the proverbial bull in the china shop, accentuated Candace's iffy position. "Steady on, Deke!" someone counselled. "No hurry!" Wonderful, his name was Deke. And his groggy, smirking salutations to the fellas were illuminated by the waxing false dawn of candles. Each man lit the wick of the next with his own; the candles had paper drip-guards around them, like those at childhood Christmas Eve masses. This inspired her to fix the friendliest face to this business by likening it to Christmas in June: they were plainly celebrating a holiday and had promised her a fantastic gift.

Soon the entire glade was etched in a haggard glow whose outskirts flickered against the surrounding trees. A stronger blotch of light preceded a sharp-cheeked, sharp-chinned, veiny-eyed visage, stringent with authority. "Welcome, and lovely to see you again, hope you've had a nice nap, no ill effects? Deke's told us all about you. We're delighted to be of service."

When would Deke have told them anything? During that interlude when he was pumping gas and she was scoring coffee? Hard to picture him even owning a phone. "And allow me to thank you for the favor you're doing us. We've had no previous opportunity to prove our mettle helping someone like you."

What? Occult eccentrics were one thing, but first-timers in this particular hocus-pocus? She hadn't signed on for that. Nonetheless, she was too woozy, too suggestible to scorn the eager attentions of these outpatients, and staggered where they led her, at arm's length from the irises. The men fanned out to make her the denim midpoint of a linen crescent.

She was insensible to whatever cue set them to chanting mumbo-jumbo in unison. Deke alone broke ranks, earning a glare from the bony-cheeked honcho for overstepping rank, to whisper in Candace's ear, "Now meditate on him. Call his name." His words percolated a tad slowly into her awareness, partly because of residual sedation, partly because of his rancid fumes from salami and wine.

Mercifully, he withdrew to reinforce the chorus, and lacking other options, why not contemplate Skyler? Crying out his name wasn't in the cards, just creeped her out. To recall Skyler, though, equaled steeping herself in despair, a heartache that pulsed like a backbeat to the emphatic chanting. The rut wherein her life foundered had never afflicted her as acutely, between the tar-pit of her day job and the minuscule odds of escaping it without Skyler. This English sojourn was a mere stopgap measure, fell pathetically short of satisfying her wish never to go home again. Why not cut to the chase, embrace obliteration?

She sought for images of Skyler as temporary refuge, and how come she could only summon up his photo on her nightstand, the paper-thin simulation and not memories of him per se? Tears and whimpers hit her unexpectedly, as did the resurgence of bell-racks in the mitts of every other cultist, who'd handed his candle to the dude beside him. Her bedazed aversion to watching their antics made it more startling when the brouhaha abruptly ceased and the burning candles tumbled into the irises. Jesus Christ, had the flowers been doused with kerosene? They didn't smell like it, but blazed up alarmingly.

The company of firebugs took this in stride, of course, had their chins in the air, mouths agape, as if to taste raindrops. But then their lips quivered and they started mouthing syllables that amplified in erratic spurts till the voices knitted loosely into a tune. Candace was confounded. They couldn't have been that well versed in her history, such that it was a joke of cosmic proportions for the ragtag outbursts to consolidate as "You'll Never Walk Alone."

Ironically, she felt more alone than during Skyler's funeral or subsequent throes of depression. The blaze amounted to light pollution effacing the stars, turning the sky a vacuous black, appropriate to her nihilist mood. Several bell-racks dropped from nerveless fingers. The song gabbled on, its choristers popeyed, slack-limbed as if in ecstasy or absence seizure, and it induced totally novel abrasions inside her, emotional or spiritual, she couldn't decide, and was she squeamish, or indignant, or terror-stricken at them?

These riddles would go forever unsolved. The choristers hushed up as one, like wildlife under threat, and only the crackle of incinerating irises was audible as a shadow eclipsed the bonfire, the white robes, her; how anomalous for something to cast a shadow without light behind it. Its unhasty pace, its viscous gray touched off a flashback to that hawk's or stray dog's shadow blocking the skylight in the barrow. Should she run for cover? The conjurers trembled in place, manifestly overawed at their own success. Their amazement mushroomed into rapture as the shadow receded, while amid the flames a silhouette arose like an actor cranked up through a theatre trapdoor, or a jack-in-the-pulpit in time-lapse photography.

Once the head and shoulders had cleared the fire, it starkly underlit them, and to her profoundest shock and confusion, they belonged to naked Skyler. His blank expression was that of a death mask, betraying no cognizance of her, and her heart lodged in her throat as she willed that simulacrum with all her intangible might to quicken, to smile on her. The sheer impossibility of this sensory input she shunted to the back burner, for she deserved him, had endured grief and privation long enough, had no defense against the visceral craving to go on with him, conjuration or not.

Since Skyler was unequivocally dead, she wasn't choosing life in the strictest sense, but was belatedly renouncing self-destruction. Her necromantic chums were beaming at her with a self-congratulatory glee, and why not? They'd delivered, and what's more, their eyes glistened by firelight, pegging them as old softies. Should she pay them? Would they charge her? Issues of money, of working versus marrying for it, had partly fueled her journey here, but right now money seemed the most abstract and irrelevant force in the universe.

Her willpower must have been formidable, because the figure in the flames was shaking its head as if dispelling naptime cobwebs, a little too vigorously, for the mask of Skyler whirled off into the unnaturally smokeless inferno. The visage beneath was of red embers and cinders, with hissing coals for eyes, molten slag for cheekbones, and there was some smoke, puffing from ragged nostrils. Candace's intellect was reduced to a cinder too, but that guttering pinpoint afforded an inkling of what had happened: these clowns had managed to summon a "summer god" this morning, who in his mordant fashion was honoring tonight's petition.

Nor did he disdain playing the amorous spouse, spreading his arms to hug her after advancing a couple of steps, a difference of inches that blasted her with the heat of Skyler's body, white-hot rather than its usual SPF-50 pallor. Deke and his cronies couldn't have dreamed of this outcome, were patently unequipped to save her, yet she'd expected better from them than ongoing rapture, as if unshakable in the conviction they'd granted her heart's-ease. In fact, they'd resumed belting out "You'll Never Walk Alone" much more jovially.

The first bars prompted a pause and a presumptive grin from the conjuration like the bending of an ingot, before it advanced and Candace smelled her eyebrows and cardigan singe. Hold on, though, what if that mask hadn't been a macabre concession to her, what if this was Skyler who'd been cremated in the limo crash? Either way, he was reaching for her past the robustly blazing greenery, to dole out the dissolution she'd solicited like a broken record, though never foreseeing she'd be literally consumed by the past.

It may have been Skyler, or "summer god" impersonating Skyler, who susurrated, "They're playing our song!" But she'd already swooned from his furnace-door exhalation and was smoldering briskly.

The Uncanny Comeback of E

Damn Dan Weston and his "parlor tricks" revival. Whatever gets into him when he throws a party, it can't abide people just eating and drinking and laughing. He's no control freak at the bureau, the laissez-faire opposite, if anything. At home, though, midcentury-modern decor sets the stage for a host hooked on the regimented fun more natural to the New Rochelle of *The Dick Van Dyke Show*. Nowadays, honestly, who can tell the trendies from the unreconstructed? But I digress. Dan foremost shoulders the responsibility for Ellery's shattering transformation and ensuing prodigal success, and indirectly for the sordid denouement.

Ellery, poor devil! He could never have imagined the zenith and nadir of his breakneck course. Not that imagination had ever found an inch of traction in him. Dan, in fact, taught himself hypnotism because of Ellery's cringeworthy incompetence when party games called for creative participation. That evening, Dan staked his repute as MC wholly on the strength of his beginner's luck as amateur Svengali.

Actually, Dan's had been only one note in the greater orchestration of bending over backward for Ellery (henceforth E; we're conditioned at the bureau to save space). We pursued this policy out of respect not for him, whom we'd never normally have befriended, but for an esteemed coworker who'd finagled his nephew the job, entrusted us with "looking after the kid," then split for lusher pastures. By the time E was effectively "one of the gang," we realized what an onerous row we'd been tricked into hoeing.

Rule One of our social contract, in keeping with shared affinities that transcended work, stated, à la *Fight Club,* "Do not talk about work." E flouted this rule with stone tone-deafness to unflagging efforts at changing the taboo subject, even unto blunter discouragements, among which I contributed, "But we're not here to grouse about the coffee machines, are we?" He was, in short, a hollow echo of the old-school "company man," minus the initiative and commitment.

The trouble was, he had scarce fodder for chitchat otherwise: zero interest in movies, books, scripted TV, which he justified by swearing he'd always been thus. The stuff of fiction was evidently too wearying and rich for his consommé blood. He did sit through sports and reality shows, though retaining little beyond an impression he'd sat through them. To him, apparently, these types of escapism were best for letting his eyes track motion while he zoned out. He bought newspapers to clip coupons. He had no hobbies, unless collecting pushpins off boardroom floors counted.

At the soirée, E was, true to form, a bottomless fount about internal affairs in departments where we knew nobody. Those of us who'd brought girlfriends were especially uptight that his babble would send them packing. Hence he was a shoo-in as Dan's first "volunteer," if only to muzzle him. He was neither resistant nor receptive to being hustled into the armchair of honor. His opaque gunmetal eyes were stolidly neutral: not windows onto his soul, but shutters over it.

To promote ambiance, Dan had draped lace mantillas atop the pole lamp overlooking E and every other lampshade, casting nearby visages as spookily underlit, gracing the ceiling with grotesque curlicues. The device was hokey albeit authentically midcentury, reprising a ton of film noir, fomenting wonderment that Halloween galas of yore didn't usually end in housefires. At most, E's pumpkinseed face expressed resignation to the scrutiny of faces masklike yet more animated than his in the eerie light, as arranged along porch gliders Dan had dragged from outdoors. He correctly surmised E wouldn't complain of point-blank audience crowding him.

Diehard-retro Dan induced trance via gold pocketwatch swinging on a fob; E went under with alacrity. According to received wisdom, susceptibility to hypnosis is a byproduct of high

IQ, so E must have had a fuller deck than we and likely he could appreciate. His chronic lumpishness was incongruent with untapped brilliance, and now his droopy eyelids and gaping mouth made him a poster boy for death warmed over.

Dan put him through elementary paces of raising an arm, singing "Jingle Bells," brushing an illusory spider off his lap. One of the girlfriends objected to jabbing him with a needle on grounds of "sadism," although Dan's command to feel no pain was a sure bet. Dan bowed complaisantly and moved on to fielding audience requests. Liam leapt in first, as always, like an old sitcom alum. He recommended the subject swing Dan's faux-rotary landline over his head and scream like a chicken. "I'd have said to swing a rubber chicken," he jibed, "but that phone's a good substitute."

Dan nixed this as "uneducational," and I, with those reflective pauses for the mot juste that try some people's patience, proposed E describe an exciting episode from his past, however long ago, back to infancy if need be. Dan awarded my flair for "education" a curt approving nod.

He rephrased my directive in mellow, zombie-friendly terms, which took a minute to penetrate the docile surface, lubricate disused wheels into creaking action. E assumed a more centered yet drawn demeanor, suddenly sadder and wiser, and had he been a more likable character, I'd already have regretted my suggestion. His hundred-yard stare bored beyond us, the wall behind us, the horizon, into a gulf I balked at contemplating. His breathing grew labored as if the air around him were too rarefied, too strange. He flinched and blinked like a wayfarer trudging into a windstorm as wet leaves buffeted his face.

Then his unrest lapsed into the speechlessness of an overwhelmed spectator, and we were dumbstruck at his rigid agitation. The poor guy couldn't have affected anyone this forcefully his whole life, and here he was missing it. Moreover, once Dan brought him around, that unique moment would "belong to the ages" the same as ancient history. And while Dan had been bowled over like the rest of us, kudos to him for grabbing the tiller and steering us back on course by asking E, "What do you see?"

"The whole family's in the bomb shelter," he intoned, more impassioned than when he wasn't mesmerized. "There's a fan going, to blow away any poison gas that gets in. It's not loud enough to drown out the air-raid siren outside. The shelter's a tight squeeze on account of the sandbags all over and the bunks and the shelves of food. Everybody's jittery, and the missus tries calming the kids down by reading from *Alice in Wonderland,* but that don't do the cat any good.

"As soon as things start to settle down and Pop peeks out the hatch for the heck of it, the first whistle makes everyone freeze, and bang! An explosion, smack dab in the neighborhood! And not ten seconds later, bang again, and again, each one's louder and the shelter rattles, and then they sound like they're right overhead, one after another, blam, blam, blam, can't even hear the whistles in between, and they shake dust from the ceiling and cans off the walls like the roof's about to cave in, and the kids are bawling and the cat's yowling and the light blinks off and on and stays off and the bombing goes on and on, and every second in the dark you think this'll be the one that blows the place up and how can it keep going on and on?"

E's lungs must have been inside-out by now. After that marathon sentence, he was panting like a racehorse. His brow was dotted with sweat and in the theatrical lighting resembled a planetarium. A vein was throbbing in his temple. Would we be complicit, morally at least, in the event of a coronary?

Dan, as dutiful host and decent human being, stepped in before E had stockpiled the oxygen to broach his next syllable. "Galahad!" Yes, that was his Christian name. By consensus, referring to him by his patronym was a kindness. "What you're describing, it's gone, over and done with. It can't hurt you." E's breathing slowed, and I was probably just reading skepticism into that squint he gave Dan; the dangling gold watch must have bedazzled him. The guests vented a collective wheeze of relief as E reverted to normal wheyface.

"You will forget everything you said after I asked what you

were seeing." Dan picked his words as if skirting verbal boo-bytraps. He also went with the shopworn snap of fingers to render the subject "awake and refreshed," who did sit up a little straight-er and smile a bit less faintly than average.

The general easing of tension was short-lived, though, for a sharp reek brought everyone to their feet, except E, who regarded the wisps drifting above the lampshade beside him with the cus-tomary detachment. A heartbeat later, the hair-trigger smoke alarm injected its earsplitting bleeps into the impending chaos. Dan virtually short-circuited at the cacophony, hulked there as if poleaxed. Liam's statuesque girlfriend analyzed the problem and sprinted from lightbulb to lightbulb, swearing like a stevedore, flinging smoldery mantillas to the floor.

Andy from payroll knocked the alarm off the ceiling with his left brogue and stomped it out of commission with his right, nip-ping decibel-crazed exodus in the bud. But the party broke up within a quarter-hour anyway. How could Dan top practically torching the house and getting us killed?

Come Monday, E's monologue dominated breakroom palaver whenever two or more of us convened minus him. Funny how delving into somebody's underlying persona can reveal as much about the delver. Andy, with his steel-trap brain for figures and sometimes ungentle default to expediency (viz. his squelching of the smoke alarm), wasn't your garden-variety New Ager. Nonethe-less, he argued, hadn't E recounted adversity from the Blitz? And hadn't Dan bade him regress until something exciting cropped up? And since E obviously postdated the Blitz, mightn't his perfor-mance indicate he'd regressed clear back to a prior incarnation?

Hearing this from pragmatic Andy didn't make it any more plausible. Or was he pulling our legs? He bristled at aspersions on his sincerity and challenged us to a "scientific" showdown (nor did anyone scruple to lay odds on the outcome). If E had accessed a past life with such a vivid chapter, could it have been the only one? "Come on, Danny boy, in for a penny, in for a pound," Andy harangued, well informed how that moniker riled Dan like a red hankie. "You owe it to me, yourself, and him, repeat the experiment, prove your hypnotic mettle, transport us to another thrilling day of yesteryear."

We really did respect Dan's qualms about inflicting more trauma upon E, none the wiser he'd ever been "transported." But as Andy pointed out, a mere snap of the fingers would restore him to unwitting banality. As for why E should voluntarily go under again, Andy forwent even the pretense of a rationale and simply asked if he'd mind Dan rehypnotizing him in his cubicle after hours. E shrugged and drawled, "Okay." He didn't visibly care how he filled the vacuity of his leisure time, and since we were his self-professed "pals," why not play along?

E's cubicle was equally bereft of job-related clutter and personal touches, bespeaking no clues about his role at the bureau, though it testified eloquently to his blankness, like an outline of him in negative space. Our navy-blue blazers, yellow neckties, class-ring garnets lent relative brio to his achromatic surroundings, not to mention Dan's gold watch, which appeared to be an entrenched affectation. Or else he, the inveterate ham, was always hoping for an opportunity like this.

Six of us huddled behind Dan in the unlit cubicle. As he swung his pocketwatch in front of E's face, it glinted with the fluorescent glow it caught from over the partitions, where a few grinds were burning the after-five oil. The previous session may have primed the pump; E subsided into stupor at the speed of heroin. For this encore, Dan sought wording that wouldn't conduce so readily to E dredging up terror: "As we did before, let's journey into your past. Let's revisit an occasion that stirred your emotions, moved you profoundly."

Again E quivered like gelatin into stasis, scales melted from his sights, he gawked into a confounding void, a private leafstorm buffeted his wincing face, and Dan, a stammer undermining his sangfroid, bid him describe what was happening.

"I'm with the sergeant," he related in that unwonted briskness, "getting out of the cab. He takes his leave from the captain inside with a snappy salute and shoulders his duffel. He hoofs it into an apartment block, not too swank but nice and solid, and already he's pretty much lost his swagger, just enough left to chew out a pissant deskman giving him flack about going up to his own home-sweet-home unannounced. Can't that damn pipsqueak see his stripes? The sarge is a bundle of nerves all right, so maybe as well the elevator boy don't look at him.

"From the elevator to his door feels like a long, slow haul. How many years since he's been down this corridor? It's become strange to him and he's sorta shaky, and on the other side of the door there's a wife, a family he hasn't seen in ages, how's it gonna sit with him seeing them again, and them him?

"Then his mitt takes over and rings the doorbell, maybe he mislaid his key in a foxhole, and being home he's glad as he's never been before, in a way nobody could be who hasn't been what he's been through. And it's calling the shots when one of his kids opens up and goes to raise a holler and the sarge clamps a hand over his mouth, shhh, mum's the word, and then his daughter shows up carrying a platter of something, and he shushes her too.

"So the kids hang back at their end of the hall while their mom in the dining room at the other end is asking what's going on. She comes out before he's gone a step, but he's not jittery anymore, a ton has disappeared off his shoulders. She's still beautiful, not exactly first bloom of youth but beautiful, as she's always been in the fifteen years since I first laid eyes on her, beautiful just as he left her as if no time has passed, though it also feels like forever and they couldn't know if this day would ever come or not.

"They hug and smooch to start making up for lost time, and how they feel for him to be home safe after this war is something nobody but themselves, and only for right now, could ever understand, except they're too preoccupied to step back and understand it. The kids at their end of the corridor scram into separate rooms so they won't see each other getting teary-eyed and to give the folks some privacy, and in fact there's not a dry eye in the house."

I expected E's prior incarnation was hanging back with the

kids, but what a privilege to be the sarge's pal right now. E was under a strain again, though, sniffling, tears rolling down his gopher cheeks, raspy asthmatic breathing. Dan needed no further excuse to snap his fingers.

Now I was wishing we were among mixed company so somebody's girlfriend could wipe the tears off E's cheeks. None of us qualified as mothering types, and nothing short of direst emergency would call for such personal contact. He "awoke refreshed," same as before, but with a novel wryness asked, "Have I been crying?"

"No," Dan lied with bureau-careerist fluency. "But you ought to check for dust in here or some chemical that's irritating your tear ducts." E nodded (as best I could judge) tractably. He tugged a Kleenex from a white plastic dispenser and daubed under his eyes. Thank God he bought, or anyhow didn't contest, Dan's blarney.

The mystery of E, meanwhile, had only become more consuming: on the upside, reason enough to convene at Hurley's, the bureau-adjacent tavern, not E's kind of place, if he had any kind of place. Every sizable burg should boast its old-fangled counterpart, sawdust on plank floors, a dented brass rail along a massive bar, whereon the Early-American carven graffiti induces reverence, though new incisions (sacrilege!) earn the vandal summary ejection.

Already we'd blundered with inexorable momentum onto a slippery slope. Attributing E's blather to past-life regression was barmy. Yet his "alter ego" was fascinating grist, beguiling us into behaving as if he were real. Our midcentury figment, we inferred, had been a Yank under an English roof during the Blitz, enlisting after Pearl Harbor and returning Stateside postwar. For all the drama surrounding him, though, he was, like E, a cipher: a recording witness to history, a bystander lacking agency. But how could a nebbish have commandeered ringside seats for even two such potent moments?

We felt like dupes, squiring each other down the garden path of the occult, and also like heels, omitting to brief E on his *cris de coeur,* telling ourselves he'd freak out and veto further research. Meanwhile we lobbied Dan to lose his qualms about psychic wear and tear on E, swing that pocketwatch again, do justice to whomever E used to be, categorically more than an onlooker. There had to be more to him than there was to E!

I was plying Dan with Hurley's most persuasive cocktails when past our booth strode Gaston, en route to the Men's. We flagged him down and urged he join us on the rebound. In two minutes he came bearing a fresh round of cosmos. He'd been on ten days' vacation in Cannes, where he had pals who put him up; we nodded for the umpteenth time at his idea of bragging rights. This was his first half-day back, mostly wasted deleting spam and wading through voicemail, which would drive anyone to drink, he carped, after getting used to the Côte d'Azur.

Since he'd missed the whole business with E, we filled him in. He slurped alcohol, swished it around pensively, gulped, and leaned forward to speak, which he didn't till peevish Dan and I reached for our drinks. This "holding pattern" was Gaston's MO, whether because he cogitated at a glacial pace or relished the limelight. "Ellery, eh?" he sniffed. "More to him than meets the eye, but what? We'll never get anywhere stalling midstream." For me at least, his Delphic utterance had been worth the wait, if it really was a vote to revisit E's "preincarnation." And Gaston's pursing lips implied he was methodically digesting something we'd said about E that had meant nothing to us.

On the pretext E was our "pal," he received notice we'd pick him up Sunday to come see the playoff on Liam's 110-inch screen. "Sure," E consented with a microblip of cheer. This ruse to replant him in front of Dan's pocketwatch had been Gaston's, who excelled at stage management, in contrast to Dan's penchant for parlor tricks. Liam's girlfriend, the only one of us who might ever have qualified to play the sports we watched, was also there.

E moped through the first half with the same woodenness that characterized him at work. The girlfriend tried engaging with him, even flirting valiantly to fluster him out of his torpor, and his bloodless flicker of a smile may have signified discreet appreciation or may have insinuated, "Dames is poison." I think we all wished she'd treat us like that sometimes, but we offered her overachiever nature no challenge.

Good thing for Liam she was a jock at heart, or his team-booster decor might have put her off. I was no stickler for elegance, but the Yankees and Packers slipcovers, placemats, drapes put me off, dwarfed though they were by the Carlsbad proportions of Liam's postindustrial-loft man-cave. Operationally, our setting didn't matter, yet it seemed a tad crass for delving into the supernatural, or earth-shaking history, or a bygone life's turning points. Dan's gold watch was no sooner out than it shone like a sore thumb.

Still and all, once halftime was underway, Liam hit mute, and his darling Tracy stole off to a less distracting distance. "Galahad," said Gaston (and how that rang like a gratuitous taunt), "I was away, you know, both times you were hypnotized, and I was wondering, would you mind being a subject again while I'm here?"

E shrugged. "Why not?"

"I'm sure we'll be done before the game's back on," Gaston promised, with a falter midsentence as if expecting sales resistance, then realizing he needn't have said anything. Amazement impelled him to ask, "Aren't you curious about what goes on when you're in a trance?"

"Not especially," E droned. "Nobody wants to hurt me, so what's the difference?" Well, if E related to humankind on the simple binary basis of who would or wouldn't injure him, we were free to proceed in good conscience, weren't we? E came across as even slighter by his lonesome on the big couch in the low-lit cavernous den, where the arc of Dan's swinging watch ended with flashes captured from the lambent TV behind him. Dan adhered to the routine of sending E into that more eventful past, with somewhat more refined instructions: "The war is over. Describe a memorable incident from a civilian frame of reference."

Our regressive soul bucked the habitual turbulence, gunmetal eyes roved and narrowed as if searching a bottomless gulf, jaw twitched sidewise as if tuning in an elusive wavelength, and the eyes widened like a voyeur's on the verge of beholding unpleasantness. "What's happening?" Dan pressed.

"Don't rush me, I'm not adjusted to the dark yet." Nope, this wasn't the E we knew. "There go mister and missus in a humble putt-putt for hire, with a canopy like one of those surreys with the fringe on top. The pond they're on has palm trees along the shore, and he kills the motor in a nice secluded spot." E scowled and retracted his lips to dig with a fingernail at an incisor's gumline, gave up after a few seconds with a huff of annoyance.

"He's an okay-looking Joe, no Adonis. She, on the other hand, is a glamor-puss, a bombshell, a little undernourished, what the fashion rags go for nowadays. He tries waxing nostalgic about 'cruises to nowhere' like this from their salad days, but she gets hinky and starts fussing about a pile of money he's got stashed, and then a gun falls out of her handbag, they both grab for it and she drills him, an outcome to which she was maybe reconciled from the get-go." His tongue poked at that same tooth, soon relented.

"Then it turns out the spot's not very nice or secluded, because her accomplice boyfriend, a shifty-eyed creep with a cowlick, is lurking in the bushes. But when he expresses reservations about the capital offense bleeding underfoot, she pulls the gun on him, makes him weigh dead hubby down with chains and dump him overboard, and pretend to be him when they return the boat, slouching off in a dead man's coat with his fedora shading his face. Meanwhile I hadn't pulled any triggers or sunk any corpses, but I was still feeling unclean like, and I knew from experience things would only get worse."

"What experience? And where were you during all this?" Dan demanded, a question I was wishing he'd voiced in previous séances. "Did you work for the boat rental? Were you another customer?"

"Naw," E scoffed as if Dan must have been a rube.

"Hey!" Tracy shouted, though I reckon the other guys, like me, heard her from across a vast, muffling distance. "The game's coming back on!"

Yes, technically, that's why we were there, and flustered Dan snapped E out of it. E blinked with the usual fleeting invigoration, and before relapsing into dullness, spat out something immaterial to us, perhaps a tactile holdover from his pre-existence, like a speck of popcorn stuck in his teeth for decades.

Tracy alone avidly enjoyed the remainder of the game, the salty snacks on the NBA All-Stars coffee table, a couple more Coronas. E reverted to mouth-breather viewing, sans the stressor of female attentions (I gather she decided he was our hobby, not hers). We guys languished in a metaphysical funk, even if nobody would phrase it that way: the appeal of melodrama, of sensationalism, had us reacting to E with a double standard of disbelief and captivation. We were emotionally invested in his preincarnation's travails, queasy at his submersion into rough company all too soon after seemlier war-related activities.

We were more concerned for him than for flesh-and-blood E, wayward as that sounds, and anxious to learn what became of him, whether he ever rebounded into "polite society." Gaston still studied him through that lens of unexpressed reservations, which merely colored, without diminishing, his curiosity about E's "alter ego." E was progressively fading into a blind spot in our solicitude, whereas the opposite was true for the psychic or psychological phenomenon under his skin.

And tangentially, I brooded on reincarnation more that upcoming workweek than in my entire life, till Dan's hastily organized Saturday night shindig, at which, we naively dreamed, one more trance might somehow resolve the saga of E's ex-self where we'd begun it. As long as we were casting better judgment to the winds, fine, let's say we are products of metempsychosis. Too bad then about that clunky regression therapy, the piecemeal inefficiency with which expired biographies have to be reassembled. If only we had the wherewithal to carry life-lessons from the last go-round into current embodiments! Or not.

Considering the innumerable influences in anyone's life-course, how to apply the lessons of a former to a subsequent identity? To bypass whatever led to a precursor's downfall might only ensure future disaster: get married younger, don't marry so young, stay single, take career more seriously, don't be a workaholic. Overlaying any such broad dictum onto the pattern of someone's fate would be like fine-tuning clockwork with a mallet.

My qualms only strengthened the case against exploiting E. How was another sweaty bout under hypnosis supposed to benefit him? Or were these bouts beneficial in a respect we'd yet to fathom, and not necessarily to E per se? The insistence that self-illumination was always constructive struck me as simplistic. As I peeped across Dan's living-room at E on his quiescent own, like a phantom nursing a can of PBR, hardly indenting the teal velvet sofa, I was at a loss to picture how he'd ever profit from an awareness of past-life escapades.

He did, nonetheless, illustrate the sentiment that we're each ultimately unique by dint of the damages we've sustained, our cumulative reversals; nothing else may better separate identical twins. But from what remove can these distinguishing marks impinge: antenatal or clear back to preincarnations? Might E's passivity have stemmed from traumas unknowable to him? He was a more dispiriting sight than ever at prospects that the dark horse of transmigration may have trumped both nature and nurture in fixing his destiny.

His interactions with other partygoers were few and brief. Everyone except him, apparently, understood why he was there, and it wasn't to bend ears about bureau gossip and gripes. When Dan moseyed over to solicit a repeat performance from his "really proficient hypnotic subject," E fazed me by swigging his lager as if crossing something off an agenda, giving people's girlfriends a casual but incisive once-over, and asking, "Nobody else wants to have a go at it?"

Dan's mumbled answer contained "afterward, maybe." He was evidently as fazed as I. E's conduct in anyone else would have raised no eyebrows; from him, this was willfulness. Be that as it may, he set empty can on polymer-mosaic coffee table and sat up amenably. Were I less sober, I'd have read some arch amusement into his focus on the swinging timepiece.

Most of us guys were listening for a keynote to define the man E used to be, though Gaston's more owlish airs hinted at listening for something else. Tracy and the other guys' dates comprised a breakaway faction by the kitchen doorway, occasionally rolling their eyes toward us as if our fascination with E were not only our hobby and not theirs, but grossly weird to boot.

In more mundane lighting than before, probably thanks to Tracy chastising Dan about flammable mantillas over lampshades, our host addressed E with a reprise of nervous quaver, despite days to prepare. He directed E to revisit a dramatic point of no return, a watershed moment after which nothing would be the same. Beyond the typical wincing in the brunt of leafstorm, Dan's proposition made for more fitful grimaces, as if it were too finicky a target, or incongruous with the way E's "forerunner" codified his midcentury CV.

Sporting an expression I'd parse in anyone else as "take it or leave it," E intoned, "We're in front of the Glendale station, middle of a windy night, nobody around besides our blond, kinda square-headed pal, not your textbook pretty boy, liable to go to fat if he gets the chance. But we're not alone after all. While our cagey friend is pacing up and down the deserted platform, his nemesis, the lame guy in trenchcoat and Stetson, heaves out of the shadows, draws a service pistol, keeps his distance though, isn't on blondie's radar yet.

"The lame fella's tall and rugged, not ugly, more like hardboiled. It wouldn't end well if you called him a gimp. Too bad that draggy foot gives him an unsavory aspect. With every step it's like someone's stropping a razor.

"Then a black sedan parks by the station. The driver stays put behind the wheel, sizing up the terrain with googly eyes. The guy's not right. He's got a coldblooded babyface, like. Blondie meanwhile has become antsy, wanders over to his car and away again, champing to get something over with.

"The lame fella mobilizes, and blondie hears him coming, and as they approach each other, an express rockets toward the station without slowing down, whistle blasting. 'No, wait!' yells blondie at the lame fella, says he's here to warn him, but nothing carries over the engine racket.

"The goon in the black car is aiming a long-barreled revolver out the driver-side window, has a bead on the lame fella, but blondie gets in the line of fire to keep him from getting plugged and takes a slug while the train racing by muffles the discharge." E's mounting excitement has attained to the pitch of a sportscaster or racetrack announcer.

"Blondie is knocked off his feet but lurches up like a real trouper and launches himself at the black sedan. He lands on the running board and holds fast just as the car reverses and careens into the business district. Our casualty is tussling with the driver, grabbing at the wheel, and the car skids out of control, nearly flattens a couple on the main drag, and smacks head-on into a street-lamp. Blondie gets thrown on his ass by the impact, and ten seconds later the car bursts into flame.

"By now, the guy in the trenchcoat has hobbled up to the accident scene, and a girl who's sorta mousy but pretty enough scampers up to him. He didn't do it, he tells her. A cop comes along, examines blondie, pronounces him DOA, of course. When the cop steps away, the lame fella takes his place and the girl wants to know who's gonna tell the stiff's wife. He says he will, and the two of them schlep off as the rubbernecks crowd around."

Our noblesse deemed it only fair to let E breathe deep after his breathless exposition. Once he was respiring normally, gazing vacantly into some private void at the end of his nose, Dan voiced our impatience at his lengthening silence. "Well? What happened next?"

"I got up and left. What else? I'd had a large Coke. The smart money beats the rush to the bathroom. I never stay for the credits." The sweep of his eye encompassed us all, and not merely Dan, a departure as startling as that eye's soupçon of disdain, as if we were clucks. Then the lassitude resumed, and was it strictly involuntary? It set in abruptly, like the clang of shutters. Nobody was more shaken than goggling Dan, his ringmaster status no longer cut-and-dried: was E in his absolute power or not?

Gaston was staring dumbfounded too, but with the shock of affirmation instead of chagrin. He worked his jaw back and forth as if unsticking the lid of his word hoard, cleared his throat and elucidated, still eyeballing E, "I didn't mention it earlier because you wouldn't want me saying I told you so, but I've had a nagging suspicion everything Ellery described I'd heard somewhere before. It didn't click till tonight, and that was by the grace of dumb luck when I was channel-flipping last week. You'll never put Ellery's stories together into a life that makes sense. They were never part of anyone's life."

"You mean he was bullshitting?" translated no-nonsense Andy. "Very creative, I'll give him that."

"No, wrong on both counts," Gaston parried. Tracy had tiptoed over, to suss out why we were pale and rattled. "We're all aware Ellery's the farthest thing from a film buff. Dan, would you kindly ask our friend here, whoever he is, if he ever attends the cinema?"

Dan put it to him and received the pert answer, "Yeah, I go to the movies. Almost every night. Except when I've been to every theatre and none of 'em has changed the picture yet. Those nights, I got nothin'." And that "nothin'" was manifestly a chronic, if not permanent, condition, spanning the Blitz to the noirish end of the '40s at least.

"Dan," Gaston followed up, "Can you ask if he's ever seen a film called *Act of Violence*? Did it make an impression on him?"

"I dunno," E's inner moviegoer shrugged. "I never remember their names once I've seen 'em. I go by the ads in the paper to tell if they look like something I already been to." His disposition had grown edgy, a whisker shy of snappish, his undertone defensive. Okey-dokey then, his leaden frown seemed to mock us, any more stupid questions?

"Volatile" was never an adjective I'd have attached to E. In the rigors of trance, though, he was morphing into someone for whom sitting calmly was an option he might strenuously reject. How to corral him if he ran amuck? "Dan, if you're satisfied for now," I exhorted sotto voce, "maybe wrap up this session?"

Dan nodded gratefully amid his foundering, and reeled off E's standard wakeup protocol. Tracy cut in with her two cents before Dan snapped his fingers. "Shouldn't you let him remember all this stuff he's been telling you? Doesn't he have a right to know?" If she'd been heeding E and not Dan at this juncture, the wolfish way he was sizing her up might have made her less intent on sticking up for him.

"No," opined her boyfriend Liam, who'd seen E leering at her. "What right would that be? The right to know he's the reincarnation of a schlub with no apparent life, who goes to the movies every night or he's 'got nothing'?"

Liam had cut to the bone all right. The vain or needy consumer of regression therapy never balks at numbering a hero, a celebrity, royalty among his erstwhile versions. But statistically, wouldn't most subjects' past lifespans be at least as boring as those underway? Sad-sack E's pre-existence had been so bleak and monotonous that nothing stood out in retrospect beyond the vicarious deeds of celluloid characters, their fictitious lives conflated with his pathetic own. I had to side with Liam: would a nerd like E be well served to discover he was the sequel to an even worse nonentity?

Tracy's fiery glance at Liam warned they'd have it out later for contradicting her in public. I'd have been more interested in this interpersonal flashpoint, had E's gasping re-entry into modern sentience not rung false with its blinking scan of our faces, as if to confirm we were buying a charade. I was inexplicably spooked, and while I can't speak for anyone else, unease may have motivated Andy and Gaston to stage a tag-team inquisition, to establish E was genuinely E.

Gaston, pacing before E like a TV lawyer on a short tether, listed three movies (the titles of which I've misfiled) plus *Act of*

Violence, and asked, was E familiar with them?

"No!" he denied, fidgety with confusion at this line of questioning. Good-scout Tracy fetched him a tumbler of water.

Andy swooped in, spitballing that E might have watched movies when he was a kid, after school with pals or with his folks after supper. Mightn't he simply have forgotten portions of his viewing childhood?

"No!" E repeated with a vehemence at odds with the nerd we knew. "Never!" Merciful heavens, an outburst! His posture bordered on confrontational, as if barbs might erupt through subcutaneous latency: how dare we accuse him of wasting hours on Hollywood piffle, of not being straight with us? Were we not informed of his lifelong disregard for motion pictures?

The ladies minus Tracy were yukking it up in the kitchen, the serial clink of glasses to convey they were insulating themselves with shots against our icky vibes. For us, however, the party had outlasted its function, had run aground, was reduced to awkwardly reassuring E we'd intended no disrespect, were just bringing him into our chitchat (without deigning to fill him in about his "alter ego").

E's rejoinder was a thin smile in a vaguely philosophic vein. He raised Tracy's tumbler with a pause like a subliminal toast, sipped, and thrust the tumbler away sourly. He snickered at Tracy, "Honey, I was hoping you'd have handed me a stronger type of clear liquid."

Tracy, agog at E's lewd grin, batted an SOS at Liam to the effect, Is that how he was looking at me while he was under? Liam meted out a nod I'd have missed had I blinked. Maybe they wouldn't have a donnybrook tonight. She blathered, "Hey, I just realized it's getting late, we'd better be off. The dog has to go out. Or the rug will suffer. The little blackmailer, ha-ha!"

That opened the sluiceway, as first deserters always do. The splinter group in the kitchen was openly grateful that the onus to keep downing shots had lifted. E went along serenely enough with designated chauffeur Andy, who reported that E rode inert as a box of donuts till they pulled up at E's apartment complex, where he flatly enunciated, "Nice party. I feel like a new man."

E debarked without elaborating and did remain his old self in having to push the Wrangler door twice to shut it properly. The "new man's" farewell to Andy may have reflected new fondness for cryptic declarations. Yes or no, he put his best foot forward by quitting the bureau Monday. To his colleagues, and quite conceivably our superiors, he tendered no ampler an explanation than of having "things to do." He bid people adieu and containerized his meager belongings with the blandest pokerface.

Actually, that wasn't 100% true. I stopped by E's cubicle to wish him luck, got nowhere conversationally, and settled for watching him chuck his credit-union calendar of historic lighthouses into a half-empty W. B. Mason box. He then picked up, vacantly hefted, and set back down the quart-size mayo jar of pushpins rescued from boardroom floors. He was bequeathing this sole oasis of primary colors, I deduced, to his cell's next inmate.

As his hand retracted from the jar, I did a double-take at E's flare-up of alarm, briefer than a flick of Zippo flame. It partook of helpless remorse at a rash leap off the deep end, or else the helpless distress of an abductee wrested from someplace safe and routine to God knew where. Ephemeral or not, I'd never observed such raw emotion on E's doughy features, and how tragic that his capacity for profound feelings had been quickened, I feared, by the same agency ruthlessly burying it.

I was laboring under the premise, rationality be damned, an insurgent personality wore lethargy like a disguise, quashing E's feeble attempts at self-assertion. Whatever had held the insurgent down before, he was raring to go now, after decades in purgatorial suspension, and wouldn't stand on ethical ceremony in optimizing his renewed consciousness. Or, I reined myself in, had E simply succumbed to cold feet while impulsively flexing some strength of personality that Don's psychic excavations had somehow freed?

And speaking of Zippos, E's sidelong look effectively fumed, Why was I still hanging around? Blank-faced, loose-limbed, he fished a pack of Camels from his desk's top drawer and flicked a silver lighter at a cigarette dangling with practiced laziness from aloof lips.

"You can't do that in here!" I protested, more in astonishment than worried he might get in Dutch. Exerting more of a presence didn't make him more lovable, did it?

"Don't sweat it," he chaffed, winking as smoke got in one eye. "I'm out of here tout-suite, right?"

I nodded, saluted farewell minus handshake or other physicality, and ducked out. I was partly freaked (at E and/or his paranormal squatter), partly loath to get mixed up in E's infractions. I'd walked in guilty enough as a member of the cheering section for mesmerist Dan. Plus, E wanted me gone; I was keen to oblige, as were my colleagues in their turn. Thus E folded his tent sans fanfare, in an impudent tobacco nimbus that soon faded from topicality because we were cocksure we'd seen the last of him: out of sight and mind, whoever was manning the helm of his body.

How flat-out wrong we were! For a pencil-pusher, the name Galahad Ellery was laughable. For a novelist, it was fine. We'd been E-less about nine months, an apt stretch for staging a rebirth, I guess. Wherever he'd gone, the book review Dan shoved under everyone's nose came from our Sunday paper's leisure section, but had been sourced from a national wire service. Neither headline nor editorial insertion promoted E as a hometown boy, a sad testimony to the negligible traces he'd left behind.

The reviewer flaunted her youth by extolling *From the Gutter to the Deep* with a fulsome vivacity totally inapplicable to the E of our acquaintance. With centrifugal abandon she slung terms like "meta," "recombinant," "ironic," and "Borgesian," which isn't even in my Webster's. The breadth of moods, themes, allusions, the bold collision of genres, the underlying postmodernist cool were intoxicating. Was E this generation's archetype of the "overnight sensation decades in the making," to paraphrase Sinatra? As lucky bull's-eyes went, she didn't know the half of it. In giddy conclusion, she smelled a Pulitzer!

I tried construing this development through the rosiest-tinted glasses. Despite Dan's injunctions to forget everything hypnosis dredged up, going under in itself may have incurred psychic repercussions, unblocking E's wellsprings of inspiration, of individualism. He had us to thank for liberating his potential (to lend the most benign optics to using him for our amusement). And if he were "woke" to our shenanigans, no surprise he'd cold-shouldered our so-called friendship.

The least I as a former pal could do was contribute a few pennies in royalties by cruising to the mall and buying E's opus at Barnes & Noble. Righteously virtuous at spending $25 on a hardcover, I plopped onto my couch, flipped to Chapter 1, and here's what greeted me:

> He was old and he fished in the Gulf by himself in his rowboat. He'd gone almost three months without catching a fish. A boy had been with him the first month or so. But after that the boy's folks kept him ashore, telling him the old guy had to be unlucky in the worst way, till they sent him out in another boat that brought in three big fish the first week.

I wasn't a movie fan like Gaston, or the midcentury expert Dan claims to be, but I did retain enough from university English classes to recognize Hemingway's *Old Man and the Sea* when someone plagiarized it.

I'd no idea at whom to be primarily aghast: the editor and publisher for being oblivious to the obvious (if indeed it was obvious to millennials) or for justifying larceny as some intellectual gimmick. Or at E, whether he'd purposely or unconsciously cribbed from reading assignments of student yesteryears. Or was E's "precursor" conning the undereducated public and publishing industry alike, too loosey-goosey in their understanding of "literary experiments"?

I'm morally opposed to peeking at last pages, flouting the reader's social contract with the writer. But E had broken that contract right out the gate, so I brushed off any onus about riffling to the end:

Did it matter where your body went when you died? The bottom of a well or a hilltop mausoleum? You were gone, you were down for the nap everlasting, you didn't care about the unpleasantness that put you there. I belonged to that unpleasantness now, more than moldering Red did. More than the old guy who would linger quietly, whose hands were folded over his chest like they were already clasping a lily, who'd never hear from me where Red was. His faculties had petered out, his heart would soon join them, and then he'd be down for the same nap everlasting. En route to the office I imbibed a couple of stiff ones at Hurley's. They didn't help, just the opposite. They brought the girl to mind, but I was dead and buried as far as she was concerned.

My discomposure mushroomed. This damn well wasn't Hemingway; it wasn't original, passed for pastiche at best, on that much I'd wager without the bookishness to peg source material. The last paragraph made no sense in light of the first, on stylistic or other grounds, and what mishmash of hijacked prose could have sanely connected them? Here, anyhow, were the earmarks of E or his "forerunner" from our sessions: a pathologically needy soul who conflated the input of printed text and movie screen with the blank slate of his own barren isolation.

The "novel E" had laced his finis (again, accidentally or not?) with a couple of telling details. The workplace-adjacent Hurley's was explicitly on his radar, though never, to our knowledge, on our ex-coworker's. Nor had ex-coworker E been prey to the female mystique, which did, however, plainly figure in plagiarist E's universe. And how much of his forlorn self had he revealed by referencing a girl to whom he was "dead and buried"?

I swung by Gaston's, divining he'd be best-versed among us at IDing passages from fiction popular enough for Hollywood to option. If he preferred not to be thus pestered, he shouldn't have loaded his condo with posters of Bogart features, lobby cards from RKO musicals, framed selfies with celebs at Cannes and Sundance, et cetera. We toasted E's "succès fou," as Gaston called it, with absinthe on the rocks. His bonhomie then hit some grimacing snags as he scanned E's closing lines, mouthed phrases with bemusement or maybe scorn.

"Nap everlasting?" he quoted, leveling his frown at me as if I'd lent E that coinage. Did Gaston deem it incriminating or "infelicitous" (a pet word of his) or both? He stalked over to a floor-to-ceiling bookcase, reached on tiptoe for a lurid blue spine, and leafed backward from the back cover with the reverence of a monk for a reliquary. "It's an eight-thousand-dollar book," he explained; I retreated several cagey paces. He then went, "Aha!"

For "nap everlasting," he expounded, I should substitute "big sleep," as if that were a dead giveaway for all but the subliterate. I deviously scoped out the name on the dust jacket. Chandler, yeah, I think I'd heard of him.

Gaston elaborated that E's preincarnation—"let's designate him 'pre-E' for convenience"—was more complicated than the lonesome moviegoer we'd cross-examined. The novel's first and final pages bespoke a grab-bag of well-digested reading, reproduced and stitched together to the best of a stalwart recollection. Pre-E's ethical fibre, on the other hand, could not have been so robust for him to sign off on brazen piracy. Okay, I interjected, but was Gaston comfortable building on the thesis reincarnation was for real? Because, honestly, I wasn't.

His brow furrowed dismissively. "Fine. Let's speculate instead that Ellery, after a lifelong aversion to books and cinema, was suddenly compelled to spend nine months not only cramming his fallow brain with literature, but also furiously regurgitating it onto paper, in a manic bid for the renown he'd always secretly craved." Gaston was often laps ahead of me thinking likelihoods through, and damn him for being so gleeful about it. "If you really believe our Ellery had the untapped talent to pull a best-seller out of nowhere . . ." Putting it thus, reincarnation wasn't a great deal more incredible.

Reshelving his prize collectible, he cracked a smile either sportive or patronizing. "We can test on Friday whether his behavior supports one theory or another. Look on the hutch. Next to the cocktail shaker. It's a clipping from today's paper." I must have had tunnel vision when I bought E's opus. The Barnes & Noble would have had a poster up for his in-store reading, as touted in the Community Calendar. Again, no editorial acknowledgment he was a local hero.

After work Friday, the gang, including Tracy, foregathered for happy hour at the Applebee's in the same mall as the booksellers. Our second and third pints were symptomatic of a malaise that I, at least, could ascribe to the insoluble riddle: was it E or "pre-E" we'd presumed to know too well, or both? Was there only ever our E from the bureau, or one person with two consecutive lifespans and an amnesic hiatus of death?

A pox on those lulls in the conversation that gave my dysphoria elbow room; everyone was brooding into their lagers, with whatever reservations. My forebodings were, in the event, on target, though venting them aloud would have accomplished nothing. At this point, trepidation was purely natural. His farewells to us at the bureau had not been redolent with warmth. We may have been tottering into a lion's den if E had come to characterize us as tormentors.

Andy announced the moment of truth was looming and commenced herding us toward the door. We didn't get far. E might have been amused at how we bunched up and crashed into one another on finding him at the end of the bar, but he was too busy peering into his bourbon, the way we had into our beers, to notice us. And many previous bourbons seemed to weigh on his shoulders.

He rotated his wrist a few degrees to check his watch, gulped the balance of his drink, swung off the stool as if it were his high horse, and jumped a little to behold us ogling him. No change in demeanor betrayed we'd ever met before, though he did unabashedly ogle Tracy back.

"Ellery!" cried Dan, with the immediacy of tossing out or grabbing at a lifeline, couldn't say which. "It's your old chums from the bureau!" E nodded and waved a desultory inch or two of greeting, still unable to tell us from Adam. Not that I was sure whom we were accosting, either.

"Well, I must be pushing on," he salaamed with alcohol-fueled exaggeration, begging the possibility he'd have remembered us had we not been slightly blurry. "Gotta go sing for my supper."

"See you at the bookstore!" chirruped Liam in a flailing effort to be upbeat, despite seeing as well as anyone where E's sightline tarried.

Tracy sidled from our ranks and into E's peripheral vision. "I'll be happier after a pit stop." She slid out past E before his gaze could catch up with her, and called, "Save me a seat, please!"

"Pit stop. Good idea," E agreed. He loped off without further ado. While she'd lit out for the mall facilities with the transparent purpose of making tracks away from E, he'd have sooner achieved relief in Applebee's restroom instead of following Tracy's lead.

We moved out more indolently in the same direction, toward the Barnes & Noble. I'd have tutted at the consumer throng's destitute imaginations, squandering "date night" at the mall, but here we were too. We were almost abreast of the long corridor that banished the public toilets to discreet isolation, when from its twilit maw burst a scream that arrested us like the rev of a chainsaw. "Oh, fuck!" Liam bellowed. "It's Tracy!" I like to think we'd have bolted as quickly to the rescue whether her scream was somehow distinctive to him or not.

We were the vanguard of a rush down the corridor where two witnesses were already on hand, fortyish Cyndi Lauper wannabes whose backs were against the wall and who wore the confused rictus that goes with not knowing how to feel. The epicenter of their confusion was Tracy, saucer-eyed and hyperventilating, her frilly blouse ripped from collar to sternum. She was transfixed on E, crumpled on his side, blood welling from his ear, obstructing the corridor so that the women would have to step over him to flee, and that was tangibly beyond them. They might have been afraid of Tracy or for her. I'm no mind-reader.

"Tracy?" Liam ventured as if to penetrate a fragile child's

trauma, yet no more inclined than the glammed-up bystanders to overleap motionless E. "Can you tell us what happened?"

"Of course I can," Tracy well-nigh spat, miffed at his kid gloves, though no muscle in her look or body budged. "Before I'd even gone in the bathroom, he comes up behind and grabs me by the shoulders and spins me around. As soon as we're face-to-face he starts tearing off my top, and I hauled off on autopilot and slammed him upside the head. I reacted before I could tell who he was; he was an attacker, that was all. But when he went down it was like a sack of laundry, nobody there, not now."

Liam, sundry strangers, and I transferred our gawking attentions to the pseudo-Laupers for backup. They nodded like persecuted bobbleheads. Someone among the onlookers must have peeled off to summon assistance. A mall cop elbowed with ex-Marine swagger between Andy and Gaston and reframed Liam's question to Tracy, minus the coddling. While Tracy repeated herself verbatim, the uniformed galoot squatted over E, fingered his wrist and carotid, and verified our suspicions.

Liam shook off the general paralysis to take a giant step past deceased E's legs and drape his varsity blazer across Tracy's trembling shoulders and exposed bra. The uniform glowered as if about to lambaste Liam for interfering with a crime scene, but held off when Tracy busted out sobbing and pushed Liam away, which I read as a sign she was scared of involuntarily clocking him next.

A pair of EMTs in festive paisley scrubs squeezed by us with a defibrillator on whatever misguided pretext. They went through the same motions the cop did, and more, seeking to "wake the dead," then radioed for a stretcher and some city-payroll police. And thus crashed and burned the meteoric career of littérateur E.

The realm of belles lettres may embrace a prodigy, but loves a scandal to pieces. Critics and the press posthumously vilified E as zealously as they'd exalted him, and ransacked his masterwork for myriad intimations of abnormal psychology. As such, Tracy was never in dangerously hot water for defending herself, for intrepidly retaliating against sexual assault. There were witnesses, and I had to credit mall cop with the smarts to detain the pseudo-Laupers till police arrived to record statements.

"Novelist E" acted, at any rate, in woeful ignorance of how vigorously modern tempora-et-mores would condemn his "direct" approach to women. Condoning nothing, I can lament the cluelessness with which he channeled his untested freedom from perhaps two lifetimes of inhibition and torpor, like a feral kid in a candy shop. On the other hand, who could he ever have been, to fancy his conduct was within civilized bounds?

No friends or family rushed from the woodwork to defend E's character and condemn his death as wrongful, not even our esteemed ex-colleague who'd foisted him on us originally. Maybe he only ever wanted E out of his hair. Nor did we care to apprise him of E's role as party entertainment, in which he perniciously converted us into believing the novelist-cum-attempted-rapist was no longer anybody's nephew: the nebbish's ongoing presence was skin-deep at best.

As for Tracy, the court of public opinion prevailed and she was spared the ordeal of trial by jury, getting off in chambers with a suspended sentence. Bully for her, though I still harbor a modicum of pity for E, or whoever he was, who finally broke through his shell of smothering inaction, won the liberty to act on impulse, and see where it got him. Or given the direction that liberty took, maybe a repressed soul would have been preferable for all involved.

I wonder how far he'll get next time around (and could I wonder anything more academic?). May no future Dan inveigle him into parlor tricks that upend his placid world and galvanize the potential of his "inner man"! Or who knows? Considering the countless vagaries shaping every life, it might prove the ultimate making of him.

Nos Morituri

A climbing boy can't hope for no better than this! I thought sure my situation was sunk after my voice cracked and I shot up in height like a thistle. Practically overnight I couldn't fit up the flues no more. But the master sweep he likes me, he says, and in earnest of securing my fortune he's made me Jack-in-the-Green this May Day, now I'm tall enough to wear the wicker.

No matter how you slice it, nothing do beat May Day—the one holiday for us in the year—Christmas, Twelfth Night, Easter, that's when we're busiest, like as not. But come May we get to make merry, parade down the High Street, the boys in soot head to toe, banging brushes and shovels together, while the prentices dress like elegant damsels and skip up to gentlemen and badger coins out of them. Then we sup on Her Ladyship's beef, plum pudding, and beer till we're fit to pop, and share out the coppers amongst us.

To be the Jack, though, nothing's better, the sinecure of every eye is what the master says. Ten feet tall inside the cone am I, cutting capers while the boys dance rings around me, with nought of me to be seen but shoes and pants cuffs and there's the slot for my eyes, the rest hid in barrel hoops and wicker decked every inch in ivy, with a crown of flowers and brilliant streamers. I've never been prouder by half, and when the burden of my shoulder harness makes me stumble on the cobbles and I tilt to and fro, people only clap and laugh the harder.

Being as I'm the sinecure, I was a trifle worried, as Kilcullen's sweeps promised a ruction if we showed ourselves and "filched what shillings was rightly theirs" is what they said, and me a defenseless walking bower. But the master he bade me pluck up my courage, inside the ivy-clad Jack I'm safest of anybody, good as in a fortress.

I rest against a postbox as the prentices call a halt so they can reach their baskets on ten-yard poles up to people's windows. Myself in the glass of a shopfront catches my notice, and I was expecting to admire how big and green I was. Instead, the sight of me is like waking up in a bed of nettles. I feel mocked and sullied. I can't suss why, as all the laughs from everybody is just a bit of fun. Everything I do is to make the folk laugh, and I ought to be content with my beginner's luck.

But it's wounded dignity as afflicts me, and it's from looking in the glass at my shape, a cone with flowers and such on top, and smarting at how they're wrong to belittle it, as if that shape was really me. I can't make head or tail of myself no more, and I'm hot and sickish, despite I've had nary a snort today. There's a roar in my ears like I'm next to a sluice so I can't barely hear people shouting and calling, miles away they seem.

It's then I smells the smoke, right under my nose as it were. I heave off of the postbox, and gorblimey but there's a red-hot glowing punk sticking through the wicker, nigh poking me in the breadbasket. The wicker's old and dry like tinder and my nose is stinging from the smoke as thickens in a trice. I can't barely keep my eyes open nor have the good of 'em in guiding my hands to the brand, as it's blazing and I daren't try pulling it free.

I spin about and yell for help, and do myself the more harm by fanning the flames with my antics. I can smell my knuckle hairs singeing, and my cheeks are like to be in the blast from a furnace! Kilcullen! This has his lot's stamp all over it, and them too craven to stand by and take credit! But why should they when their work's done and they've queered it to the hilt for our crew? No Jack, no May Day!

Most everybody I see through the eyehole has got the horrors, but is afeard to come too close and scorch themselves—except, that is, for the master. Dumbstruck I am and have to look twice to believe it, he's covering his mouth the way you do to stop up laughing. And big plans for me, he said to my face!

I stagger off, to nowhere I know of, and I stumble on a scrap of wall above the drop into a cellar entrance. "Nos morituri te salutamus!" Where'd I get that guff? If I could have set myself upright again, that mumbo-jumbo has me too mixed up to think straight. Bloody hell, I'm on fire! Over I go, bang goes my noggin on the flagstones!

~~~~~

I rail against the bastard Britunculi, threaten them with Empire's scourge at its most vengeful. No use! They laugh off a wrathful throne a thousand leagues away when they have their god on their side and their sanguinary duty to please him. Do these savages even have a word for "thousand"? Yet how good their ears must be, to hear me at this height.

Once they'd dragged me up the ladder, naked, drugged, trussed, and dangling from a rope like an Egyptian crocodile, a priest in unclean white robe unbound me, as his two blue-stained, tattooed bodyguards leered approvingly. I contended in vain to regain my footing as the priest tossed my silver-knobbed vine-wood staff at my feet, a gesture bursting with contempt for the authority it symbolized. They filed out and fastened the hatch behind them with willow osiers, worried about me breaking out no more than the livestock staked to the loose plank floor. The light weakened before I could shake off my stupor.

I know what's in store from Caesar's *Commentaries,* and can but bitterly deplore Britannia's lack of civilizing progress in the hundred years since. Nor do I doubt Rome was victorious at Mons Graupius, sealing the natives' defeat from end to end of this benighted island. Scant consolation to me! But is mine the fault when moody Fortune separates men from their cohort and leads them into ambuscade? As centurion, I alone was spared torture and mutilation, earmarked for this most exclusive fate, albeit one I share with swine, sheep, and cattle. I marvel, grudgingly, at the pious dedication that went into hoisting a cow up here.

The wicker switches of these walls are sturdy and tight-woven enough to withstand pushing, tugging, cudgeling, yet contain squarish gaps through which a leg, an arm, a head could fit. I gather they're meant to encourage drafts and maximize my exposure to a cruel, lustful mob. Ruefully I admire the vista these apertures afford, of the sheer hillside below my deathtrap of a perch, and the placid lake surrounding a massive, drum-shaped island stronghold, and the inlets of ocean hemmed in by rugged bluish peaks, everything the starker with the onset of dusk. Down by the lake, only the tribesmen, dirty, restive, coarsely clad, mar the landscape.

Given time, I might have bashed through the hatchway with my staff. But I smell smoke and hear the scraggly priest invoke his gods, harangue his votaries in their bleating excuse for a language. Even if I breached the wall, how then to get down? In fumbling like a spider for toeholds and grips on smoldering wicker, I'd merely tempt my tormentors with a comical target. The tethered beasts, with their keener noses, already paw the floor with nervous hooves. At the sight of them, twin bolts of rage and disdain jolt me. Am I no better than these animals, to wait stupidly, terrorized, for immolation?

No, I will act, and I will not hobble myself by thinking too many steps ahead, gauging my infinitesimal odds. I will make of my desperation a goad. As the reek of brushfire parches my nostrils, curlicues of smoke begin sifting up between the floorboards. The priest has led his grubby cultists to the foot of the hill, the better to jeer me. He seems unfazed by their inattention to his pronouncements. Tipsy worshippers swill from horns; equally drunken fools have donned my butchered men's armor and test its durability by belaboring one another with slingstones and clubs.

If their chieftain carouses in their midst, he's indistinct from them at this remove. Nor do women and children mix with the menfolk; perhaps experience has taught them to steer clear of besotted horseplay. Perhaps they're entrusted with tending and stoking the fire under my feet. The tethered beasts have taken to venting raucous distress, in its raw ugliness not unlike the uproar below. They dance in place or trot the widest circles they can on hooves recoiling from the heat.

High time I scoop up my staff; the spiraling vines carven along its length are hotter than the soles of my bare feet. The stokers are apparently shy the skill to distribute their inferno evenly beneath the floor. Children indeed, I'd wager! Ironically, this chamber, though separated from the barbarians' source of fitful illumination by mere flimsy boards, is steeped by nightfall in sludgy darkness. Flames crackle at the underside of the floor as if knocking to come in, but till they do, the dimness here is the same with or without windows, so blocking them will little hinder my vision.

The piteous animals are doomed no matter what, and their agitation would only interfere with my impromptu designs. Thus caving in their skulls with my silver-headed staff qualifies as merciful. The cow I spare for now; once the sheep, pigs, and goats have lost their naive bids at evading me, I drag their carcasses to the apertures overlooking the rabble and thrust their broken heads outside with exertions rough enough to wedge them into hanging there. At first the roisterers cheer at the droll spectacle of dead beasts poking their heads outside as if beseeching mercy, but grouse and catcall when it dawns I've spoiled any view of me.

Orange lines between the boards lend a faint glow to this wicker oven just after the fear-crazed cow becomes sole survivor of her barnyard. The smoke billows in now, adds a dense haze to the murky twilight. The heat stings my feet if I don't keep picking them up. How much worse to face this nightmare with feeble, undisciplined bovine wits! Bearing witness to the slaughter of her stablemates cannot have been a calming influence. Unlike them, though, her fate will be one with mine.

With the gouge-like end of my staff I stretch, fray, and sever the slit in the crude leather harness by which my fellow victim is chained. I grasp her collar, spring onto her back. The smoke makes my head swim. As my bawling mount totters about, her momentum building with her terror, my weight must be anything but reassuring. I am forced to accept I will come out of this ordeal no better than she; but the point, I also accept, has never been to survive. Rather, I demand the satisfaction of ruining this sacrifice to uncouth gods, rendering devout efforts fruitless, robbing these savages of their enjoyment.

Soon lather scatters from the cow's slippery flanks; I must dig in my heels to stay on as she bucks and skitters, and I thank Faunus she hasn't lost her balance. Bludgeoning her rump with my gory staff impels her straight onward until the wall turns her aside, and such bursts of sharp, piloting pain may serve as humane distraction, if she feels the pounding waves of heat as vividly as I do. Shallow breaths avail nothing against the choking smoke, and scores of flames spit up between the cracks. The inferno may have compromised the walls below, weakened them overall. I must take it on faith they have: much further delay and one or both of us, or the floor, will collapse.

As she skids around after near collision with the wicker, I swat her with all my might, send her unswervably as a ballista stone at the wall overlooking the tribesmen, and through it in a shower of twigs and sparks and carcasses. We hurtle into the chill night air. Our wretched audience is dumbstruck. In less than a heartbeat we must plummet, crash, burst like wineskins against the rocky ground. Yet before our forward impetus peters out, we hang unnaturally in midair, the swollen moon at eye level, the lake a taunting furlong too far to land in.

The water isn't too far to escape our fantastical reflection, though, and that of the blazing wicker cone behind us. Whatever inconceivable agency is involved, I have a mad but unshakable conviction that we pause to enable its dour scrutiny of our would-be pyre. And instead of outrage at my captors or alarm at impending death, I share in its offense at the wanton abuse of the geometry alight. How dare these puny bipeds arrogate its primal elegance for their idiotic bloodletting, desecrate it with scurrilous superstition? I do not understand my rancor, but it is as real as anything else, or more so.

To the power that has made me its vessel, I sardonically exclaim, "Nos morituri te salutamus!" And on saluting that which has deferred but not averted my death, I carry its righteous disgust with me to Hades as time resumes, and before I can count to one, the earth rushes up and I suffer a red instant of pulverizing obliteration.

~~~~~

I am flustered and embarrassed and foremost relieved that the overrides finally activated. Imprudently or not, I alone can test the projector. Who, if not the inventor, ought to brave the unpredictable risks? I should have anticipated, though, that tectonic rumblings from the Interland Sea would trigger surges in the power grid and induce the cascade of identities. Luckily there were only two before the playback circuits switched off!

What comfort to behold these ageless granite walls, their blocks of restful gray like interlocking loaves (What is a loaf? From whom and when did I pick up that word?). How uplifting to reside in my own body again. From my private alcove I find serenity in watching the librarians whisk between the books on countless shelves and those on the obsidian tables, shiny with glow from the crystal globes. Let me not dwell on the sordid personhoods in which the projector immersed me!

And praise be to the books, those priceless, imperishable transcripts of thoughts and experiences compiled over millions of years, those histories and perspectives of our Great Race and of myriad others whose minds we wrested from the remotest past and future. In strict frankness, though, the unquestioned attachment to any such bulky medium must overtax the loftiest genius for conserving space. We have burrowed as close to earth's mantle, and built towers as close to the stratosphere, as safety permits. Our knowledge threatens to hem us in like silverfish between bricks.

To document mentalities as electrical impulses, appropriating only the space for an instrument to store them, eliminating the onus of fetching minds against their wills to make them jot down their biographies, should accord with impeccable logic. And I did receive approval to proceed, but must do so in frustrating fits and starts because it remains my primary occupation to swap bodies with future-dwellers, collecting knowledge the wasteful old conservative way.

I am uninformed of any experimental approaches to data storage on the Southern Continent. We are all the same Great Race, but the Southerners, freighted with the duty and obsession to guard the trapdoors sealing off our conquered enemies the Amorphous Ones, are perforce of less contemplative, inventive dispositions. I unclasp the headband of the projector from around two of my eyes.

My own vagrant penchant may have dictated the cascade's specific playbacks. I am confessedly an overzealous researcher into the echoes, the distortions of us that crop up repeatedly in the folklore, rituals, material cultures of those species we've infiltrated. Will we imprint the idea, the subliminal trauma of us on the brains, the genomes of these organisms as they evolve? Too bad my fascination vies with revulsion at our ugly portrayals by ugly inferiors! Still, how delectable that our questing intellects cast shadows a million centuries long upon successors too obtuse to fathom a hundredth of that span.

I retract my neck and pincer limbs and feeding stalk to arrange myself most compactly atop my conical body, in its corrugations like a rolled-up map of the sublime thousand-league delta that empties into the Arctic Sound (but what is a league?). I extend a meticulously polished claw to flick a windblown speck of ginkgo leaf off the obsidian tabletop before basking in the black reflection of the most of me I can see at once. Is the Great Race not the crown of creation?

I gaze in rapture, then wake up mid-scream on my pallet below the Fresnel lenses. It had been a tranquil night, out at sea anyway, affording me the luxury of a catnap. I yank the nightcap from over my eyes, which I then squeeze shut against burning my retinas in the lamplight. I breathe deep to slow my heart. Thank God I'm miles from anyone, thank God I got wind of this vacancy months ago, before family and neighbors could vie with one another over who would have me locked up first.

Based on the fruits of my eavesdropping, I was a deal more tol'able in the throes of amnesia, about which of course I cannot judge, than when I became "myself again" and the nightmares and hysteric fits ensued. Why must I dream of monsters and ancient eras? Why must I dream of being a monster? To slither about as a legless, wrinkly cone with giant crawdad claws, that's not too much to get over, likewise the nagging fantasy that the impossibilities I dream really happened to me. But my skin crawls at musing that if I were inside the body of a loathsome creature, then logically enough, it was inside mine. And that leaves a stain on my composure, my flesh, no human agency can cleanse.

I stagger to my feet and peer out to sea, choppier now, breakers grumbling as they hit the rocks. Countless whitecaps appear when the beacon swings around, disappear when my back blocks its hot beam, reappear several more seconds as the beacon revolves onward. Not till this late date do I grasp how this, of all solitary livelihoods, drew me because the lighthouse is a cone, a cone for me to inhabit even as I seem to have grown perversely used to inhabiting a cone during those amnesiac years. As such I suddenly gasp under an insufferable burden of entrapment, not by dint of my abode's isolation or remoteness, but by the inescapability of the monster that the shape of this lighthouse represents.

Worse yet, worse than the taint of that thing infesting me, is the unbearable understanding of that gulf of eons between its day and mine. My head cannot hold the acute, overpowering realization of that span, no human head could, and to have it lodged between my ears must climax in the detonation of my brain, blasting my skull into ruddy shrapnel. That is why I press my face and fingertips against the cold, moist window and ponder how much impact would be needful to break it and liberate me. Would a running leap do? I bet it would.

"Nos morituri te salutamus!" I hear myself yell, which utterly confounds but does not deter me one whit.

A Dip in the Bog

Moray had virtually built his house upon contradictions and reflected on them little more than others did the ground beneath their cornerstones. He'd gone abroad to free-float like a thistle seed, yet here he was planting roots. He sought isolation, though achieving that meant people underfoot every waking hour. He'd fixed his sights on a future detached from past baggage, even as he waded into an antiquarian morass. And though he aspired to mundane, silver-haired maturity, he drifted ever further into the nebulous fantastic.

His toothbrush was the first indicator of occult infiltration, but who was ever receptive to the portents in a toothbrush? No, by then he was blinkered by realism, too preoccupied by brick-and-mortar decisions to intuit what else was taking shape around him. Initially his had been a quest for mere R&R, with an option on "broadening himself." And what more apposite to tour than the Highlands, outsized glorification as they were of his Nova Scotian rockbound shores and glacial moraines, a more "magnificent desolation," to quote some ancient astronaut?

Like the majority of his province, his blood was reputedly Scottish, and while no "old country" lore had enriched his childhood, Scotland was the foreign clime most "about him," made for a grander heritage than hunkering, stolid Halifax. Cocksure that overplanning would kill the spirit of this lark, he leased a BMW in tidy, tourist-lodestone Edinburgh, with no set aim but northward. His millions had always bridged logistic pitfalls for him; cash-strapped "Celtic fringe" should be no different.

By the time post-industrial Dundee was behind him, he'd gotten the hang of wrong-side driving, could relax and savor topographic majesty till he grew glutted on countless heaving hills, purple with heather, green with conifers. Cascades bisected slopes; looking-glass lochs and coves doubled them. Had he been a sightseer of weak resolve, he'd have braked every thirty seconds to take snapshots and put ten lousy miles behind him for the day. Just as well his irascible mind's eye demoted the hills metaphorically from riven church bells to a slovenly giant's crumpled Kleenexes.

His footloose, high-rolling modus operandi met with no snags the while he pinballed between Fort George, Inverness, Urquhart Castle, Culloden, Aberdeen, and scragglier settlements up north. Communing with himself for second-gear hours, he wondered if his growing ennui with the scenery stemmed from solipsism. 'Twas ever thus with him, perhaps, and integral to toughness in business, resilience in relationships. If nobody or nothing else was real, what could "get to him"? TBD: was more forbidding countryside dimming his spirits, or did satiation make him accentuate the negative in a consistently majestic landscape?

The farther he drove, the deeper was he entrenched in the rut of self-absorption. As he downshifted to rattle across the afternoon's hundredth cattle grid, it struck him that his journey's purpose had morphed from admiring ancestral terrain to taking dead-serious stock of home truths. It was clear, at this distance from daily routines, he valued memories of friendship above friendship per se. And a lucky thing, really, since his nearest and dearest were all consigned to the inactive file. He'd outgrown youthful pals, those with whom he'd launched businesses had become enemies, ex-wives had vowed to remain friends, but where were they? Memories had more staying power; shadows, yeah, though irreproachable Platonic shadows.

To his left, colossal clouds with black underbellies prowled low, grazing hilltops, looming predatory as if aching to pounce on cars. Even more conducive to brooding were the scraps of black plastic sheeting snagged on barbed wire along every mile of road and flapping ominously. For the inner man to harmonize with such external conditions was discomfiting, but self-awareness felt surprisingly good, a release of pressure like ears popping onboard a plane. So what to make of feeling drawn to forlorn roofless cottages, remnant chimneys, cellar holes in the lee of scarps, surrounded by bogs?

Not his fault if personal insights and the debris of forced clearances conflated themselves in his head! But this excursion was an act of clearance: no point passing judgment on his past without evicting its deadweight, to which end his own contemplative retreat would be vital. And where better for that than the unpeopled heath, that house pit right there, for instance, restored to livability per his dictates? He knew his actuary tables: time to reset his life-course before he had insufficient future to repay the effort!

He could elicit no reason not to get what he wanted, when he wanted it; he'd never have succeeded otherwise. From the roadside he got on the horn with his lawyers, forwarded GPS coordinates, issued orders to track down the landowners, badger them into naming a price for 50 acres, clinch the deal. With that, hey presto, a text announced he was a country squire while he manfully dispatched a parfait glass of cloying-rich cranachan. Even signatures on deeds were rubberstamps online nowadays, no facetime required. Hell, the seller might be toasting his windfall in this very dining room of Moray's seaside hotel (not that anyone seemed hard-up or a pushover).

Until his ruins reacquired the architecture to deflect harsh weather, he persevered nomadic, overnighting in waterfront bedsits, off-season ski lodges, twee market towns. This immersion in Scottish stomping-grounds, unfortunately, dredged up doleful associations with his Scottish extraction. Perhaps out of errant whimsy, his folks had saddled him with the forename Glen, guaranteeing a liter of Glen Moray from one or more waggish associates every Xmas and birthday. Every other occasion, partygoers joshed how some Highland geography was named after him. This, after suffering the nickname "Moray Eel" all through grade school. No wonder he'd never gone in for ethnic pride.

His abode, with neither postal address nor paved driveway,

became habitable enough while still under noisy construction. It had a well, plumbing, a septic system, a pellet-burning woodstove and relined flue, a generator outside sharing a cement slab with a propane hookup to the kitchen, hardwood floors but no rugs, windows but no curtains, shelves but no mementoes. And damned if he was going to send for any of his Halifax clutter when it could only trip him up as he groped into existential murk toward overhauled selfhood.

Making peace with his Scottish legacy was the plain-as-day baby step in that direction, and even that was laden with obstacles. His operational HQ and indoor campground was the library with bookshelves and no books, wainscoting and no furniture; from a mattress on the floor, via laptop, he monitored his stocks, investment properties, outlay on the rehab around him. The hammering, sawing, drilling of carpenters, drywallers, electricians handily defeated the purpose of his cottage as sanctum sanctorum. The racket of these Scotsmen flustered any inner Scotsman of his into pell-mell retreat.

Nothing against them, but nobody's name or face, no certainty of their total number, had stuck with him. It did at least dawn that his activities might qualify as cultural appropriation. Despite his name, genes, purported family history, could he pick up being Scottish where emigrant forebears had left off? Or had they forfeited his claim on belonging here? Such riddles faded out in pace with the ruckus as he patrolled the walkable limits of his domain; without the jarring impingements of people, Scotland felt more securely his.

From behind the ridgetop along his west boundary towered three wind turbines like alien titans, and Moray pondered, who were his enterprising neighbors? Beyond the dry platform of his houselot, in morass too abysmal to drain, a derelict RV was in over its axles, doomed to submersion, a mystery for next millennium's archaeologists, and no less for him: how had it crossed a hundred yards of oozy peat without benefit of terra firma, let alone a road? What telltale of crime might be locked inside to titillate those archaeologists? And gazing toward his reconfigured croft, he pondered its final tenants: under what circumstances had they decamped in the nineteenth, eighteenth, seventeenth century?

Hell, between antiquity and now, the homestead was doubtless steeped in misery, injustice, violence, malfeasance, but what square mile of planet Earth wasn't, given genus *Homo*'s million years? Whether those iniquities had sunk into his wetlands or fused with his chimney stones, he'd had no hand in them, he was the fresh start incarnate. The past had no truck with him, did it? Two snub-nosed, grouper-jawed galoots, apparently brothers or cousins, were whitewashing the plaster frontage. They weren't overtly "foreign," would have excited no comment on a Canadian street. Conversely, why shouldn't he walk among them like one of theirs?

He couldn't nail down why that notion was so gratifying, or why it was more gratifying to watch the kinsmen whitewash, as if that had symbolic meaning beyond conscious grasp. Frustration at his dearth of self-understanding trumped any sociability, goading him to slouch by the workmen with his head down, mute lips compressed. No snub intended; his egoism had simply crowded them out of the picture. They carried on with practiced indifference to bad manners.

On account of insistent drizzle later, the workmen knocked off and Moray locked himself in. The solitary evenings brought him closest to contentment, the fulfillment of getting his money's worth. Everywhere inside, for all the tarps and dropcloths, was weathertight. No drafts or ceiling drips infringed on mulling and rejecting guilt over hurting loved ones, cheating clients, the unavoidable downsides of furthering self-interest. Going forward, should any people figure in his pursuits, or, forget how mad it sounded, should he really commit himself to home quarantine, see what came of it?

Ah well, he was getting drowsy. Table the matter till morning. He brushed his teeth and otherwise called the day quits in his unfinished but serviceable bathroom. Its floor of spruce plywood and a pair of bathmats was beginning to try his patience, but it was snug and dry as the rest of the house. In bed, listening to the rain, he smiled complacently and wondered who'd been putting those silly thoughts of isolationism in his head, as if he might be other than alone, concocting a presence detectable solely as a power of suggestion.

The grate of van wheels against loose gravel, the grinding of diesel engines roused him like a cockcrow at dawn. Bad form to laze in bed while labor was underway, or maybe his dignity shied from visions of workmen busting in on him in his pajamas. Huh? His toothbrush was wet; how off-putting! Everything else in the bathroom was tumbleweed-dry, even the cup-holder, its cup, its slot for the toothbrush. The bristles had dried every night before, so what was up? They were soaked, as if someone had beaten him by five minutes. Of course nobody else was home. Work crews were only arriving now.

Squeamishness toward the toothbrush was brazenly illogical, so he refused to let a vagary of temperature, humidity, barometric pressure, "one of those things" in any case, push him around. Okay then, it didn't taste like some stranger's nasty mouth. Still, an unclean aura persisted till Moray chucked his Oral-B in the wastebasket. Never had he encountered even this much of a hiccup in causality's mundane proceedings, and he reflexively blocked it from his ken as he would a fart in a shareholders' meeting.

But the fact remained, he was out a toothbrush, and replacing it meant hitting the road. He hated flouting his brand-new resolve to stay put, and moreover admitted to misgivings about leaving the contractors to their own devices. He'd done likewise, though, without harm to former homes (inured as he was to such peccadilloes as workmen using his toilet instead of the port-o-john), as if his blue-collars wouldn't be out of sight, out of mind once he was on the highway, which indeed happened.

Twenty minutes north was Thurso, the last populous burg en route to the coast, hyping its ramshackle charms online to entice tourists away from less remote destinations. Moray commended its pluck; how could the shops not have tons of toothbrushes for the prospective hordes? The farther he drove, the freer he felt of a borderline-palpable pressure, akin to that buoyancy his first time on this road, when he'd originally beheld his house pit. Not knowing what to make of this sensation, he chose to sideline it. On to Thurso!

As predicted, scoring a toothbrush was a cinch. At a quaint High Street druggist he grabbed half a dozen. Safety in numbers, better safe than sorry: such chestnuts were his bywords. He also found himself longing for the day he had a factotum for nuisance errands or a speed-dial directory of stores that delivered. And didn't he deserve credit for catching himself out on his conflicted agenda, simultaneously demanding isolation and a corps of enablers at his elbow? Actually, that double bind was susceptible to special pleading. He wouldn't interact with staff, not meaningfully, they were more like plumbing, part of his hermitage's operating system.

Anyway, mission accomplished, so why not relax over lunch in town? But typically, innocent afterthought became the springboard to aggravation. The clean, no-nonsense Scottish equivalent of a trattoria externally looked cavernous within, probably from lack of patronage. On the upside, nobody stood between him and snappy service. Or might the cuisine's shortcomings be common knowledge locally?

Moray cleared his throat and his leaden footfalls echoed around the foyer an irksome minute before a plump, abstracted teenager emerged from nether warrens. She seated him, presented a menu, and skedaddled. He scanned its overambitious contents and decided he'd be safest with mac-and-cheese. But where was she? Three entire techno-dance hits of the '90s stoked his displeasure via overhead speakers. And then from kitchen or office (the acoustics made it impossible to pinpoint), a torrent of castigation flooded the soundscape, a bit too muffled to follow. In its rare letups, a dispirited girl, presumptively Moray's server, squeaked mealy-mouthed excuses.

Good heavens, whether the termagant were chef or manager,

was she not concerned that a customer was not only in earshot but chafing neglected, his good graces clearly less important than her strident diatribe? After a lull, the girl lurched through a swinging door with a porthole in it. She acted none the worse for being savaged—water off a blasé duck apparently—and tendered no apology for the wait. He took the highroad and ordered without venting snippiness. She went MIA for another galling stint of techno; by the time she produced his food, he'd normally be examining the check.

He raised his fork, blinked incredulous, swiveled about to protest this misguided idea of a joke. Self-consciously he shut his mouth. For a sluggish girl, she had a gift for lightning getaways. Not to begrudge his limp salad its square inch, but the plate would contain twice as much of what he'd selected had half of it not been heaped with fries. Fries and macaroni? Really? He jounced up and swiped a menu off a stack at a condiment station. Rereading more carefully, yep, fries were included, begging the question: if someone ordered fries, would they come with a side of mac-and-cheese?

His fare, what he could swallow of it, was mediocre, but why expect higher standards to prevail in this disaster-zone's kitchen? The waitress spared them both the shuck-and-jive of asking how everything was, and sometime after he'd shoved his untouched portion to the far edge of the table, she rematerialized to chirp, "All done?" He affected sangfroid in rasping, "Check, please." He'd been here an hour already.

She pulled "the damage," which he'd calculated ages ago, from an apron pocket, and on the spot he thrust a twenty at her, bluntly requesting his change pronto as he was "running late." Did she even hear him? Arguably not, as he clocked her completion of a sixty-second task at ten minutes. But tipping in the UK wasn't bound to hard-and-fast rules, was it? He totted up her gratuity as a penny for each minute she'd been lollygagging, and pitched ten contemptuous pence onto his placemat. Then he slunk out to dodge her acid glare or the ghastlier time-waster of a squabble.

Cruising homeward, he overwhelmed self-reproach with the mantra, What an idiot he'd have been to reward rudeness and incompetence! Stiffing her did not automatically make him an upper-class twit. Still, his eyes were earthbound as he trudged by the outdoor workmen as if they'd revile the elitism writ plain on his face. Artisans indoors were making an undefinable racket in the single, claustrophobic upstairs chamber, a "finished attic" of dubious usefulness. Thank God he could beeline to the library unbeknownst to them: no gauntlet of shame when their implicit Spidey sense for outing upper-crust buggers commenced tingling.

And once he'd conceived of such a psychic faculty, it was no great leap to read into unevenly drying varnish an accusatory stain creeping up the library's wainscoting. The resentment, the condemnation of some disaffected crofter, or generations of them, was rising like damp from foundation stones saturated with their sweat, tears, poverty, failure, in solidarity with their descendants, as if they had more against Moray than cold-shouldering laborers, undertipping a server. Jesus, even if moisture were seeping in, how did that morph into the X-Files? He inhaled between clenched teeth, essentially a reverse hissing, an outward show of ousting thoughts inscrutable and therefore pointless.

Back to killing cloistered hours while hired men were about! In his bid to burn home-soil bridges from the comfort of bed, he deleted his devices' address books, speed-dial listings, emails, social media apps, excepting contacts with lawyers, brokers, accountants—and these not out of friendship. He and they were cordial, but they were basically flesh-and-blood interfaces with his assets, avatars of his portfolio. The data he dumped, moreover, had mostly languished untouched for years. This purge busied him till he had to switch on the lamp beside his mattress to see his stocking feet.

Soon the clangor overhead tapered off and three sets of feet clumped downstairs. The front door slammed. Out the square window, too small to clamber through in case of fire, three silhouettes flickered by. Right after, a fourth pair of clodhoppers thundered down. Moray's focus drifted as he rubbed away laptop-screen eyestrain. The fourth man's exit went unregistered, but must have occurred during that hiatus. Never mind; he was hungry, no surprise since he'd bailed on half his lunch. Cottage pie (and what more suitable to a cottage-dweller?) from freezer to microwave was of comparable quality and stress-free.

No creaks or bumps in the night warned he might not have the house to himself. But when he got up well rested, early enough for breakfast in his skivvies before workmen arrived, how else to explain why the fridge door was open a hand's width? White light spilled out and shone in a puddle fanning across burgundy tiles. He swatted the door shut, incensed, and then alarmed at recalling yesterday's fourth workman of the unperceived departure.

A search of the house, kebab skewer in his fidgety grip, only reaffirmed the assumption he'd been alone the last twelve hours. And bloody hell, the window of opportunity for breakfast *en déshabillé* was down to toasting bread, especially since his other morning-friendly foodstuffs were spoiled. As it was, one ear was on constant guard for wheels on driveway gravel.

Were he less devoted to sober logic, he might have entertained the nonsense of fridge meltdown as payback by ghostly residue from the bog or chimney stones for his one-percenter behavior. Or had his conscience, under the same pretext, struck him absentminded after he'd rummaged ketchup from the Hotpoint? Balderdash! Why would conscience bug him now when it hadn't, for instance, amid fracking millions out from under First Nations territory?

He managed to shave and dress before greeting the vanload of upstairs-bound artisans, and today he performed a head count. He eschewed bringing up the untowardness in the night. No profit in chipping away at his authority by furnishing excuses to debate his stability. Then off to Thurso, for the second ill-starred day in a row, to restock the larder. He patted the dashboard GPS like a favorite pet; it steered him unerringly to Tesco as if he were to the moorland born.

To his relief, the fridge had been rebounding from its mishap. Less propitiously, ahead of him in the checkout was yesterday's waitress, gabbing with the thickset cashier. Had he backed out to switch lanes, he'd have been horribly conspicuous; as it was, she acted oblivious to him. Play it cool, eyes on his cart! She was harping, to his blushing unease, about "these foreigners carrying on like they owned the place." Ulp! That was a standard complaint, though, in a tourist economy. Not necessarily a jab at him!

But hold on, he *did* own the place, or anyhow a place up the road. Plus, if he wanted to get technical, he wasn't purely a foreigner: as a Canadian, he was as much a member of the Commonwealth as any Brit. He had his rights and privileges here, if not a UK passport. By this stage in his brown study, the waitress had cleared off, and the cashier startled him into the breach by querulously urging, "Sir? Sir?" He'd have to research whether Tesco delivered.

Not a mile beyond town, a bag in the trunk capsized, as one always did, and lest he go nuts from the incessant thumping as things rolled about, he locked his attention on the scenery. Scant solace came of this, as nothing beyond the windshield was more compelling than that flapping of black plastic streamers in the barbed wire. He couldn't shake the suspicion they had it in for him, would eagerly inflict welts and lacerations, were imbued with that same animus he couldn't placate by waving around a title deed as proof he belonged.

In brooding over how to defuse Scotland's oppositional spirit, he backpedaled to "going native" in terms of his selfhood's makeover. Mightn't he feel more accepted after installing tokens of goodwill throughout the premises, tartan drapes, tweed placemats, framed photos of traditional Highland life, pipe-and-drum music for his future stereo? Mightn't flaunting these make him Scottish in better standing? An afternoon antiquing and sifting through gift-shop tat ought to do it. Worth a shot!

He stowed the replacement perishables in his blessedly good-as-new fridge, unstowed some for lunch, boomeranged back to

Thurso. Auspiciously, no further run-ins with the waitress ensued as he ransacked emporia with names like Hunky-Dory, Northern Lights, Caithness Crafts. He bought everything on his wish-list, and more: a Celtic harp for a pedestal somewhere, a sporran to hang on the parlor wall, snowglobes of Viking ships with plaid sails or clueless fishermen hooking Nessie, rugs with prints of the heath, of nouveau-style thistles, of other inhospitable landscape features.

Wending home he observed, as if scales had fallen from his eyes, numerous footpaths slanting up desolate hillsides, criss-crossing the dry hummocks of bogs. They were superimposed onto nowhere and went nowhere. Who maintained them, and why? They had an abstruse quality, rarefied by distance into seams more than trails, as if he'd penetrate layers of geology, or history, by training binoculars on them. And suppose he clambered to a given seam and hallooed into it, would the burr of some premodern Gael answer?

If any did, odds were decent, he reckoned, of that phantom's kinship to him. The basic math of genealogy professed as much, forging a profounder connection to his inner Scot than souvenir-shop kitsch could. To recap the obvious, he had two parents, four grandparents, eight great-grandparents, sixteen great-great-grandparents, et cetera, and throw uncles, cousins, and their precursors into the mix, how many generations would he have to backtrack to rack up a thousand relatives? So yeah, he was very plausibly descended from the bastard or bastards who evicted the tenants of one century or another from his modern-day croft.

His initial sympathies were reflexively with the dispossessed. Had he grown up under the conditions of yesteryear's bastards, though, he might have wound up the worst of them. He shied from reviewing many of his own sound business moves. Besides, any resonance with bygone landowners was restricted to the domain of his imagination. The crap in his trunk was for real.

He waived his backroom seclusion to spend the afternoon adorning every available wall and surface, as if strategically deployed tourist dross could radiate ethnic integrity into him. He didn't meet with grief till the sporran he'd suspended on a tack in the parlor wall plummeted with a soft thump as soon as his back was turned. He winced at the sprinkling of plaster on and around his cultural fetish, under an eye-level pockmark.

Nobody ambling through with tools or fittings had injected any comments on the decor; not their place to acknowledge it, apparently. As if he craved their approval! And he certainly didn't rate the approval of the rangy native leaning against the kitchen doorjamb, biting his lower lip. He wore a denim jacket so threadbare it looked bleached; his cheeks were like swarthy quinces, his beard like a black goat's. His broad forehead's off-putting random dimples vanished as his windburnt features crinkled into mordancy. "Ya didnae use a studfinder?"

Moray was no carpenter. Whatever this hireling referred to was no part of his experience. Hence he stared speechless, awaiting an explanation of the item in question. But the hireling, eyes downcast, only loped past him to the front door, mumbling he was "overdue for a wee dip in the bog," heaping cryptic slang atop handyman jargon. Was there an air of tension in his wake? Should Moray feel bad for failure to engage warmly with the help?

As the cottage neared completion and daily routines fell into corresponding shape, he fathomed in ever fuller scope the paradox of keeping up a hermitage by recruiting more and more people to service him. A flock of architects, builders, indoor contractors had already beaten a path to his middle-of-nowhere. To guarantee his survival, his sanity in the wilderness, would entail scads more "support personnel" on tap: postmen, deliverymen, housecleaners, muckers for the septic tank, miscellaneous suppliers and repairmen.

And thus he recouped the status, the muscle, of his putative SOB forefathers who'd ordered the clearances. Since salad days he'd taken for granted the privilege of inducing less solvent others to do his bidding, within Canadian society's benign strictures. These shows of dominance were devoid of malice and consideration alike, which in Scottish context meant diverting salt-of-the-earth folk miles from their convenient rounds to please him. He was justified in getting his way solely because he could: a rationale of the might-makes-right variety, no different from the lairds of old with their eviction notices, and what was the percentage in crocodile tears?

His acceptance of an autocrat's traditional niche conferred, oddly, no satisfaction or serenity. He could study no element of his campy decorating scheme without an upsurge of malaise, of apprehension; and in sync with his simmering unrest, or in preternatural disdain for all the patronizing kitsch, moisture and mold were brashly climbing the ground-floor walls, spreading gray fingers from the baseboards up. The guys tiling the bathroom floor, pumping insulation behind the joists upstairs, wiring the alarm system pretended blindness to the spongy walls, maybe treating them as no more their business than the ridiculous decor. He refused to believe the spoilage might be illusory.

Still, at a loss to explain his foreboding and the rising damp, he balked at pondering or mentioning them to anybody as if they were one and the subjective same. The difference between self-containment and loneliness grew more distinct whenever a workman hustled by as if Moray weren't there. He began to wish he hadn't deleted social contacts from his cellphone, the option of transatlantic perspective, anchoring him to normality. Sounding boards to help articulate his jumbled emotions, reduce them to disposable twaddle, would have been therapeutic. No matter if friendships were past their expiration dates; it was call-and-response he coveted.

Instead, his ties to humankind grew more tenuous as his morning headcounts of workmen diminished by the day. Someone, though, must have been a chronic laggard, for Moray always tallied one more departing than had entered. That fourth pair of boots pounding down the stairs, the night the fridge stayed open, leapt to mind. On no rational basis, he conflated those disconcerting boots with the extra laborer each eventide, whose attire gave Moray, but nobody else, pause. In fact, the others never interacted with him, as if he were immaterial to them, even less of a presence than Moray.

The suspected fridge-raider's wardrobe was timeless, nonspecific to any era. He was compact, small-boned, his gait forward-leaning. His straight-cut trousers' cuffs bunched around clunky boots. His vest had more the generous cut of a sleeveless jacket, and off one shoulder hung a short cape the dimensions of a plastic poncho, down which trailed a length of stocking-cap, perched raffishly above an utterly nondescript face. Nor were the garments' colors memorable, as if fabric and flesh shared an earthy monochrome. He didn't strike Moray, though, as expressly uncanny; were those muted tones only a trick of the twilight?

Meanwhile, as the company of concrete, if aloof, Scotsmen dwindled, Moray sought to refill the void in good recluse fashion. He crowded bookcases with (and diligently pored over) scholarly tomes on Scottish history and Scottishness generally, and curio cabinets with antiquities to spark museum curators' envy: monstrous claymores, chunky Pictish torcs, chainmail from a soldier of Braveheart, dazzling illuminated Gospels, Iron Age chariot hubs. Moot that he was enriching the black market, arrogating national heritage, the better to style himself an exemplary Scot, plant more committed roots. Virtue to him was the fortitude to meet any price from anybody who had what he wanted.

Exposing irreplaceable treasures to moldy, dank environs likewise triggered no twinge of conscience. And perversely, the more he collected, the more aggressively the squalor spread. Black mold was barely visible to a head-on view, but at an angle reared like stark silhouettes of Mammoth Cave stalagmites. Pastel coats of paint blistered furtively like loose cellophane over islands of caseating plaster. From Lord knew where nagged the "intrusive thought" that the creeping grunge was an earthly symptom of spiritual rats in the walls, an occult infestation enticed by, and despising, Moray's bid to buy into Highland identity.

In the court of his embattled mind, he objected to any interference with becoming whomever he chose, as if that were anybody's

affair! Worse, these rats born of past injustices had unfairly target-
ed him for the retribution due his forebears. Whatever their guilt,
and yes, he and those landowners had their parallels, he'd racked
up no misdeeds here. He was the victim of a misguided vendetta,
wasn't he, but how to seek redress from occult persecution?

To err on the naturalistic side, mildew and damp might be
typical fallout from new construction's tonnage on boggy ground,
a variation on the creaks and shudders of a house settling. Nobody had reacted to the seepage with alarm, which could mean he
shouldn't either. Then again, when the last two artisans packed up
their gear one October dusk, they offered no explicit valediction,
but the spring in their step was redolent of good riddance to this
chapter in their careers, and the hindmost of them turned on the
doorstep to begrudge Moray a dour "good luck!"

Behind them lingered the implication Moray should hang onto every scrap of luck for dear life: because he was on his own out
here, or because of escalating water damage or less mundane har-
bingers? Before he could solicit clarification at the doorway, the
breath stuck in his throat. Two men had gone out, but three had
their retreating backs to him. The foremost pair plodded side by
side to their van. The third, whom the others paid no mind,
swerved onto the heath.

Moray was unheedful of vehicle doors slamming, engine turning over, wheels on gravel, any pro forma farewells, as he tailed
the dim outline in the gloaming. And no need for major caution,
as the figure never looked aside or backward. None of its face
showed, but its short, flapping cape and the swing of its stocking-
cap were telltales enough of the trespasser who'd violated his
fridge. Moray desisted once the ground squished up around his
trainers, and squinted after the entity whose pace hadn't slack-
ened at all, who was already fading into the murk.

If the idea was to lure Moray into the morass, this virtual will-
o'-the-wisp was going about it with supreme indifference, as if unaware of being shadowed. A mere mortal who'd really learned the
terrain, Moray supposed, could blaze a trustworthy path through

it, navigate with impunity in the dark. Scarier to him was the trail's apparent terminus, the vague white mass of the abandoned camper, as he beheld on raising his sights a little. He couldn't verify whether its presumptive occupant had gone the distance, didn't discern white door swinging open. Chalk it up to nearsightedness or advancing nightfall, the caped invader altogether dropped from view.

The incredible suspicion abided, though, of someone squatting in a partly flooded, inexorably sinking RV. This mad or fugitive vagrant, judging by his familiarity with the land, had been on site months or years before Moray. More unnerving yet, Moray's homestead had furnished the squatter a kitchen to pilfer, and with the day-labor out of the picture, how much more brazenly might he exploit domestic resources? Who was Moray to rule out face-to-face confrontations or worse? Thank God for state-of-the-art security system!

More pressing issues recalled him from the realm of morbid speculation. He was shivering in the frosty gloom, his cheeks stung, his fleece pullover was no match for the serrated wind, and his clammy toes were uncomfortably numb. It behooved him to scamper back to the warm refuge of his own making, mold and moisture notwithstanding. In the vestibule, though, definitely punch in the code, safety first!

He'd begun spending nights in his actual snug bedroom, betwixt library and bath. And tomorrow he'd greet the dawn without construction racket impending, hurray! On Swedish memory foam custom-fitted to his spindly Elizabethan four-poster, he slept as soundly as ever he did, waking periodically, listening in vain for any noise of intrusion, dozing off again. On top of which, nothing tripped the alarm for the duration.

Therefore, come morning, he could only gawk incredulous at the testimony of his eyes, an experience fraught with the shock of the new: he'd never felt compelled before to distrust his senses. But impossibly, without letting slip a decibel, without cannonballing his shallow sleep, every square inch of glass in every bookcase, cabinet, and cupboard had sundered into myriad fractions, casting glittery sunbursts over expanses of floorboard or carpet. Stare, blink, shake the cobwebs from his brain till doomsday, the impossible refused to budge.

Rather than dwell on intractable wherefores, he fast-forwarded to the follow-up requisite in any event. The house-cleaning agency with the snazziest ad online ought to have somebody manning the phone by now, insofar as the sun was up. And indeed, a chipper dispatcher would see to it ASAP, with directions to the cottage already on tap, maybe via hinterland grapevine. Moray hung up beaming, gratified by money's power anywhere to iron out difficulties, press people into pretty much anything.

An hour later, his complacent smile wavered at the advent of one subcompact junker with a punctured muffler, teetered on collapse as the car disgorged a solitary chubby girl, and capsized into the abyss when his myopic gaze identified the dotard waitress. She must have gotten the boot from that trattoria and rebranded herself a charwoman. He bit his lower lip as she slouched in, but none of the anticipated snark or peevishness flared up. Mercifully, she must have forgotten or never really noticed his face. Or was she faking insouciance out of pacifist or less benign motives?

Regardless, he saw to it their eyes never met while he escorted her around the offending floorscapes. She was there solely to expunge the pulverized glass, but be absolutely thorough about it! She nodded in stolid resignation, as best he could infer, and he breathed much easier after leaving her to it and escaping outdoors. As he moseyed on autopilot, the clatter of the ex-waitress lugging dry-vac, supplies, tools of the trade from the car impinged faintly as from far away, surely didn't merit turning around to watch.

Padding gingerly into the wetlands (where else was there?), he homed in on the damned RV, the single swatch of contrast in the drabness. Two opposing notions vied to occupy the same head-space simultaneously, as if some psychic broadcaster in the RV were messing with his wavelength. First off, though he'd always acted as if nobody was as real as himself, the unreal tableau of a bog-bound camper extended this solipsism from everybody to everything. The mired RV, the proper stuff of mirage, persuaded him that the world of anything so barmy could exert no power over him; nor could anything he did in, or to, that world matter.

His brain also hosted a proposition that the past was the one reality, or at least the only one to which benighted humans had access. Archaeology, paleontology, geology were at heart flawed lenses, grubby windows onto an actuality hiding in plain sight. Strictly speaking, the senses reported nothing save the past. They enabled people to function in the so-called present, but light and sound traveled at finite speeds, well short of instantaneous, a truth emblazoned across every night sky. The starry yonder of the here and now travels millennia from its points of origin, is a mélange of long-dead epochs. And that camper was a spyhole in its own right into bygone circumstances, hopelessly cryptic in the absence of context.

Moray could credit that the past was verily ensconced inside, like the contents of a time capsule—or personified as the tenebrous "extra man"? Going by motley attire alone, the RV's putative squatter wasn't a personage as much as a composite of downtrodden generations, deathless victimhood personified. Shamefaced, Moray yanked the reins on his galloping reverie. How could he, in the name of self-respect, stoop to such sophomoric guff? He had also, to his chagrin, rambled into the mire a clothesline's length from the camper. Don't panic! The ground must have been less treacherous than he'd surmised.

Amidst gathering the nerve to retrace his inexplicit route, he weathered shock as a flurry of hammering rattled the vehicle. Were the embellishments of keening and grunts coming from his own throat or the shuddering camper, out of whose windowsills and doorframe water was briskly leaking, as if under pressure? Realistically, no one could be inside and desperate for rescue from implausibly rising waters; hence there was nothing to do here. Yet the curtained, dirt-encrusted glass in door and window thwarted him from checking for sure, and as he about-faced and bolted, his upstart conscience ineffectively harried him for criminal negligence.

He was muddy and sopping by the time he scrambled up the gradient to his driveway. The outbound path he'd unconsciously threaded high-and-dry had evaded his powers of observation. He repeatedly tripped over stones, blundered into potholes, misjudged the solidity of hummocks. Lucky thing he hadn't belly-flopped into quicksand! Indoors again, he kicked off his trainers, stormed into the bedroom to strip and towel off. Now that danger was behind him, anger flared up: at the RV for beckoning him astray, at the imbecile who'd parked it there, at himself for sleep-walking into and blundering out of a morass.

On donning terrycloth robe and slippers, he surveyed the sparkling carpet around him, and his rancor mounted to encompass the loutish girl still on the premises. A miracle he hadn't laid down a trail of blood! Glass from the chiffonier for tartan ribbons, tams, ghillies, other vintage garb glittered impudently, inches from his feet; it was halfway hoovered up at best. Her piss-poor work ethic was equally tangible in crunching glints underfoot straight through to the kitchen, where she was packing her gear and helping herself to a bag of crisps and a can of lager on the granite countertop.

She was indubitably real as a feckless moocher of his pantry. Otherwise his epiphany at the RV about the unreality of everybody else, the inconsequentiality of how he treated them, accorded him carte blanche in venting at her, "What did I tell you? Are you suggesting you've faithfully discharged your very explicit instructions?"

She bent but didn't break under his bellowing, raising her eyes not quite to the level of his, daring a minuscule shrug and sad-sack pout. She also didn't, to Moray's mushrooming ire, unpack as much as a Swiffer. "You believe this is good enough? Fine! Get on your knees and rub your bare hands around the mat by the sink. Since you're all done, it must be spic-and-span and you won't bleed any. Go on!" Christ almighty, now he understood why her ex-boss had felt compelled to chew her out. He also understood how addictive the rush of bullying inferiors must have been for his forefathers.

"I got another place to be at," she mumbled with the feeblest soupçon of insubordination. She shuffled backward with her double armload, the vacuum-cleaner hose dragging afore her like a limp tail. He hungered to clout her one, push her down face-first, make her bloody herself, but the voltage of his outrage anchored him to the spot till her bungling exodus, prolonged by dropping and retrieving things, cut off the current. She shambled to her junker without shutting his door. Mobility restored, Moray strode over, slammed it, then wished he hadn't when it dawned on him to yell after her, "Lazy millennial brat!"

He phoned the service and gave them a piece of his mind before she could whine her self-serving side of the story. The balance of this first degraded day at home alone, he slogged away coaxing shiny particles out of carpet pile and floorboard seams, wielding damp paper towels, shoeshine brushes, other improvisations. During every breather, he lapsed into gaping at the contents of glassless cabinets, slackly disappointed that they excited nothing inside, no tribal pride or warmth of belonging. They were like body parts stitched willy-nilly to him, and he rejected them like botched allograft tissue. Or were they rejecting him?

Hell, something had made the glass explode, some natural cause, obviously, unless he weren't fantasizing sub rosa malice in the gleams of primitive farm tools and weaponry. And the row of snowglobes in the parlor—did lamplight lend them a semblance of baleful spider eyes? Even the harp, on provisional display sideways on a bookshelf, projected a menacing sheen, as if strung with garrote wires. His every collectible couldn't be haunted, that would be crazy, but was he exhibiting the symptoms of a budding animist?

Small comfort there! Just for stiffing a waitress, wherein he was perfectly justified, the water table itself (speaking animistically) had welled up in righteous indignation and moisturized his walls. Therefore, after verbally, almost physically, abusing her, he should have been awash in an indoor riptide. But he wasn't, because animism was a crock on a par with spooks, to belabor the self-evident. Too much time unmoored from normal social patterns was breeding opportunistic figments, like monsters in that Goya drawing. What next he had to do in modeling the "new him" was get a better grip on himself, blinker and bridle his free-ranging imagination.

Till dinner he reviewed his portfolio online, a nuts-and-bolts distraction from the less workable reality of walls that sweated mold. The ex-waitress was harder to shoo from his antsy attention. Like hell was he contrite, given her carelessness: by sheer luck his bare feet didn't look as if they'd been rubbed against a grater. Let delinquency slide, these kids would never learn; the ship of polite society would sink like a sieve. What was there to argue?

Insofar as she had a point of view, was the onus on him to second-guess she had a learning disability or psychological scars? In which case, her employers shouldn't have tossed her into the labor pool without attaching a caveat about cutting her some slack. If "blood will out," as the proverb went, she was hands-down a daughter of the soil, progeny of the dispossessed who hadn't the gumption or ingenuity to vacate. Genes and genealogy being what they were, however, maybe she'd come of lordly bloodlines, and he of paupers fleeing debtors' prison—not that either scenario imparted absolution for her shortcomings.

Lulled into tranquility by market values and net changes, he narrowed his view to exclude mildew-streaked paint, and heated up canned haggis for supper. Now there was cuisine to rile the ghosts of any Scottish purists, but none, he smugly noted, dashed his plate off the kitchen table. Moray afterward cleaned up in the sink, as he'd dirtied too little to run the dishwasher, and he was Scotsman enough to hate wastefulness. A jarring, reverberant banging erupted to accompany the faucet, doubtless attributable to the pipes under the sink. Christ, did plumbing have to join the list of domestic headaches?

He finished up, but the din didn't relent. Nor did it originate in the kitchen. If noisy plumbing were the problem, those pipes ran bafflingly behind that parlor wall where he'd failed to nail up a sporran. The pockmark hadn't gone anywhere, and the pounding hearkened remarkably, in pitch and tempo, to that from the RV. Coincidence to be sure, an accident of acoustics, and he could prove it by putting an eye up to the peephole, expecting thus to diagnose the problem.

He didn't freak out at the eye gawking back at him: admirable sangfroid, if he did say so! Reason dictated the wall contained no pockets wherein anyone could lurk. And on the extreme off-chance of a workman getting immured during construction, he'd hardly have waited till today to bang out an SOS. Moray had to be staring down a distorted reflection that jerked up and down at each hammer beat, like a rearview mirror undergoing fitful adjustment.

That was it: he was ogling a shard of mirror, maybe a segment of the unquiet drainpipe. And it was unforgivably squalid for something so newly installed, tainting the flesh around the eye a dingy gray, the eye itself a dull, rheumy dun. Moray shrank from the unflattering peepshow in disgust. His could have been the eyes, the skin, of the weirdly attired worker who'd beaten a path toward the sinking camper, who may have been locked inside when it flooded. Tomorrow he'd get to the bottom of the reflecting surface in the wall. For tonight, best to derail trains of thought that led to guys drowning in RVs or immured in the parlor.

And no sooner had his mind ceased to dwell on it than the cacophony let up. The moral: focus wisely! In a capacious leather armchair, with the pockmark at arm's length but mentally a world away, he curled up and cracked a weighty tome on tartans. Best-faith efforts to concentrate fell woefully short. Five soporific pages elapsed, he nodded off, and nobody heard the thump as his book slid to the carpet.

Naps before bedtime often conduced to dreaming, and canned haggis may have guaranteed a nightmarish upshot. And in spite, or rather because, of the depravity his dream-self was perpetrating, Moray was exultant, in nowise critical of his own sadism. The cradle over which he loomed was seemingly plunked down in his cottage, except the floor was earthen, strewn with hay, the walls were black with peat smoke, and the drafty chill was redolent of barnyard animals. In the cradle, the ex-waitress was manifest as both biologically adult and larval, helpless on her humpback, naked upon second glance, puffy skin a bloodless white.

To his initial surprise, it was he cackling as he poured an apparently bottomless ewer of ground glass over the girl, powerless to escape or defend herself, churning arms and legs in the air like a tortoise, a beetle. More comical still, her skin was sticky, and the glass, adhering like sugar, pierced it to inflict countless bleeding nicks. The larval girl was, understandably, bawling at a despicable, earsplitting volume. Fine and dandy, this was exactly what the dumbass slob deserved!

Professing such ugly sentiments produced a unique calm of self-awareness, of reconciliation with the swine he frankly was, an acceptance of his demons minus any urge to curb them. He could close the book on remolding his selfhood, for he finally realized, six-plus decades along, that who he'd always been was A-OK. Then that same din from behind the pockmark, from inside the RV, resounded more harshly than ever, emanating now from the dust-encrusted windowpane overlooking the cradle.

The monochrome man with the stocking cap was tapping like crazy, though the opaque glass made IDing him an educated guess. Apparently he was out to catch Moray's eye, nothing more, subjecting him to a look both judgmental and manic. In that look, though, was a gravitas well suited to passing sentence. The bawling hadn't abated, and had the larval squirming created the momentum to rock the cradle? Oh, if only! The cradle was afloat and rolling gently in turbid, swirling water above his knees, to which he'd been insensible because its iciness had summarily numbed his legs.

One rap too many shattered the glass at last, in which instant his panic snapped him out of dreamland. But what the fuck? Frigid, mucky bog water really was lapping at his groin, and where the cradle had floated relative to his dream-self, the book on tartans was bobbing around. He screeched and lunged out of the chair he'd settled into contentedly, and went from bad to direly worse. Nestling so long had put pins and needles in total charge of his legs. They were responsive as logs; swimming for it wasn't an option. Before the glacial eddying dragged him under, he glimpsed the walls crumbling like soggy cake, which should have dispersed the rising tide but didn't.

Days later, the exasperated propane dealer came around because Moray was blowing off phone messages and invoices; the house had devolved a good deal already toward its wonted condition as two endwalls and a foundation harboring weeds and rubble. Moray had fetched up between collapsed frontage and mud-spattered BMW; his indeterminate tenure in freak floodwater had pickled his hide, bleached him and his clothing to a drabness amounting to no nameable color.

Moray's tannic-smelling corpse was remanded to his nonplussed Canadian lawyer, with terse, equivocal paperwork from the coroner on cause of death. Hardscrabble scavengers accelerated the cottage's dissolution by stripping copper pipes, masonry, fixtures. Antique treasures and kitsch alike had been claimed by whatever esoteric agency had fomented the destruction, or at any rate were never seen again. The exception would have been a snowglobe of a Viking ship that a shepherd's foot accidentally poked from muck around a spring, a mile downslope from Moray's, but too far removed in time and space for any connection with him.

The house pit was good for inducing malaise in legend-trippers, and to all intents became ownerless again, resuming its traditional role as sad footnote to the clearances. Glib rumor had it that the site was haunted by the ghost of an "American millionaire," but no anecdotes about supernatural activities or specific Yanks fleshed out this bog-standard lore. The past had swallowed Moray with a vengeance, but hadn't the same appetite for the camper, which never subsided below fuel-cap level and whose unwelcoming windows kept gloomy vigil on the ruin.

Lead On, Vergil

This guidebook has been refined and updated numerous times since its long-ago first edition. Its present version should serve the excursionist for many years to come, in particular its foreign audience, among whom Americans and Australians must figure prominently in light of their "homing instinct" for the "mother country."

In deference to the primary author of these walking tours, Vergil Thorncroft, we begin our series of scenic strolls in his birthplace of Dudwich, quoting from his original text (except for each attraction's parenthesized hours of operation). Dudwich was an important center of the wool trade during the Middle Ages and a haven for Flemish refugees from religious persecution.

After you have wrapped up any pressing business, as this will be an exceptionally absorbing ramble, begin in front of the Guildhall (open Monday–Wednesday 10 A.M.–3 P.M., Thursday, Friday, and Sunday 11 A.M.–1 P.M., 2:30–4 P.M., closed Saturdays), one of the best-preserved such buildings in the British Isles, dominating the Market Square and its abundance of quaint storefronts beneath overhanging half-timbered upper storeys. The hall boasts excellent linenfold oak paneling and a fifteenth-century hammerbeam roof, and formerly housed the county's English-Speaking Union. Nowadays it is a museum where the visitor will find interesting prehistoric, Roman, Saxon, and medieval artifacts.

Proceed from the Guildhall to the left and follow Mote Street, turning right on Muster Street. You will be tempted there by various antique and curio shops behind Georgian façades, though too much lies ahead to tarry yet.

~~~~~

Wow, this guidebook is strong on technical terms, but they've "refined and updated" any feel for actually "being there" clean out of it. It's as if I've been tricked into halfway writing the book myself, trying to reanimate freeze-dried language, filling in the blanks with my own gut reactions. And what the hell is linenfold paneling? A hammerbeam roof? A glossary would help, since I haven't a clue what I'm supposed to be gawking at, unless the book dismisses me as an ignorant cluck for not knowing these things already.

Still, the book came with the room, or anyway, it was in the nightstand drawer, like some Bizarro excuse for a Gideon Bible. Might as well make the best of it; in for a penny, right?

~~~~~

Turn left onto Epsom Lane and after the splendid Regency-era terraced housing, built out of the renowned local brownish-yellow sandstone, you will be impressed by the majestic Perpendicular-style parish church of St. Fremund, looming suddenly beyond the townhouses. The Earl de Grisaille and his soldiers were said to pray here before embarking for Agincourt. You will admire the linenfold rood screen and the breathtakingly restored hammer-beam ceiling. The Earl donated the spectacular stained glass, the most sumptuous for a church of its size in Northern Europe, after the victory at Agincourt. The baptismal font, which may predate the Norman Conquest, is entrancing.

~~~~~

Methinks this Thorncroft presumes too much. Cocksure of him, taking for granted I'll be tempted or impressed by anything on his dubious authority. Did it never dawn on him he might rub people the wrong way, dictating their emotional responses, minus any fun particulars to justify those feelings? Who was the Earl de Grisaille anyway? What makes this church more Perpendicular than another? But contrary to better judgment, I can barely tear myself away from this beat-up stone punchbowl, which must constitute the "font."

~~~~~

From St. Fremund's, retrace your steps as far as Fleece Alley and go left. You will be charmed by the black-and-white Elizabethan residences with their overhanging upper storeys; this street is scarcely the width of a car. It curves to the right, and soon you catch glimpses of the Millpond between extensive fragments of the ancient Roman wall. We will return to the pond later.

For now, continue until the street ends at Abbey Green. Linger a minute in the shade of the venerable cedars of Lebanon, where you can contemplate the ruins of the Greyfriars abbey from the thirteenth century, of which only the fifteenth-century Perpendicular apse escaped the destruction wrought by Henry VIII. Finish crossing the green, and stroll right alongside the lush herbaceous border, exiting through the substantial Drovers' Gate, constructed by the Normans atop foundations of fourth-century Roman defenses.

Beyond the gate you enter upon Drovers' Road, and on the left you will observe the Tudor-era Hank and Shears alehouse, where Oliver Cromwell and his troops reportedly enjoyed refreshment. If you're hungry, stop in here for a snack lunch (daytime hours, 10 A.M.–1:30 P.M. Monday, Wednesday, and Thursday, 11 A.M.–2 P.M. Tuesday, Friday, and Saturday, Noon to 3 P.M. Sunday).

~~~~~

Finally a sympathetic idea from Thorncroft, and thanks very much for permission to eat! A "snack lunch" doesn't sound especially filling, though, and I observe the book didn't include permission to order a pint. In fact, when the barman inquires what I'll have, the cat's got my tongue till he loses interest and waddles off, not that the beer taps are at all confusing or complicated.

Eventually I flag him down and order a Scotch egg with chips, the most intriguing choice on the menu board. A glossary of exotic foodstuffs in the book would be a further courtesy. When my plate arrives I'm little the wiser about what's in front of me, and I taste precious little of it because I've abruptly developed a compulsion to gorge at full tilt.

The barman eyeballs Thorncroft beside my plate and buttons his smallish lips as if it's not his place to say anything. Okay, fine, but the book's shortcomings are obvious, so don't pretend you're suppressing a news flash. All the same, his behavior's a bit off-putting, so away we go.

~~~~~

As you leave the pub, head left on Drovers' Road. You will pass quaint sixteenth-century Flemish weavers' cottages, converted to almshouses during the reign of Queen Anne. No great distance beyond these, as you approach the outskirts of town, you will admire, on your right, the tastefully proportioned brownish-yellow sandstone manor house, one of Sir Christopher Wren's lesser-known gems. After belonging to many generations of the de Grisaille family, it was sold to a London businessman in the 1930s. It is not open to the public, but if the present owner is out front, he may agree to show you his fascinating collection of memorial brasses.

In any case, once you have paid your respects to the manor, the tranquillity of a tree-lined country lane as you stroll Drovers' Road will enchant you, until you stop next at Palmers' Chapel, an outlying relic of the former de Grisaille estate, now a property of the National Trust and temporary meetinghouse for the English-Speaking Union (open Tuesday–Friday 10 A.M.–5 P.M., Saturday–Sunday Noon–5 P.M., closed Mondays). Be sure to inspect the Crusades-era misericord seat and the unique linenfold cope chest.

Upon bidding the Chapel a fond adieu, continue a further hundred feet on Drovers' Road and turn right onto Old Tannery Way. You are on course again to the center of town. Have you dreamt of remaining in Dudwich indefinitely?

~~~~~

Au contraire, I'm sorely tempted to remain on Drovers' Road and take my chances on the next town, but my baggage languishes in Dudwich, so there I must repair. And far as I know, the next town bears the onus of an equally exasperating tour in the book. All these über-quaint English villages are really sinister labyrinths at heart, aren't they? But that's been the lesson of every other Masterpiece Mystery episode since forever; the English don't trust their idyllic little burgs one bit themselves, do they? What did I ever do to Vergil Thorncroft?

~~~~~

As you come to Dancaster Bridge, a twelfth-century specimen of sturdy Norman design over the River Dan, gaze on your reflection in the invitingly serene waters, which arise from a limestone cave fifty yards to your right. The bridge derives its name from marauding Danes who camped nearby one winter.

On the other side, Old Tannery Way becomes more thickly settled. Your eye will be drawn to the Abbey Chapterhouse while you are still some minutes away. By dint of its striking Perpendicular architecture, Henry VIII confiscated it for royal functions and feasts, sparing it the dismal fate meted out to the rest of the Abbey. Earlier, it had been commandeered as a staging area for archers en route to Agincourt, and was subsequently a garrison for Cromwell. It is open to the public (same hours as the Guildhall). Do not fail to appreciate the masterful linenfold altar and the stunning quantity of Renaissance brasses, widely praised as the most diverse assortment in Western Europe.

At the intersection after the Chapterhouse, go right on Bellwether Street, where you are immediately greeted by the black-and-white Tudor façade of the town's oldest inn, the Hook and Haunch. Why not stroll in for a half pint of bitter, in surroundings largely unaltered since Dickens supped here?

~~~~~

Half a pint? Only half a pint? Was Thorncroft some kind of temperance Nazi? And for one of these authentically quaint joints, it's chilly as a morgue, as if the AC is working overtime to keep the ambience from spoiling, or the limestone cave that feeds the river is directly under the floorboards.

Actually, just as well I ordered a half, despite every intention of imbibing more. The beer isn't reviving me; it's making me colder, and the moonfaced, crater-skinned barman isn't helping with that tic making the bags below one eye flutter on noticing the book in my hand. Maybe it marks me as a tourist and they simply don't cotton to tourists here. I don't see much else on which to base an economy. No matter, I've had enough of the Hook and Haunch, half a pint was plenty at that. Lead on, Vergil!

~~~~~

No sooner have you penetrated a neighbourhood of overhanging black-and-white upper storeys, where Bellwether Street narrows to the width of a single car, than you are delighted to renew your acquaintance with the spacious Abbey Green. Its magnificent cedars of Lebanon were planted as saplings during the Regency. Forging a path through them, turn left along the lovely herbaceous border. You are momentarily awestruck as the grandeur that is the cathedral of St. Blitha-sur-Lees dwarfs all else.

~~~~~

Just what the hell is an herbaceous border? He's harped on this before, and damned if anything lush or lovely graces this landscape. Does he mean that straggle of weeds aspiring to imitate a hedge? Weeks of scruffy curbside growth the lawnmower couldn't get at? Table that line of questioning, I'm on the guidebook's virtual conveyer belt into yet another bloody church.

~~~~~

Though Dudwich has not been the seat of a bishopric since the early sixteenth century, its glorious Perpendicular cathedral comprises the loftiest example of its style in the English-speaking world. The sublime hammerbeam roof, the exquisite linenfold chancel, the Gothic piers chock-a-block with gleaming brasses to honor the fallen at Agincourt are revered by cognoscenti the world over. But all these are practically upstaged by the opulence of stained glass, a gift of Henry V, and consisting of some ten thousand leaded pieces.

Our humble town is rightly proud of its cathedral, the transcendent jewel in its diadem of acclaimed antiquities. You should savour your proximity to this miraculous annex of heaven on earth, for when will you ever experience the like again? And what an ideal place to say a prayer for your benighted soul.

When you are done here, turn left outside and follow your first right down Mercator Way. Browse a minute in one of the antique and curio shops occupying the refurbished seminary, another lesser-known triumph of Sir Christopher Wren. Gilchrist's is popularly regarded as the most comprehensive and trustworthy emporium.

~~~~~

Hey, Gilchrist's is right here. Couldn't hurt to take a breather from the marathon, pick up a couple of souvenirs for Mom and the girlfriend. Jesus, what a ton of bric-a-brac, I can hardly see straight. Now here's something, a shelf of brass candle snuffers shaped like heads of birds, monks, cats, devils with comically gaping mouths. They're portable, whimsical, and if luck is with me, cheap tokens of affection. I grab a half dozen at random—they're all fabulous enough—and saunter up to the putative Mr. Gilchrist behind the cashbox. Fingers crossed, I start to ask how much they cost, since none of them have price tags.

Wait, why am I shuffling backward midsentence, how literally must I read the book's instruction to browse a minute? Time's up, is it? When will the book give me permission to panic? Mr. Gilchrist, or whoever it is, watches me in resigned silence, or rather, homes in on the book under my arm as if he's lost business this way before, and nothing to be done for it. I, in the event, feel sorry for him. "I'll try to swing by later!" I lie, as the bell in the path of the opening door jingles. Am I tossing false hope to him or myself?

~~~~~

At the end of Mercator, you will observe the rear wall of the imposing Guildhall, and turning left, you follow the downhill curve of Bourneway, which approximates the outline of the Roman wall around the town's original nucleus. You catch your first whiff of the River Dan as you admire the lovingly restored black-and-white Tudor houses with upper storeys overhanging both sides of the street, which is scarcely wider than a car.

At the bottom of Bourneway, the glinting of the stream, beckoning through the cedars of Lebanon in the riverside park, captures your attention. The Dan broadens into the Millpond here, which used to serve the thirteenth-century mill of brownish-yellow masonry. The mill has been beautifully reconstructed and is open to the public (same hours as Palmers' Chapel), but is not on your schedule.

Exercise care stepping over the herbaceous border above the water's edge so as not to damage any of this botanical treasure trove. Now cast me away, onto the lawn behind you, for someone else to find, and jump in the lake. You will sink like an anvil, you incurable philistine.

~~~~~

My God, at least let me trample the damned herbaceous border! I so badly want to, but not even that is conceded to me. Whoa there, I love Dudwich, love it, I tell you! Nope, that avails me nothing. "Shit!" I succeed in yelling, no ban on that, and though I'm obviously in earshot, none of the park's several pensioners or moms with prams pay me the slightest mind, no tut-tutting at my profanity, no nothing, as I leap headfirst into the silty, stagnant-tasting drink.

The Muybridge Cocktail

The golden age was never the present one." Thus read the old-timey sampler, courtesy of departmental 3D printer, hiding the sherry stain on his office wall. Intervening years had expunged beyond recall his reason for flinging the snifter. Hundreds of possibilities! Listing the savants credited with that adage, though? Nothing easier: seventeenth-century historian Thomas Fuller, eighteenth-century statesman Ben Franklin, twenty-first-century pop-icon Martin Newell. Newell, in turn, had paraphrased it as Aristotle's—quite the centuried run, and never truer.

Listergil would defy those bygone sages to disprove his age the worst: Florida reduced to a stick figure of its former breadth via polar meltdown; superpowers waging wars over aquifers; upkeep of roads, bridges, infrastructure in general down to a defunded joke. No wonder he'd cleaved to academe, to archaeology, to the subfield of archaeochemistry as firewalls against distressing head-lines.

But shitty as the world had become, some few constants from halcyon yesteryears lingered, e.g., the caves with the most cele-brated Ice Age art continued owing their discovery to backcountry youth tumbling headlong into them. And even the woodsiest tykes nowadays went nowhere without their technology, so once some Cantabrian girl had put her foot through mini-sinkhole, slid under, and dusted off her providentially unharmed self, she shone her phone around. It chanced upon engravings of owls beside the mouth of a posterior chamber, and she exclaimed, as the Twitter-verse listened, "Dos pájaros!"

Just like that, she'd irrevocably christened the cave. Newsfeeds sowed her texts and photos across the globe, such that the moni-

ker "Two Birds" was good as etched in stone hours before kinfolk
and neighbors extricated her. She might well have considered the
kids who'd stumbled onto Altamira and Lascaux as primitive as
Cro-Magnons, yet wasn't she a link in the chain of their tradition?

Listergil's department won the contract to send the geofizz
team and drones over to Spain. The owls, disarming as they were,
weren't the big deal, compared with the frolicsome horses and bison of the chamber they guarded. These were masterful, vibrant,
and, above all, pristine: no mortal eye or corrosive breath had as-
sailed them for 15,000 years at least. And to preserve their lustre,
they'd undergo documentation almost exclusively via the instru-
ments and lenses of saucer-sized drones.

He respected that, really he did, but video of the chamber
floor excited him into invoking "tenured clearance" before the
crew arrived. Few comps beyond privileged access at sensitive
sites accrued to top academic rungs, and who would never make
the best of it, given chintzy university salaries? His would be the
sole CO_2 to impact, albeit minimally, the mystically vivid pigments, for the sake of assaying a green-stained steatite bowl.

That residue could be of an offering to wildlife gods, or of a
limner's lunch, or of immense value in proving a pet theory that
involved shamanism, precocious artistry, and drugs. The bowl was
exactly where it ought to be if he were on the right track, if he
were to make a golden age for himself. In his thirties he'd dated
an assistant prof in Art History till her gushing love for eighteenth-century Wedgwood drove him bananas. She did, however,
impart a life-changing factoid about the perceptual accuracy of
troglodytes.

On French and Spanish cave walls, charging buffalo, galloping
stallions were portrayed with all four hooves airborne, scrunched
up together beneath the belly. This correct record of locomotion,
common knowledge in the Paleolithic, went by the boards post-
glacially; ten millennia of pictorial falsehood were only rectified in
A.D. 1878 by Eadweard Muybridge's camerawork. More tellingly,
unaided human vision was never up to detailed observation of

speeding beasts, could hardly have gotten it right without stop-motion photography, hence begging the question of how "primitive man" pulled it off.

And Listergil wagered he had the answer. Shaman-centric communities, on their UNESCO reservations, had changed little since their first late-medieval descriptions, and shamanistic practices everywhere had underlying similarities. Therefore the herb-and-fungus pharmacopeia enriching magicianly bags-of-tricks now was probably also *de rigueur* way back when. In which case, Cro-Magnon vision may not have been unaided, and perfectly serviceable speculation had it that shamans and muralists had been one and the same. How else to study animals in motion than by slowing down time, and how to do that except with a mind-altering formula?

As for why shamans' art had to capture true-to-life motion? Maybe that demonstrated their thoroughgoing control over the animal kingdom, or the potency of luck they disbursed to tribal hunters. Listergil didn't care. More compelling was the inference that the formula was a jealously guarded trade secret, its ingestion strictly limited to the shaman class. Can't have just anyone monkeying with time, subverting the social hierarchy, undercutting shamanic crowd control!

When a shaman went on duty, then, he'd take the drug, observe the herds, retire to his subterranean sanctum and apply pigments, with or without an audience. The bowl and its leftover dosage had to stay in his sight, lest the curious laity sample any untended contents. Whether the shaman at Dos Pájaros had forsaken the bowl due to absentmindedness, someone's medical emergency, or enemy onslaught, it had been an object at rest from the Upper Pleistocene till whenever Listergil's white-gloved hands accosted it.

The inalienable good news: botanical species in shamanic brew may have gone extinct, but the molecules comprising them certainly hadn't. He shrugged off his lab-in-a-backpack, everything he needed to analyze and synthesize archaic dregs, and paused with key in hand before the bombproof hatchway, a largely symbolic component of official defenses against nighthawks. He about-faced to savor a vista unspoilt by human endeavor, perhaps recognizable to Ice Age eyes. The crinkled heights were forested, while lower slopes were yellow and brown with parched August grass, and at several elevations, sheer limestone outcrops beetled like layers of cake stripped of frosting.

Quite the drowsy place for a tumultuous breakthrough, since today's covert R&D would assuredly trigger a seismic paradigm shift. Whether science, industry, or the intelligence community (if any useful distinction separated them) were the beneficiaries, theirs would be a modality for data collection, forensics, security ops calibrated to nanoseconds, completely independent of satellites, microchips, any technology. Play intrepidly close to the vest, he'd soon be in position to swan-dive off the academic stepladder into an Olympic pool of wealth.

But first he had an hour's work cut out for him. Don infrared goggles, spring the hatch, lock it behind him, clamber down the polymer companionway, activate his black-market blockbox to fool detectors into signaling no ambient changes. He broke out the carbon-neutral lantern and repacked the goggles, submitted to onerous latex gloves and filter mask (to safeguard shamanic elixir as much as cave art), and in the stark white light met the stern appraisal of the life-size sentinel owls.

Chances are, they were at eye-level for the pre-teen who'd announced them to the world. For him it was disorienting to peer down at images meant to intimidate, flanking a turnstile-high triangular aperture like parted curtains of limestone. The birds were delineated as vigorous strokes, as if slashed into the rock, and to further their grotesquerie, their folded wings were toward the onlooker, their ogling heads twisted round in unique owlish fashion. A crick in the neck for eternity: rather a mean-spirited depiction!

Clasping rucksack to his chest, with lamp dangling off one wrist, he salaamed into the inner sanctum, where wonderment overcame him, despite his hardnosed purpose. Bison, horses, stags, aurochs on the rugose walls were stampeding straight at him, as if spooked by the lamplight. Their incendiary ochre, yellow, black were stunning enough in themselves, and he couldn't begin to guess the effect of this bestiary on hunter-gatherers for whom hocus-pocus by torchlight tilted the fickle balance away from starvation, who sought desperate intimacy down here with their gods and cosmos.

Another scholar might have marveled most at the miraculous accuracy of four hooves in midair; for him that was a prod to deal with the momentous business in the soapstone bowl. Handheld lidar blazed him a path that inflicted no telltale bootprints or harm to subsoil artifacts. He knelt at the bowl like a pilgrim before splinters of the True Cross. Scraping at the thickest-looking residue with a penknife, while gingerly steadying the bowl *in situ,* constituted the whole of his protocol that would have borne any semblance to his granddad's archaeology. Afterward, the suction tube slurped up a decigram or two of powder he subjected to a gauntlet of compact devices.

In paltry minutes, the powder's components were IDed: he transferred phials from analytical to synthesizing gizmos, and his giddiness mounted. Whatever liquid filled the final 25-cl test-tube, and yeah, it wasn't necessarily his "Muybridge cocktail," never did the recipe stump the machinery, nor did lethal toxicity ever trigger digital klaxons. Impatience vied with a compunction to honor this sea-change moment with pensive contemplation. He begrudged decorum a few antsy seconds, then yanked off the filter mask, swigged 10 centiliters. What bitter, slimy swill! He capped and pocketed the phial.

A cave devoid of macroscopic life, where change proceeded at a literal geologic rate, plainly wasn't ideal for tracking his perceptions of kinetic fauna. Privacy trumped other priorities, though, to avoid being perceived himself if the potion, like peyote, induced puking or delirium. A suspenseful half hour later, nothing worse than minor sweats, flushed cheeks, a faint headache ensued. Whew! He was on the verge of taking this drug trial outside when

his vision mistook a disturbance in the space before him for motion. Padding forward for a closer once-over, he blocked the
lamp's direct radiance from the mystery in its shallow alcove. In
the inkier shadow, paradoxically, more definition and contrast
came to the fore.

The drug, no doubt, accounted for the pressure pulsing in his
ears and eyeballs, the peripheral floaters he gamely ignored. The
drug might also have led his brain to collate flint protuberances,
limestone seams, suggestive shadows into bodily contours and
volumes, an illusory projection of details on the walls into the alcove's midpoint.

But no optical illusion could have jolted his windpipe into
constricting, or sent shockwaves of pity and amazement through
him. To have a naked man materialize within grabbing range of
Listergil's shoestrings didn't frighten him a bit. Was the drug
blunting his fight-or-flight response? Probably not: it was the
squatting man's very immobility that made him so ghastly, his
popeyed despair that declared him no physical threat. And what a
huge relief, for the squatter's grimacing panic and frustration
mingling with his despair would have to explode into a tornadic
frenzy, wreaking oblivious harm on himself, on Listergil.

Had shamanic features been less excruciatingly rigid, they'd
certainly have broadcast resentment at someone else's freedom of
movement, for the paralyzed eyes had Listergil's squarely in their
sightline, and were charged with an awareness of him.

Were the caveman clean and sane, though, he'd pass as normal in modern company; granted, he'd be no social magnet at
parties. His skin was nearest a gunmetal gray, maybe due to the
shadows, or to the ashes and grime embedded in his pores. His
nose was long and pointy like a crow's beak, his chin was small
under half-inch stubble, his hair approximated a stellate, mud-
stiffened blast. Green smudges at the corners of his mouth captured the hue of the bowl's contents at their freshest, and his fingertips, splayed against the ground, were red and black with
ingrained pigments.

To Listergil the horror ratcheted up on recalling that 10 centi-liters of the potion infiltrated his own bloodstream. Its mecha-nism of action was more bizarrely abstruse than ever, so much more on grasping the nature of its effects. Instead of retarding the subjective perception of time, it literally retarded time for the us-er, decelerated him into a temporal eddy, safe from all worldly alarms as it were, and, it went without saying, beyond the limits of drug-free optic nerves to register him. And whether out of hubris, curiosity, or accident, the Pleistocene madman must have guzzled a massive dose and was still "tripping," trapped in his private time zone till the potion wore off.

Wasn't it likely enough the cave had been forsaken, sealed off even, when the shaman's worried people checked on him, discov-ered he'd vanished, and concluded he must have offended "higher powers" who'd annihilated him? At least Listergil hadn't blithely "overmedicated," would pose his colleagues no riddle of apparatus left behind and he never to reappear. Right? He indulged one more probing eyeful of this "living fossil," endured a jolt at reading into paralytic stare a note of pleading and of warning too; rationally or not, he feared that lingering meant courting the shaman's fate. In an access of angst, he made to turn and bolt, but couldn't.

As if they constituted a closed circuit, the two of them were fused in place, locked in each other's sights, Listergil sharing gut-level knowledge now of the prehistoric artist's helpless panic. Bad as anything else was the implication he'd been reduced to parity with this crazed primitive, for all his lecture-hall praise of the har-dy, inventive Cro-Magnons. Hold it together! He had 15,000 years of scientific progress, of cultural sophistication to ward off the de-rangement that tried corrupting him via primeval chestnut irises.

Meanwhile, Listergil lost track of time, kept phasing in and out of cognizance. How much less than 10 centiliters, how minus-cule, must the proper clinical dose of potion have been? Had the shaman rashly swigged his standard "Muybridge cocktail" or ex-perimented with a different formulation?

At some juncture that seemed no different from any other, he felt himself expelling a breath as if his lungs had stored a zeppelin's capacity for eons. The circuit with this victim of Ice Age OD had shorted out, no need to ponder why, suffice to say 10 centiliters had run their course, just go! He spun around and bolted as if the bison and aurochs on the wall were giving chase. Conjecture at leisure where his kit had gone! Illumination enough was diffusing from a sunshaft in the antechamber, as if he'd forgotten to batten down the hatch. He'd have sworn he had!

The polymer ladder, anyway, hadn't budged, and he clambered into the old immutable landscape, staggering blindly till his momentum was spent, only to mark, when his eyes adjusted, pronounced changes indeed. The semblance of an old-fashioned cellphone tower rose a good hundred feet from over the valley's fringe of hilltops, except a giant gyroscope surmounted it, spinning deliberately, tilting brashly at random. And hundreds of feet higher, numerous beyond reckoning and fading into the hazy distance in east-west orientation (except none were directly overhead), endless pink ribbons never touched one another, despite bending into new configurations constantly, like rivers eroding new channels in time-lapse footage. What the hell were they?

In the back of his mind the gist of his predicament was obvious, but the longer he forestalled articulating it, the better for his functionality. He swiveled around to see whether ribbons floated behind him as well, but before he could raise his eyes the hatchway transfixed him, an open pit now with a silvery rim that gave off an unsettling ruddy glow. A lazy bumblebee swooped over, lost elevation thanks to a downdraft, dipped below rim-level, and combusted in a purple flash. Listergil expected he'd fare as poorly; anything below, such as noxious gases or humidity, was evidently welcome to exit, but ingress merited capital punishment.

Listergil sank into dour reverie picturing the kind of society okay with treating nighthawks and clumsy innocents alike as bugzapper bait. Hence the babble, grunting, and raspy gasping from inside the pit broke in on him with an unreal, dreamlike quality till the insane shaman sprang onto the turf. Oh, shit! Well, he'd had to get over his megadose sometime, and for all Listergil knew, someone to focus on may have egged him into rallying sooner. Had Listergil dared pick up a rock, the troglodyte would have been easy to brain at this range, except that picking it up would have incited the troglodyte to attack, and he'd have been upon Listergil in seconds.

For the nonce, no aggression was in the offing: Listergil hoped his own face hadn't been distorted by the same terror-stricken stupefaction upon meeting this new world. The shaman, for all the familiarity with fantastic realms that should have gone with his profession, was palsied and gabbling beyond even the power of his madness to set him in motion. And then the AI units, from out of nowhere, surrounded them.

Four hovered at a prudent remove from Listergil, and four from the paleo-Methuselah, like candlepins that had gone to over-fed pot, on the scale of inflatable pool toys, and ringed around the midriff bulge with blue electric eyes. With one grating, simulcast voice their future accents scolded the scofflaws for "footprinting abusively," admonished them to "buffer" pending arrival of "the birdhouse." Jesus, as if Listergil hadn't already gathered, this present age was no great shakes either!

The naked shaman, even without understanding a word, and with reasoning ability abraded to nothing by 15,000 petrified years, must have made the same determination. He'd been venting nonstop, chimplike racket ever since the AI units had shown up and thrust the future's intolerable strangeness more or less in his face, and their caterwauling had set him to hopping frantically from foot to foot. Suddenly, at some arbitrary prompt, everything became too much and he dove back down the hatch. The flash of his incineration was bigger and brighter, but just as fleeting and complete as the bumblebee's.

What a waste! Not that science could have learned a thing that called for cooperation, let alone communication, from this Cro-Magnon wreckage. How pathetic, though, for resurrection to be so short-lived, how like the poor shaman was to a cicada, abiding underground for greater than 99% of its lifespan, only to greet the sunshine and, before it can get its bearings, be snuffed out, whether by predation or naive blundering. The AI units had fallen into nonplussed silence, their programming in an apparent dither at the novelty of self-immolation. Thank you, raving caveman, for the diversion!

Listergil came to a snap decision, was willing to wager on a future age's goldenness, saw scant choice but to bail on this one. He snatched plastic test-tube from vest pocket, uncapped it with his thumb, told himself he surely had psychological resources superior to those of an unbathed savage, was vastly better prepared to wait out epochal stasis. Hadn't he transcended however many decades without worse effect than gaping lacunae (a mercy, admittedly) in his memory? Before the AI units could rebound or receive new orders, he toasted his optimism: the age when he'd resolidify would have to be a golden one, because he was about to empty the phial. Bottoms up!

A Box from Blackstone

"Look at me now, I know something that you don't,
But that's the way we all go."
                                        —Tim Smith of Cardiacs

If I went back to 1900 or so, I like to think I'd run into the pre-teen Howard Phillips Lovecraft exploring the woods where our house went up circa 1920. Our overgrown bungalow with a colonnaded porch is, after all, a scant half-mile from both his childhood addresses on Angell Street. Yep, Providence's own master of twentieth-century weird horror was a regular nineteenth-century kid playing at wild-west or private-eye or whatever fun-and-games with neighborhood chums (when he wasn't studying Latin or chemistry). Chances are nil of unearthing any "smoking gun" of his, a time capsule or whatnot, when I dig in the garden; no illusions there. Still, I want to rent a metal detector someday, just out of general curiosity.

But once Clarice and I had bought into the worst part of town for property taxes, I tried getting my money's worth by resorting often to the local resource of Blackstone Boulevard. The boulevard's glorified median strip amounts to a greenbelt with trees, benches, a central footpath. I'd pick up the path three blocks east of our house and trot to the end and back, passing Butler Hospital where Lovecraft's parents died, and Swan Point Cemetery where he, his parents, and immediate kin repose. After Swan Point, the trail terminates in a turnaround by the Pawtucket line.

On the same side of the road as the cemetery, for upwards of the last mile to the edge of town, a rugged wall flanks an unpaved, scruffy verge with its own inches-wide filament of a path. Behind the wall are some surprisingly mature woods, and the wall boasts some surprisingly megalithic capstones, bringing the deceptively casual-looking assemblage to a height of seven feet in places, and begging the question of how such tonnage was hoisted in the 1880s, or why.

When I took my hour-long constitutional after lunch, I'd observe a wiry old lady, tatty and drab except for a bright red beret, stalking alongside the monumental wall, spellbound on some esoteric mission. Pausing on the greenway, I watched her skip over to seemingly random pockets and seams between rocks, peering into them as into a nickelodeon peephole, or sliding a skittish hand inside. Outwardly she was never more perturbed coming up empty than a robin pecking in vain for worms and flying away.

Early on I'd mention her when Clarice came home from the studio. Clarice wears the public face of our fledgling business; I'm the tech-head behind the curtain. With semi-jesting acerbity, she admonished me not to squander company time spying on the homeless. I, lest I forget, was privileged to telecommute in my sweats, and she didn't get to add postprandial hikes to her lunchbreak.

Now that's the thing in a town this ancient, though Clarice, after eight hours downcity, is seldom up for any magnitude of hairsplitting. Especially factoring in shabby gentility, i.e., ingrained Yankee cheapness, distinguishing old money from indigence can be difficult, even a few conversations later. And maybe that's par for any shallow genepool. The Providence Art Club, for example, has canned more than one green waitress for shooing ragged millionaires from the buffet at Sunday openings (whereas a clean shirt equals carte blanche to guzzle free wine).

I did flout workday discipline further by crossing to the unkempt verge, to snoop into intramural cavities every dozen yards or so. Whatever could be the prize? In short order I learned inspecting apertures was as absorbing for me as for the septuagenarian, because I was deaf to her approach till she was right beside me, asking without aboveboard dander or defensiveness, "Are you a relative too?"

As opening lines went, few had caught me more off-guard,

and her matter-of-fact delivery threw me further. "Whose relative am I?"

She tutted as if playing dumb were beneath me. "Look, I may not be overjoyed about it," she archly confessed, "but you are within your rights." I was still fumbling for words when she cocked an index finger toward the cemetery beyond the woods. "You and I both know there's but one person of account in there." Yes, I tactfully omitted to mention, if you ignore governors, Civil War heroes, and captains of industry, which was fine by me. Ergo, no contest whom that process of elimination would leave standing. "Ah, but which crack in the wall did he choose?"

"There's the rub," I ventured.

"I have Phillips blood on both sides of my family, which may have called on me to do this. And if you're not a relative, how else would you have heard about . . ." She waved peremptorily at the wall, as if disdaining to belabor the obvious, or say overmuch around uninitiated ears. Here was a fidgety incarnation of how everyday Providence amounted to a relentless, if largely subliminal, Lovecraftian presence inconceivable to outsiders.

"I've a Phillips or two up my family tree as well. And a bunch of Hazards," I adlibbed, recalling another lineage of his. Well, a lot of us stuck-in-the-mud Rhode Islanders have those surnames among our roots. It clinched no argument for kinship to Lovecraft; and however prominent Phillips DNA was in her background, that offered no guarantee she wasn't crazy. On the other hand, if a delusion of kinship to Lovecraft made her happy, who was I to knock it?

"All right then, no point pussyfooting. I already said I'm not mad. You've as much right to the box as I," she conceded, though with a grudging pout.

"So what have you heard about the contents of the box?" Sure, technically I was dissembling, since I hadn't disabused her about our common bloodlines, but again, yes, they might ennoble my veins. And in such extended kindreds, anything this similar to buried treasure had to breed reams of theorizing.

But she wasn't having any. With a more jaundiced eye she huffed, "I've never heard of any particular contents, nobody knows what's in there, and anyone claiming otherwise is a liar or an impostor."

"No, you can't play it too safe!" I parried in my capacity as impostor, digging my pit of duplicity deeper, intimating I'd been the wary one testing her. Not as if I'd introduced myself with a fake name, though, or done worse than humor her, really. "It's not against the rules to guess what's inside, is it?"

Her shrug was dismissively understated. "Keepsakes to salt away for some abstract posterity. Offerings to those classical gods he venerated as a boy. A tribute to his parents over the wall, someplace where the groundskeepers wouldn't dispose of it." Wow, for holding speculation in contempt, she was going out on very creative limbs. "We can't speak to why he'd wedge a box of something between stones in a wall when we can't even say if he was a kid at the time or on his last legs."

"I'm new to this sleuthing business." That statement wouldn't jar a polygraph needle. "Most of what you've said has never occurred to me."

"Fine then, you're all caught up with everything I know. Happy hunting." Her smile was brittle. "I'll be dying without issue. Whatever I don't share will go to waste."

"Don't worry about me," I valiantly assured her. "I can't commit to meaningful effort here. Work keeps me too busy. This is your side of the street. I wouldn't dream of horning in on you. I was just dabbling when you came along." I took my diffident leave as she nodded deliberatively, as if weighing my probity anew.

Not that I wouldn't be keeping tabs on her from my side of the street, i.e., the greenway. I set out on my daily walk after lunch or not at all: why bother, except to maximize chances of monitoring this daft quest for a most nebulous grail? She was fixated beyond ever noticing me, or perhaps astigmatic. If we'd both bought into the possibility Lovecraft had stashed something in the wall, we also implicitly rejected the possibility of someone beating us to it, or that anything inserted before his death in 1937 wouldn't have disintegrated.

Plus, she'd been correct to reweigh my probity. I did, several times, confirm the coast was clear and conduct a spot search of crannies, to gratify a vagrant impulse, with no greater rewards than an empty pack of Marlboros, a bouquet of wilted condoms. And a bit more errantly, I blew an extra hour on the clock trailing the elderly delver to settle whether she lived in poverty or a dynastic seat. The red beret made for an easy mark.

I'd have been rather more truant from my desk had her multi-family dwelling not been a block from home. Unfortunately, I went away none the wiser about her financial status. The most modest apartments hereabouts can fetch premium rents, and many have converted to condos. She might be a fixed-income pauper subsisting month-to-month, or not. Nonetheless, this bush-league skullduggery was instructive, reinforcing a truism of our zip code, whose insular residents never set eyes on most of their neighbors. In over two years I'd been unconscious of that red beret. Clarice and I weren't in a community so much as an aggregate of property investors.

Meanwhile, my own ties with reality weren't absolutely Gordian. My fascination with homegrown littérateur H. P. Lovecraft may have been no stronger than the next townie's, but the question still went begging: did my footloose reveries of walking in Lovecraft's shoes commence before or after I met the neurotic dowager? In either case, I had an autopilot awareness of my boulevard surroundings: not as if I blindly plowed into joggers or traffic where cross-streets breached the greenbelt. Imagination superimposed yesteryear's boulevard upon today's, like a mild double-exposure, and the hypothetical persona of Lovecraft overlaid mine like a translucent mask.

These vagaries were mostly fleeting and superficial, recapturing no exact phase of Lovecraft's career, little beyond a nod toward refilling his footsteps, beholding the terrain as he had. I did transcribe the most vivid scenario, which felt uniquely like a psychic connection across the decades or the Valley of the Shadow (despite his unbelief in an afterlife). Its first memorable detail was at once visceral and prosaic. My stomach hurt. I wasn't so profoundly embedded in him, though, as to forfeit my bird's-eye view of his encumbered shoulders, his sweaty brow, his dragging steps, as if his shopworn black suit were toilsome armor.

We were at the corner where Elmgrove Avenue merges with Blackstone Boulevard, opposite the gates of Swan Point. Let's not canter over to the uneven median, less taxing to stick with the fresh-laid sidewalk this side of Blackstone; in any event, there's no greenway footpath for us, only streetcar tracks. Some of my earliest memories are of sprucing up to ride the trolley down Angell Street with Mother. The tracks go all over town, their steel rails and iron spikes give off an air of permanence, of essentiality like a body's vasculature. Their routes will necessarily function long after I'm gone, which may, to credit my habitual cynicism, be imminent.

No riding for me today, though, not when each lurch of the car would deliver an acute punch to the gut. Better to weather the constant but more bearable pang with every footfall, much easier thus to emulate the Stoics. But ugh, how the old breadbasket has been acting up, and while decorum forbids blue language aloud, I'm free to grouse inwardly, Dammit, dammit, dammit! Cerberus can't wait to sink his three sets of jaws into me, he's stretched his chain and burrowed a tunnel from Hades into my bowels for the premature pleasure of gnawing on them.

That facile, pompous vein of allusion is beneath me. It must be the grippe (or worse) talking. Can the grippe linger for months? By the tracks, a fieldstone shelter tempts me, a dry grotto for rainy-day commuters, a stylish Arts-and-Crafts adjunct to the rubble wall. But no rest for the weary! Submitting to fatigue this paltry distance from College Street would be shameful, when a jaunt to Lincoln Woods and back, a good 17-mile roundtrip, was till recently nothing arduous, likewise my boyhood treks to Rehoboth.

The package in the crook of one arm is of indeterminate dimensions and poundage, which is to say, I lack the information or creativity to picture it. Lovecraft's motives and sentiments are no less inchoate as we survey the wall across the boulevard, hesitating now and then to mull a nook at apparent random, or perhaps when cramps or breathlessness call a halt. Our tailwind has barely caught up with us when we soldier on again. Around a bend, and the end of the boulevard is in sight.

To make emotional sense of the man, I have to parse his body language, his facial tics. Our indecision (or so I deduce) exasperates us. At the curb we crane our neck left and right, proceed to the tracks, repeat our precaution there and along the boulevard's northbound lane, and voilà, we can examine the wall without eyestrain. Thanks to this, the bellyache relents some but never totally subsides, and kicks back in under the pressure of cementing our decision in the next few hundred feet.

Our ailment is manifestly more serious than we'll let on, yet rather than investing trust and, more crucially, depleted funds in doctors, here we are performing a gesture, inventing a ritual with no rational hope of placating whatever is eating at us, of winning celestial intercession. Still, sometimes just doing something exerts a salubrious effect. A placebo must contain more virtue than despair. As if bowing to the arbitrary soul of this errand, we jam our undefined parcel into the nearest adequate recess.

We rock back on wobbly heels, nodding in hollow satisfaction at the mystery trove's engulfment in darkness. I was sorry Howard's heroic tenacity in the teeth of suffering wasn't more moving; I justified borderline callousness by dubbing myself too much this episode's engineer to be affected by it. Nor would Howard be pleased with the take-home lesson I, for one, had garnered. In forty-six years, the pinnacle of his wisdom was nothing he couldn't have summed up as a six-year-old, to wit, we don't really know why we do what we do.

I also can't certify how authentically I inhabited the mortally ill Lovecraft, how accurately I re-enacted the concealment of his parcel. But I'm hardly optimistic, as I was dead wrong about where it moldered. I nevermore set foot on the senior-citizen side of the boulevard, my late-blooming scout's honor was good for that much, whether or not I persistently violated the tenor of my word by spying on the pensioner's progress.

Clarice was as much in the dark about my lunch-hour double-life as the septuagenarian about starring in it. My wife had previously expressed her lack of interest, nay, derision as far as geriatric surveillance was concerned. Therefore, whatever I learned along those lines was, by her own pronouncement, none of her business. Too bad! Here was nothing it would hurt her to humor, but I was aware of this wedge, this rift between us, a degree of separation that could only increase. Then again, who has ever known everything about any other person?

As it panned out, just as well Clarice wasn't in the loop, one more witness to my foundering confusion. A fortnight or two had passed since I'd "channeled" Lovecraft caching his parcel, but to be wrong about its cubbyhole by a half-mile still ruffled my feathers. Between the cemetery's main entrance and the padlocked lesser gate of a service road, a cluster of holly trees on the widening verge imposed perpetual twilight.

In that twilight she was conspicuously atremble, and my jaw dropped, as she daintily, painstakingly extracted an oilcloth pouch, rife with cracks, mottled with stains, straps reduced to nubs, from a hip-level cleft where three boulders didn't quite meet. The pouch was of an underwhelming capacity, like a toy camera bag.

She blew off stringy cobwebs and white mineral powder, bent back the flap (which split clean off to fall unheeded), and lifted out a petit casket of olive-green steel, streaked with rust like veins in Roquefort, and maybe able to fit a gross of index cards. Without peeking inside, she reinserted it into the oilcloth and stalked homeward, too rapturous in triumph to recon her environs and catch me following. Privy as I was to her address, I could lag with impunity and convince myself I wasn't shadowing her, nope, I was merely perambulating toward my own place.

My insouciance collapsed on the sidewalk outside her building. I couldn't very well ring the doorbell, whichever it was, and railroad her into letting me in for show-and-tell. Nor was waiting for her to come out and going "Aha!" a tenable option. Loitering till something occurred to me was my pathetic default mode. To kill time I indulged a window-to-window, floor-by-floor gander, as if she'd show herself like an answer in a Magic Eight-Ball. Did she even have a window fronting on the street?

Why yes, she did, and she flung it wide to empty an overflowing dehumidifier pan from the second story into a barberry bush, narrowly missing the edge of portico roof. I was cringing with certainty the jig was up, yet she ducked back in, evidently clueless I'd been dead-to-rights in her sightline. Common sense had to infer she was more myopic than I'd surmised. Reinstalling the dehumidifier pan must have distracted her from toddling back to shut the window.

I didn't suppose she'd contract pneumonia from a draft the first week of temperate autumn. I wouldn't have supposed she'd need a dehumidifier now, either. Upon these musings trespassed a faint but reverberant pop, like the needle landing on a record. A heartbeat later, an unaccompanied tenor warbled after it, almost as faint, then amplified fivefold within seconds, implying its audience was somewhat deaf on top of purblind.

Assuming the old woman was testing out the item from the box, and assuming the box could accommodate a wax cylinder with a home recording on it, I felt safe assuming whose voice was wafting forth, thin and plaintive, though not bereft of soul. "I hear you calling me, you called me when the moon had veiled her light, before I went from you into the night," it crooned, sometimes off-key, off-pitch, which only enhanced the poignancy, without detracting from the gravitas (by the grace of Google, I reconstructed the lyrics from a few remembered phrases). The Rhode Islander's deletion of "r" from "hear" and "her" nailed the singer's ID for me.

I lost it. The song was shamelessly maudlin, an old-school weeper, and weep I did, but not, I swear, in response to the lyrics.

H. P. Lovecraft, unheard in this world since 1937, was serenading me, and did that not merit weeping quietly in public, with all the restraint self-consciousness could muster? Extraordinary that no parallel outpouring was audible from indoors! But at least I could give my callous self-image the heave-ho.

How long did I stand minutely swaying like a poplar, stunned yet basking in my privileged melancholy after the heartbreakingly ironic finis, "Do you behold me, listening here, hearing your voice through all the years between?" And how slow a death did my anticipation die before I accepted no other songs, or replays of that one song, or any further sounds would be forthcoming?

I hadn't nearly pulled myself together, was still squinting immobile toward the open window, when an inquisitor at my elbow startled me halfway to apoplexy with the simple question, "Can I help you?"

He was roughly the same height and build as the septuagenarian, though of indeterminate age, and I waffled over how similar his features were to hers. A younger sibling, reckoned that fraction of my brain not scrambling to defuse this ticking situation.

"I was just listening to some really lovely music from up there," I hedged, nodding toward the window. By dint of luck or subconscious talent, I'd steered clear of wording I'd have to walk back upon fuller disclosure.

"I missed it." The prospective brother granted me no benefit of the doubt; neither was he frankly hostile yet.

The occupant reappeared at her window. Her look encompassed us, but minus any spark of recognition, and dumping the brimful pan once again, she chirruped a succinct "Gardy-loo!" Back in she swerved, leaving me to ponder how a dehumidifier could have been so productive already. And if it wasn't a dehumidifier pan, I declined to conjecture what it was.

"Oh, it's her!" I prevaricated, perhaps a mite shrilly. "I've run into her on Blackstone Boulevard. We talked a little. You're her brother? Cousin? Nephew?" I babbled, without ceding him space to answer. "Must be pretty neat in this town to be related to H. P. Lovecraft."

"What? Who told you that?" he challenged, venting an exasperation that smacked of hearing this once too often. I nodded toward the window again. "Colleen!" he yelled in her general direction.

I was afraid he'd bolt inside and forever deprive me of once-in-a-lifetime enlightenment. "Wait, she's not related? She said there was Phillips blood on both sides of her family. There isn't?"

"No!" he snapped with gratuitous heat. "And you believed her? So it's Phillips now, is it? I'm really sick of this. It's been years, and she won't cut it out."

"But why pretend she's related to Lovecraft? What would bring that on?" To me, at least, my desperation to salvage any validity in Colleen's story was morbidly transparent. His glower starkly questioned what business she was of mine; it must have been my woebegone puppy eyes that got to him.

He sighed resignedly. "Since you obviously have to know, my grandfather used to tell us he did odd jobs when he was a kid, washing windows, shoveling snow, for Lovecraft and his mom, and we inherited some of the junk Lovecraft allegedly pawned off on him. That's where this chronic bullshit about Lovecraft started."

"Did the junk include a wax-cylinder phonograph?" I fatuously persevered.

"Maybe." His hazel eyes narrowed with trepidation ripening into disdain. Was this another line of inquiry he'd fielded once too often?

"Look, you may own a recording of Lovecraft's voice, the only one in the world. Do you realize how priceless that would be?"

"Yes, I do, and no, we don't." His sawtooth tone brooked no opposition. "Those cylinders are blanks. They're mostly in factory-sealed cartons." He made "cartons" sound like a warning shot.

I'd shunted aside the whole matter of the recording's liberation from oilcloth package in a wall. It didn't even belong in the same jigsaw of circumstances under discussion. And I refused to entertain the possibility of hallucinating a sentimental ballad. "Can your sister sing?"

"Like a blue jay." The reply was immediate, and devoid of curiosity at why I'd ask. Chalk me up a point, anyway, for establishing they were sibs. His tightlipped glare as he withdrew fairly megaphoned we'd never converse again. When he slammed the door, I blinked and cracked the varnish of dried-up tears under my eyes. Had he noticed I'd been crying? I rubbed it off, a source of bonus sympathy, maybe, but henceforth only embarrassment. I loitered a minute, then concluded he wouldn't read Colleen the riot act till I decamped.

Embarrassment, in fact, became my keyword for how that afternoon played out, or perhaps how I'd been played. Autumnal cold lent an excuse to avoid the boulevard, and more critically, the problematic Colleen. Clarice, during breakfast yet, must not have fathomed what a raw nerve she poked by teasing, "Whatever happened to that elderly girlfriend you were stalking?"

I shrugged. "Her pimp mistook my intentions. I haven't bothered with her since. She couldn't have been worth all that," I improvised, well enough for my purposes: Clarice dropped the subject with only short-term disgust at my crudeness.

The hell of it is, Clarice and I were afterward chummy as ever, guaranteed closer than if I'd force-fed her regular updates about my boulevard escapades, especially about that freakish afternoon when a dowager of fraudulent lineage treated an abjectly gullible eavesdropper to some nonexistent music. It's no less true for being paradoxical that secrecy and obfuscation can underpin a copacetic marriage. I'm more the respectable husband, as opposed to a deplorable creep, because the wife is blithely uninformed I was tailing an old lady and crying on her sidewalk. Or to flout received wisdom, hypocrisy makes the world go round!

And how should I cogently impart events incoherent to me? According to the brother, Colleen's every utterance was of whole cloth, fueling my suspicion she'd planted the parcel in the wall herself, engaging in a game wherein I may or may not have been recruited. This still did not address the reality of the song on the cylinder, or my ironclad conviction that the singer was Lovecraft.

Meanwhile, why take the brother's candor on faith? He might have been a seasoned pro at forging honest-to-God family background into a whopper about blank wax cylinders. He might have been protecting heritage or nest-egg or household privacy. He might have been zealously possessive and/or not all there, like his sister. But the impetus for Colleen's obsessive months of ferreting along the wall remained a riddle. Nothing was explicit except my disgrace at being hoodwinked, and I couldn't even affirm by whom, or why.

Like any stigma, its sting dulled as the poultice of subsequent goings-on supervened, unless chance reminders snagged the poultice loose. Shunning the boulevard minimized my risk of sighting Colleen who, despite residing one street over, hadn't impinged on my radar for two years, so why worry now? But this is Providence, socially too much of a vortex for two people to meet once and nevermore. And never predictably! Come the January thaw, the urge to walk rekindled, a precious respite between bouts of cabin fever.

Needless to say, I lit out in the opposite direction from the boulevard, due west toward Benefit Street, the Federal-era official "Mile of History." And overlooking it was one of Lovecraft's favorite views and mine, the ideal rest stop of Prospect Terrace. After his demise, the city "improved" the park with an outsize statue of founding father Roger Williams, another celebrated Rhode Islander whose exclusive club of descendants numbers about two million. If only sager heads had voted on a pose other than one arm outthrust as if deploying a yoyo, inspiring collegiate generations to risk their necks attaching a Duncan to his fingertip.

To either side of Roger, the benches in winter would have been conducive solely to frozen bums. My best alternative for a breather entailed bellying up to the wrought-iron fence on the cliff-edge of the terrace and surveying the brown expanse of lawn twenty feet below. The terrace's massive retaining wall was of tight-fitting limestone blocks, and the flagstone pavement beneath my shoes doubled as its coping. Along the base of the sheer wall was bobbing a damnably familiar swatch of bright red.

Holy cow, it was the telltale beret of none other than Colleen, totally engrossed with darting up to random blocks of masonry and rapping, on the apparent alert for a hollow ring behind the façade. Had she a screwdriver or crowbar in her frayed coat's pocket to pry out a false block and win some prize immured by who-else-but-him? I wouldn't have presumed this stone facing predated Lovecraft's death, and even if it did, probing it was vastly more quixotic than her quest on Blackstone Boulevard, such that labeling her insane was a slam dunk, and my naiveté in falling for her drivel much more mortifying.

Still, I harbored a ghastly premonition she'd someday luck out here too. On the upside, she hadn't seen me, and might sooner spontaneously combust than look up. I'd been gripping the iron rail, and realized my fingers were swelling and numb. I stepped back from the fence and just kept going, homeward bound and quashing every thought as it arose. The thaw persisted several days, but I chose instead to court a relapse of cabin fever. Till further notice, the great outdoors was hers, or anyhow wasn't worth the abashment of running into her again.

Chaining myself to the home workstation should have spared me the psychic wear-and-tear of further truck with Colleen. However, we were a measly block apart, in a precinct blessedly tranquil after the daytime leaf-blowers and other infernal machineries of anal-retentive "lawn care," summer and snowless winter, too briefly desist. Nights are never so quiet I can hear a needle drop, but consequent wax-cylinder emanations may have accounted for those tenor strains that could also have been the hum of Route 95 in the distance, or sporadic breezes through gangly pines one yard over. Cars and trees could hardly have enunciated "gladness," "moon," or "kiss," though, unless I were hallucinating lyrics.

After wound-up months of lying tense and deathly still while putative repeated spins of "I Hear You Calling Me" did Lovecraft's recording irreparable damage, I had to spring from the creaking four-poster, head full of repressed imprecations. I used the en-suite bathroom to allay wifely concerns about why I was up, and if I had disturbed her, I noted in passing, she'd fallen back asleep. I eased into bathrobe and loafers, and into a windbreaker downstairs before braving the chill April night; I pulled the unlocked front door to, but stopped shy of hearing it click.

On my compulsive route I met with no auto or foot traffic, fortunately as it transpired. I hadn't thought ahead of strategy, just trooped up Colleen's steps, chose the middle of three doorbells as likeliest for second-floor digs, and mused on whether Lovecraft had rung this very doorbell, under saner conditions, inquiring the availability of Colleen's grandpa to perform some chores. Part of me hoped this doorbell, like most doorbells nowadays, was busted, and I could honorably retreat when my sockless toes went frigid. Another part of me insisted: forget the hour, Howard was an uncontrite night-owl, what would he have said when whoever was clumping downstairs reached the door?

And on the principle that Howard, of the two of us, was the more capable, my deference allowed him to inhabit me figuratively (or me him), as had befallen on the boulevard. Colleen's readiness to open up without establishing who I was bolstered my conviction she was crazy; plus, she was unsteady with drowsiness, her eyelids laden with complaisance to the power of suggestion in a doorbell rousting her from bed. She stared vacantly with no sign of recognizing me.

I emulated Lovecraft's stern and formal stance, as if he were vitamins for my backbone, and the phrasing came automatically, helping me pretend I really was channeling him. "I believe you've been holding onto some property of mine, which I would like restored to me, please."

Colleen blinked away weariness and fixed saucer eyes on mine, and saw something in them, something more than I was aware of certainly: could I somehow have represented Lovecraft to her, or was my own mania shining in starlit eyes? Her jaw flapped soundlessly, the cords in her turkey neck bulged like cables, and her whole frame quivered a few sporadic seconds. She managed a stifled whimper and crumpled. From above, the dazzling lights for staircase and front hall were switched on. "Colleen?" called her brother.

Can shame be attached to any response as primal and reflexive as panic? Whatever Howard would have done, whoever that had been if not he whom Colleen had read in my eyes, I goggled through painful glare in my vision and legged it like a hare as the brother thudded past the landing. I was out of sight around the corner, sprinting across lawns to deaden my footfalls, before he screeched at finding her and then bellowed into the street for whoever had been there to show himself.

I exercised praiseworthy care, if I do say so, in locking the front door with fastidious slow motion instead of hastily slamming it behind me, in clearing the burn from my lungs with circumspect panting. Clarice at breakfast acted none the wiser about my nocturnal absence, and since I hadn't come clean with her about Colleen previously, why the hell start now?

As for Colleen, initially I thought the cosmic merit system had allotted me an underserved break. Three days after the "incident," I traipsed over to the Whole Foods on North Main, figuring I could shed my dread of running into Colleen for weeks, if not forever. Self-serving of me, true, though isn't that often the way with squeezing lemonade from tragic lemons? But halfway along Olney Street (the former Cat Swamp Trail), across from Hope High School (a former reservoir) with its athletic field's stone retaining wall surmounted by ivy-decked chain-link fence, I went weak-kneed spotting red beret on top of drab gray coif.

Colleen was concentrating on the wall, of course, and student gaggles on the sidewalk ignored her as utterly as she did them, as if she were invisible. Hurray, I oversoon concluded, what a load off my admittedly thick-skinned conscience. She was fine, no harm done!

I giddyapped till second thoughts triggered rip-current vertigo. That pathetic whimper, that wracking convulsion as she'd collapsed, categorically refuted she'd be gadding about in seventy-two hours. Even expecting her to survive was rather a stretch. I scarcely dared look back, but didn't dare not. The high-schoolers were a few dozen yards from where they'd been; Colleen was gone. Shellshock is no state in which to grocery-shop. I forgot a bunch of items, and I wasn't going back to that supermarket for them, ever.

Whereas she used to haunt the sunlight metaphorically, I now despair she haunts it literally. Ghosthood was her destiny, that glib pronouncement's fine and well, and the upside is, she and the brother are ignorant of my address. But I'm petrified of the other shoe dropping. She has a more impassioned motive to follow me than I had to follow her. Clarice has begun regarding me sidelong when we go out, as if worried about my paranoid behavior. I've always been a little jumpy, I remind her, feigning indignation.

My one consolation at this pass is the letup in decay of the (allegedly nonexistent) wax cylinder. In stockstill fetal position every night, till I'm favored with three hours' sleep max, I've been waiting for that retaliatory knock on the door, insofar as I disabled the doorbell. Meanwhile, many seasons into this zombifying insomnia, I haven't, to my feeble satisfaction, overheard anything that might be interpreted as Lovecraft singing.

Flouting Pascal:
An Episode from the Latest Dark Ages

"All men's miseries derive from being unable to sit in a quiet room alone." Words to the wise from seventeenth-century whiz-kid Blaise Pascal! And kudos to me for honoring them in this apartment, which is pretty much a room. That's partly why I call it The Birdhouse, and partly because it's a sixth-floor walkup: a nosebleed altitude that should oblige the slumlord to install an elevator. But the most transparent ruse exempts him. Euro-style, he prefixed second-floor units with a "1," such that I rent "5F" on the top floor. Sure he gets away with it. It's New York and the Department of Buildings has a decade or three of backlog.

In upshot, I'm a prisoner of rent control till I'm too decrepit to climb the stairs. I couldn't swing more spacious digs anywhere I'd want to be, or even a spiffier "efficiency" with a newer bathtub in the kitchen. Stocking up on toilet paper becomes second nature; erring on the worrywart side beats an emergency descent to the bodega and back.

Nor do I have to go out often. Very helpful, that, in heeding Pascal. One corner of my space is the "office" where I work online. No commuting for me; my employers aren't even based in this country. Not that I'm a doctrinaire hermit, but in terms of gratuitous outings, I'm not part of the problem, no reckless contributor to men's miseries.

Danon, on the other hand, should have taken Pascal to heart and sat in his own room instead of coming to mine, specifically that fateful Monday. He'd been high-strung since university and hit a giddy register, nigh operatic, in venting peeves and praise alike. And as it had in liberal millions, the current administration's awfulness had overloaded the circuits of his coping skills. No personal woe, be it getting canned, divorced, or cancer, had to afflict someone for 24/7 malaise to weigh onerously.

Escapism to a less out-of-control realm, or one whose disorder hurt nobody, crystallized in Danon as a fascination with gods outmoded, mysterious, obscure. In these respects "our ancestral Celtic pantheon," he practically bragged, was top-shelf. On prehistoric religion his ability to lecture was boundless, his sensitivity to people's limited interest less so. He rode his hobbyhorse the harder for fancying his surname derived from "De Danaan," an especially hallowed tribe in Irish myth. Far be it from me to berate how anyone today shores up beleaguered positivity!

Did a visitor count as unannounced when he "phoned ahead" from out front to ask if I was free? Danon knew damn well I was rarely otherwise. He mightn't have lurched in as winded had he not sprinted up two steps at a time, but was unshakable that his was a "labor-saving" practice. From the fridge I fetched the bomber of mead he'd brought the other night, and we adjourned to the guest-friendlier corner farthest from my "business center," he on the fraying couch, an IKEA coffee table between us, I in the badly sprung armchair, my back to the irksome workspace.

Our beverage I doled out in six-ounce tulips. In its favor, the stuff wasn't carbonated and kept indefinitely, and at 25% ABV, a little went a long way. In the minus column, we were imbibing a "traditional" Danish recipe with an herbal smack of aftershave. The first taste was bracing; a refill was unthinkable. Danon clinked his glass against mine and preceded our second sip with the toast, "To whichever god of our hundreds out there can deliver us from the ongoing shitshow!"

Fair enough, except I had to demur, "And there's the rub, eh? You've too many gods divvying up the universe too many ways. Weather, death, particular cities, bears, the ocean, medicine, whatever. No wonder Christianity steamrollered over them and their specialty-niche fiefdoms, demanding sacrifices, giving nothing in return. How could they compete with one omnipotent god of everything, like bathtub brewers versus Budweiser? Sure, we traded gods for saints, they were grotesquely specialized too, but they only demanded prayer and good behavior." Yes, hanging out with Danon did have me brooding on his pet fixations in my own time.

And he, true to form, was ready for me. "Whoa, you're wrong about getting nothing. We have reams of documentation, etched in stone yet, from grateful pagans all across Europe. Cures, victories, justice, absolutely delivered!" How Danon reveled in heathen boosterism! "In fact, I challenge the Christian's assumption that saints grant his wishes. Who's to say who actually intercedes when saints galore amount to Iron Age idols under Catholic haloes?" I didn't dare request examples. He'd gladly derail the evening listing them.

"I'd further insist the gods of antiquity have gone nowhere." Danon slurped mead; refueled, he resumed at a higher pitch. "They still dabble in earthly affairs, impersonate saints maybe, for their amusement, and so much the worse for us, ignorant of how they tip their hands. Our nation's sorry pass has the fingerprints of some leering trickster all over it. But which? I'm not well enough versed in tricksters to frame an educated guess. Paying them too much mind always felt like waving a lightning rod, inviting them to reciprocate. Why do that?"

"I'll concede your gods and the saints have one behavior in common: they both steal credit for the workings of chance." Do I engage in repartee or mere badgering? Damn my hair-trigger sense of guilt. "Everyone's life has to come up roses sometime."

"Roses? You're reducing the mysteries of causation to roses? No, let's talk about you. Were you not the one in a tizzy for days after that weekend on Long Island, right before you moved here?" I opened and stoically shut my mouth; no utterance of mine could stem the verbal floodtide. "Let's see, you were subletting in Connecticut and hopped the New London ferry to Orient to see that on-again, off-again girlfriend from senior year."

Yes, yes, she'd been lobbying me to visit, then made a big deal of borrowing a coworker's car to come fetch me because no mass transit ran from the North to the South Fork where she had a beach-adjacent rental. The car was a blatant clunker, a Chevy Citation, ironically apt in retrospect. She had to hotwire it under the hood while I pumped the gas in park. To my alarm, once I pressed the pedal, the gear slipped into reverse and the car slammed backward into a luxury van en route to the terminal exit.

Within seconds, the girlfriend was literally running around babbling she knew something like this was going to happen. I was in shock behind the wheel of a stalled-out lemon. A dog somewhere in the instant traffic jam wouldn't quit yapping. The family disembarking to weekend with the guy whose van I'd broadsided was already getting back on the boat, muttering something like, "Not this again." It developed I'd cut short the maiden voyage of the replacement for a Voyager that had been totaled the previous week. Though I'd have cheered nobody up mentioning it, the good news was I hadn't killed anyone.

Since I'd bought into the money-saving truism that a car in Manhattan would be a liability, my papers had lapsed, so the cop who spent five seconds assessing the situation wrote me up for driving without a license. A citation thanks to a Citation! I disagreed with his definition of "driving"—the car moved, I hadn't moved it—but just as well I was in no mental shape to pick a fight with a patrolman. My mind's a blank on how we got the car started afterward, but we wound up at her bungalow in Amagansett, the most haunted town in America, she fairly bragged, fuck Amityville!

Maybe she thought I'd dig that, but the information only made my lowering cloud of juju more ominous. I didn't doubt some local business was a front for the mouth of hell. She was due at the bistro where she waitressed; I slunk off to the beach in hopes of lightening up under the August sun. I sat cross-legged in the sand, and a benignly smiling stoner suddenly loomed over me, as if drawn to my burden of funk. His unsolicited peptalk about laughing off rough patches was a tad unctuous, but I nodded receptively to get rid of him.

I swung by a convenience store at the turnoff to the beach for a bag of chips and a Heath bar. A flyer by the register alerted the public to a serial rapist whose description and police sketch fit me to a T; that shop could have been the "mouth of hell" for me all right, but incredibly, I alone ever noticed the resemblance. Gun-shy of further "rough patches," I holed up in the bungalow till the girlfriend returned. This cooling-off period was good for putting our inauspicious start behind us. She wasn't even bothered I'd raided the pantry when the chips and chocolate failed to sate my nervous appetite.

We'd somehow never crossed the threshold to full-on sex, never reached that critical mass of arousal with each other. Or anyway, our libidos were never in sync, which went for this evening too. The flatfooted way she said let's make out made me not want to, a disappointment to her then and maybe a long-term mistake for me. Come Sunday, pleading a last-minute brunch shift, she regretted I had to thumb back to Orient; the train home from New London broke down twice amidst the saltmarshes. Typical Amtrak. A forty-minute ride took longer than *Gone with the Wind*. And we've not spoken ever after.

That did and didn't end the story. Because I wasn't on file with any DMV and the address I gave the cop was soon null-and-void and I was hardly dragnet-worthy, I circular-filed the ticket. Then during week two as a New Yorker I nearly had a coronary when a pair of cops pounded on 5F's door, but they were after the previous tenant for check fraud. The cops didn't belong to that series of events proceeding from the Orient parking lot, though coincidence had certainly bound them up in the fabric of my anecdote.

"Coincidence," Danon clucked. "Really? Cops at the door are a coincidence and every other link in your chain of calamity isn't? When there's too much coincidence, I always say there's no coincidence. How it looks to me, blow-by-blow? Nehalennia, goddess of sea journeys and fertility, took an inexplicable shine to you, and you went and snubbed her, blew your prospects of divinely mediated happiness for the weekend or maybe forever; you trivialize that as a 'mistake'? How's your love-life been the last couple of years? Dry spell, right?"

I finished my mead and smiled toothy daggers at my drinking buddy. They bounced off his oblivious hide.

"Okay." Danon drained his glass, scowled when the bottle yielded barely half a refill, dourly soldiered on. "Nehalennia singled you out during your ferry ride. Since she watches over travelers, your parking-lot kerfuffle would have gone much worse without her. That dog you heard was her mascot, incidentally, signaling her proximity. And I rather suspect your little demolition derby wasn't altogether about you. She may have had it in for the guy you walloped, or interceded for you with whichever deity the guy had pissed off; like you said, you didn't kill anyone, and this was his second accident in two weeks. I note further that driving a Voyager may have aggravated a seafaring goddess's resentment.

"I won't go out on a limb and claim the sunny stoner was Nehalennia's messenger, but to deliver a peptalk and then rub your nose in your doppelgänger's wanted poster does sound like mordant divine comedy. And just when our goddess of healing assuredly took pains to repair the rift between you and the girl, you get finicky and alienate both parties. The goddess did her big-hearted, oblique best to turn you around by breaking your train twice. But you stubbornly blundered on, and those cops doubled as couriers declaring she was miffed, you're on your hapless own, poor sap." He raised a snarky "Cheers," drank it off.

For someone who wasn't there, had never even seen the girl, he was pretty cocksure she was the love of my life. Harping on that, though, would have been as futile as disputing any of his logic, which he always defended by demanding proof the gods hadn't stage-managed events. I'd had to endure his bloviation, yet he was the restless one. As dutiful host, I tried extricating us from the rhetorical weeds. "All very thought-provoking, but aren't we off-track? Is there a go-to god for impeaching demagogues? Spell his name and I'll dedicate an altar here and now. The environment, democracy, world peace are at stake!"

With edginess unrelenting, he batted his empty tulip from hand to hand and shook his scruffy head. "I shudder to think what you'd do without me. First rookie error: your blissful naïveté. You cast a spell, there's always recoil, amateurs get as good as they give, and just because you're positive you're on the side of the angels doesn't mean you're aligned with the arc of the cosmos. Ever hear of the Poet's Curse?"

In the dimmest recesses of our acquaintance, maybe; but no worries, he'd blithely recap.

"You petition the gods to dispose of someone who, you're convinced, deserves it. After seven days, if the gods agree, the wrongdoer is never seen again. If the gods disagree, you're never seen again. Capisce? You jeopardize your very existence presuming your standards of right and wrong are on a par with divine judgment. Your second rookie error? You understocked the liquor cabinet. Tsk. And the evening so young, our banter in midflow—I, for one, am champing for additional beverages. Circumstances compelling as divine intervention combine to herd us out. Hang the extravagance of barroom markup!"

Loath as I was to flout Pascal and risk a needless excursion, resisting Danon would mire me in the crasser sin of wasting time and energy. The good news: my place was cattycorner to a Belgian joint, La Belle Abbaye, a rare checkmark in the plus-column of gentrification, mostly as beers were half-price Mondays to soup up slow trade. Despite styling their pub an abbey, the owners had opted for humdrum steel and glass inside and out, for a modernist sterility unalleviated by framed posters of Tintin and Asterix or by wooden chairs whose arms were too high to scooch under the tabletops. Clunk!

The walls fronting the street were all window, and the tables along those sides promoted the illusion of sitting in a greenhouse. Sallying forth, I had to admit, had lightened a pressure of which I'd been unconscious, though I was feeling overexposed to pedestrian traffic before the waiter loomed above us. His complexion wasn't out of the adolescent woods, yet his stance projected con-

fidence in our social and cerebral inferiority. Nonetheless, he took
our orders with a deferential bow. Danon's eyebrows lifted quizzi-
cally after our snippy garçon; then his disquisition proceeded as if
he'd flipped to a mental bookmark.

"And while I'm critiquing your hubris, what persuades you the
gods aren't on top of our political shambles? The Romans had an
aphorism for it: 'Vocatus atque non vocatus, deus aderit,' which
I've heard translated loosely but germanely as 'Do not invoke the
gods—the gods are already here.' In short, secretive divine will
may be unfolding exactly as planned."

Cold comfort as that was, on top of his insinuation the gods
were mean-spirited bastards, I wasn't about to object and delay
his progress toward some (knowing him) counterintuitive upshot.
Then he dummied up for the duration of the waiter strutting over
and noiselessly pouring our ales into chalices with inept panache.
Once the coast was clear, Danon leapt back into his screed, without a sip of the brew he'd so acutely craved.

"As my annoyance with your stingy portions of alcohol might
have implied, I'm in a celebratory mood and I intend to pull out
some, if not all, of the stops. Have you not noticed my above-
average ebullience?"

"Humph," I went, which he could parse as he liked.

"Let's cut to the pith. I speak authoritatively on the perils of
soliciting gods. I can't even remember what put me over the edge,
what with POTUS dick-moves daily, but I got fed up and dusted
off the Poet's Curse, which was too tempting because it doesn't
require samples of a subject's hair or fingernails. That was eight
days ago and I'm still here, as is, alas, the accursed. Which goes to
show what my heart of hearts always murmured: studying pagan
gods is like researching expat destinations, a form of treading water, pretending we're up shit creek but with a paddle at least, till
next election-cycle lumbers around."

Happy to hear he didn't swallow his own guff hook, line, and
sinker, albeit chances were he was only skeptical after the fact.
And as if affirming that, he postponed our toast further in unre-

formed heathen fashion, pouring a votive libation into a previous customer's stray saucer and pushing it forward as a centerpiece. "Why not?" he slung at my wry face.

There followed a clink of chalices at last, and we drank to his renewed lease on a sadder, wiser life. He gagged and yowled as if he'd swallowed a ladybug. He slammed his chalice down and snatched up the bottle. "Mort Subite!" he gasped. "Did you hear me order this?" No, I hadn't.

The waiter eventually humored our flailing come-hithers. He acknowledged Danon's grievance with token nods, but his abstracted gaze was stuck on the maroon pool in the saucer. In self-exoneration more than apology, he retailed how Danon's preference was out of stock, so he'd intrepidly substituted a Lambic of similar quality, saving Danon a few bucks into the bargain. Win-win, right?

"You do understand 'Mort Subite' means 'sudden death'?" Danon was indeed as popeyed and chalky as a poisoning victim. At this juncture, anyway, I could forgive our server's lack of rapport toward Danon's mystifying distress. Had I not connected some dots, I'd have been at an equal loss.

"It's a very well-respected brand," the poor heel floundered. "A classic. If it's flat, I'll be happy to exchange it or bring something else."

"Too late! Too late!" Danon expostulated. "The gods have spoken! Nothing you can do!"

The waiter translated this as permission to skedaddle.

Hard-pressed to exert a calming influence, I blurted, "Hold on, didn't you say we were past the statute of limitations? No blowback after a week?"

"They're gods!" Danon was atremble struggling to contain himself, to remain seated. "They can do as they like, change the rules as they go along!"

"Look, I can't explain how pulling that particular switcheroo got into the waiter's head. But you have to tell yourself, it was his whim. Nobody else's. Please be rational for both our sakes. You just said the whole hang-up over obsolete gods was a distraction from politics, no bearing on reality."

Danon's ears were clogged with panic, his mouth a spillway for it. "The god I besought was Cocidius, who presides over nature and war, whose color is red, and what the Poet's Curse clamors for is summary elimination. Why except in rejection of my appeal would I have received a cherry-red beer, with cherries on the label yet, and the words 'Mort Subite' on that label? No other reason!"

How tenaciously he ignored my point that the kid had committed his gaffe for no occult reason at all, most definitely not at divine urging. And like a fiery mayday signal, the overhang of brow between Danon's eyes, which became a button of flesh when his anxious forehead crinkled, was red as his libation. Ruddiness like a Rorschach blot was diffusing from that midpoint across his features.

Inspiration to the rescue! Or anyway, my overheating brain ad-libbed, "We'll trade, okay? I'm fine with Mort Subite, as you are with the Kasteel I ordered. I'll brave your beer of ill omen." I proactively swapped our chalices. Danon's expression perhaps flickered between doubts about my quick fix and amazement at a pal who'd take a bullet for him. He hoisted his replacement chalice, thirsty for relief, I imagined, from his tortured mindset.

Yet it was not so easily shed. He perched on the edge of his seat as if his posterior were spring-loaded. Please, let nothing thwart him from recouping self-possession, relaxing again as much as ever he did! He essayed a restorative sip, brought glass to lips for another.

A gut-wrenching thud rattled the window beside us. We twisted toward ground-zero; I pinched the stem of my chalice more tightly, whereas Danon flung his between his feet as his chair scraped noisily backward. For a millisecond a red-tailed hawk adhered spread-eagled, as it were, to the glass, where it must have crashed on maneuvers to seize a nocturnal rodent. Miraculously it hadn't busted a wing: no sooner had it registered on our retinas than its nails-on-chalkboard talons propelled it from its smudged and dusty imprint, and it fluttered off.

Almost as precipitously, Danon was up and in motion, bawling, "Cocidius! Alias Segomo in Belgium! His servants were the hawks!" He was headlong out the door, jabbering in torrential spate about unholy hunts, birds of prey tracking him down. I was on my feet, but in a quandary's paralytic grip.

Our tab languished unpaid. Of Danon's volatility the staff was ruefully aware; by default I bore closer semblance to a responsible adult. If I bolted, though, would that brand us both as runners? No one in company apron fit the hulking bouncer image, which didn't rule out their facility at pursuit and tackle. Nor was I, clinging to the Pollyanna hooey that all might end well, in a hurry to get myself eighty-sixed from a beloved neighborhood resource.

Thus I goggled transfixed out the window, hoping for the best, and during that minuscule span the window was my whole world. And constrained as it was, it was twice the size of Danon's world. I could see the hectic intersection of west-east and south-north streets, whereas his vision, blinkered by hysteria, was restricted to the avenue out front. The white hand of the walk sign extended him carte blanche to barrel ahead, or so he misconstrued. Did he ever glimpse the big black van that whipped around the corner, detained in its northbound course by the crunch of his body?

Skipping out on the check was suddenly a non-issue as I joined the stampede to the curb. I gawked with the same stupefaction as everyone, but to me alone had the fatality been a pal, and my consciousness glazed over, reducing me to an insensate daze, time in suspension, till sirens broke my shell. I apprehended only then I'd been gaping at the nameplate left of the taillight, to wit, a Voyager. The van's occupants were sitting tight behind tinted glass, not that I dared squint in to ascertain the driver's familiarity. No, no, my friend's been killed, do not let me make this about me!

At that juncture, my stream of consciousness spilled into channels more properly his, like a resumption of his thought processes *in memoriam*. From the silt of oddments he'd spent years implanting in me sprang reflections on his trenchantly apropos death, for wheels had crushed him, and wheels were ensigns of power and mutability for Segomo, Cocidius, their war-god ilk. These musings came unbidden; I'd bet I was the onlooker least in charge of his overloaded brain. And wouldn't Danon, were our positions reversed, likewise mythologize my demise?

I was weak-kneed and feverish, as if his worldview were a virus, and chronic exposure had infected me. A little hogwash can be a dangerous thing! Momentarily I was in the opening throes of police, coroner's, insurance paperwork that dogged me on and off for days. In the meantime, Danon's contagion, or else despair at our necrotizing democracy, intensified; either way I took to reading every coincidence as celestial calling card. What can I say? People tend to believe in whatever they can pretend will get them out of intractable messes.

Less defensibly, I lurched home after witnessing vehicular homicide with the sensation I'd gotten away with something. Traumatized or not, I hadn't squared the bill, haven't yet. As for the metaphysical role I conceivably played in siccing the Voyager on Danon, I hush my conscience by underscoring the infinitesimal odds of two run-ins with the same black van, unless the gods do exist. And if so, what did that connote about divine caprice and unjust spite?

With all due respect to Pascal, people can hole up in quiet rooms and still court miseries, and I don't refer to social-media folly. There are so many corrupt, shameless autocrats on whom to test the Poet's Curse, an embarrassment of guinea pigs. What's more, I can research the curse online, like anything else these days, from the comfort of my "birdhouse." The rub is to decide who couldn't possibly be of inscrutable value to the gods, who qualifies as cosmic dead weight, since starting at the top didn't exactly pan out.

Casting a whammy is a supremely idle gesture, but my best stab at shoring up positivity, so why not indulge, for temporary respite from ass-over-teakettle reality? Moreover, feeling helpless may conduce to worse mental health than could be ascribed to someone practicing harmless mumbo-jumbo. As long as I'm into nothing technically criminal or physically self-destructive, doing something must be better than twiddling thumbs, even something delusional and embarrassing in hindsight.

And for good measure, why not research appeasing Nehalennia, or magically reconciling with the girlfriend? For now, though, safety first: I adopt a hands-off policy toward Cocidius. He's sheer myth, of course, but doing otherwise would be foolhardy, wouldn't it?

After the Legions

When his wallowing tub of a Gaulish freighter docked at Pevensey, Florian's thoughts were twofold: of the tedious journey to Winchester this suboptimal landfall occasioned, and of Pevensey's vainglory in erecting colossal shoreline bastions as if Saxons would bother invading here. What a profligate waste of resources to repel a few grab-and-go pirates! How would Saxons gain even a toehold, unless Briton leaders were stupid enough to invite them en masse as, say, mercenaries?

Florian, along these lines, was no fool. Because he was heading into traditionally Belgic regions, he'd hired one bodyguard, a hulking Belgian styling himself Bauto, in the port of Boulogne; he couldn't trust two not to gang up and rob him. On the other hand, a lone bodyguard's "family resemblance" to Belgae across the Channel should ease his passage through unstable territory. Likewise, he hired horses and bought coarse-woven British hooded cloaks for the cross-country slog, instead of cozier travel by carriage, to blend in and to blunt any impression of affluence.

As further concealment, they slept rough behind hedges for the journey's two nights, not that the villages they skirted had ever rated state-sponsored inns. And after the legions' desertion of Britannia some fifteen years earlier, some towns that had maintained official inns were allegedly letting them devolve into rattraps or deathtraps infested with thieves.

Even in his pauperish guise, Florian was subjected to ample proof he couldn't have taken precautions enough. Overambitious louts impeded them at swordpoint by several desolate crossroads, declaring themselves constituted to exact tolls. Bauto had to disabuse them, and what a thrill to watch Roman training spring forth, to dismember pairs and trios of assailants with a common *gladius* as he would toddlers. Furthermore, it was heartwarming to promote a public service, improving highway safety for future travelers.

The roads were hardship in themselves. On previous inspections of the estate, in young, more sedate days, the ride had been bumpy thanks to slack maintenance, but now paving stones were sealed in mud, awash like fords, or quarried out by the furlong. Hard to credit he was still technically within the Empire where Valentinian had been emperor for three, four years. It was of no profit, really, to keep track. Now that emperors were, like everybody, Christians, no longer gods in their own right, their authority scarcely mattered more than anyone else's.

The approach to Winchester enveloped them in a diffuse shambles that spilled erratically beyond tottering municipal walls, sending forth tendrils of outlying streets as if the town were a spreading, sickly weed. Florian and Bauto led their horses upslope through unguarded east gateway into the central slums. Florian flattered himself that the inn, dominating one side of the seedy forum, had newly plastered its façade to ingratiate bluebloods of his ilk. Whatever the risks of lice and scandalous plumbing, here they'd lodge instead of his estate; why afford his disgruntled tenants a golden pass to murder him in bed?

Bauto would be invaluable in securing those tenants' cooperation tomorrow. For tonight Florian regretted the kitchen could fortify his enforcer with nothing but extremely pungent fish stew, too salty, peppery, and acrid, inducing Florian to comment the cook had overplayed the *garum*. No imported sauce, *garum* or otherwise, figured in the recipe, Bauto grumbled; the stew was simply rancid, with triple-strength seasoning to stave off virulence. Their travel rations of tough flatbread and moldy cheese and sour wine had been more wholesome.

Nonetheless, their dinner sat, miraculously perhaps, all right with them; hence complaining to the management would serve scant practical purpose. Their stuffy bedchamber, threadbare blankets, and musty pallets were likewise not nasty enough to warrant protest and the frustrating wait for corrective measures. Conditions were all the more galling because, after Florian had paid in advance with shiny new *solidi,* the innkeeper whipped out a scale, dourly indicated the coins had been "clipped," and required more. What an epitome of the unctuous, conniving little Brit, referred to by great-great-grandfather, in a letter to great-great-grandmother when buying the estate, as "Britunculi"!

The crowning indignity burst upon them in the dead of night. A virtual thunderstorm of hammering, thudding, bellowing, tortured creaking from right outside persisted though daybreak, degrading Florian's sleep to fitful at best. Only under dogged questioning did the innkeeper divulge that slaves and laborers had been pressganged to demolish the inn's bathhouse, dysfunctional since the engineers who'd serviced it had decamped with the legions. The masonry was essential for blocking up extramural northbound streets. But why the barricades? Why work by starlight? Their host shrugged, a touch impudently in Florian's opinion.

Through the boisterous night, Florian had had sundry occasions to brood on the wisdom of his initially straightforward mission. For a century, his paternal bloodline had managed the suburban British villa mostly in absentia, and tenant families had mostly forwarded annual rents without violent prompting. The current family was three years in arrears. Civil unrest, military dustups may have disrupted shipping, the availability of coinage, for part of that span, but three years?

Friends with rental villas of their own exhorted him to go lay down the law. Their holdings were in provinces firmly under Imperial control, yet delinquent tenants in Britannia set a dangerous example for Gaulish cousins to imitate. Florian, in fine, was persuaded he wouldn't qualify as public-spirited if he forswore his patrician duty. And taxes on the property, whether or not it earned him a denarius, relentlessly ate at his coffers. None of these particulars, sadly, carried convincing weight after a rotten night and borderline rotten breakfast, followed by jogging along on saddlesore horseback, in sodden itchy cloaks under a pelting rain.

Bauto rode alongside in Stoic reticence, out of respect for which Florian abstained from fuming about the barren furrows of his outlying fields, yielding only islands of burdock and furze. Within their bedimming hood, Bauto's features indulged no more than sporadic twitches at the corners of a wry frown; the unpropitious fields may already have quickened unfounded worries about Florian's willingness to pay him.

The residence lacked ells but loomed a substantial three stories, and outbuildings thronged it like piglets around a sow. It showed no exterior damage, but vented no sounds or other signs of activity. Bauto banged on the stout oaken door. Nobody answered or stirred audibly within; nor was the lock fastened. Indoors it was blessedly dry, though the chill of prolonged vacancy bit at them. Florian sighed morosely and bid Bauto search the house for truants dead or alive, for clues to this feckless dereliction.

Nothing in the entrance hall implied brigands had usurped the premises for a den. All the same, he chafed at the length of time Bauto, evidently thorough to a fault, was spending on reconnaissance. And what a waste of Florian's nerves, for when the Belgian tramped in, his report in full was a glum shake of his cowled head.

Everything domestic was in place and orderly, aside from a pall of dust. Lidded jars of dry goods lined pantry shelves, and amphorae of everyday wine and olive oil were stoppered and snug in their racks. The family might have trundled off to market day in town and loitered there three years.

Florian and Bauto went together to the equally deserted smithy and granary, the stables devoid of horses, and then the wind shifted, to bear ill tidings from the cattle byre some hundreds of feet away. Florian hadn't smelled the like since greenest childhood, during the old religion's brief revival, when his father ushered him into a Mithraeum, to his abiding confusion: should Florian have been devoutly inspired by ancient rites or bolstered in his Christianity by the callous slaughter of bulls and literal bloodbath afterward? Father never specified, and was now unforthcoming dust in his grave.

No matter; filling his lungs and muffling nostrils with his cloak, Florian waved Bauto ahead and warily trailed after. Faugh! Without inhaling, the reek was nonetheless concussive, like smacking into a shield wall. The dirt floor had become reddish, sticky mud from myriad slit throats. Cairns of scorched, putrid beef he'd foreseen, though not the savage anarchy of their butchering, or the admixture of horseflesh and portions of other anatomy, inexplicit but banefully suggestive. Neither stench nor carnage visibly fazed Bauto, too young to remember gory pagan rites; as a veteran, he was perhaps inured to grislier. A wonder the timbers hadn't caught fire!

Shaken and nauseous as he was, Florian had been brought up hardheaded, lending him the acumen to second-guess Bauto's forebodings that he'd been hired for a fool's errand. From there, might Bauto reckon on "cutting his losses," with maggots as sole witnesses? "Nothing for us here," Florian spoke up. "But your money's safe and sound in Boulogne, much more than I have on my person."

Bauto nodded, none the unsteadier for breathing unfiltered putrescence. Behind the byre they discovered a chapel, a humble whitewashed cell scarce bigger than a market stall. Beside its gaping doorway, a blood-red daub in the shape of a cross struck Florian as mocking. A whiff of the same fetor as in the byre arrested them. Bauto hunched his shoulders and strode in, to emerge before the count of ten. Florian gestured gruffly toward the doorway for clarification, but Bauto kept his own mum counsel, signing "pax vobiscum" for silence.

More vexingly, Bauto, in the pouring rain, complained of his dry mouth and requested directions to the well. Fraught moments eked by till Bauto reappeared with a dented pewter cup, which he offered with the caveat, "I've had worse. Did it always taste like this?"

Florian took the cup to humor him but lifted it no closer than sniffing range. It stank of sulfur. "No, it didn't." Florian's turn to be laconic! He handed back the cup, which Bauto drained and carelessly dropped. Florian supposed the spoiled water could explain the tenants' exodus, but certainly not the mayhem tokened by that cross of blood, so conspicuous against the whitewash. Nor would he put it past "Britunculi" townsmen to relay news of Florian en route—which, however, explained none of the mayhem, or the dust, not that he'd discussed his business with the hotelier or anyone else.

Meanwhile, what more to accomplish in the rain? They'd tied their horses to a hitching-rail in front of the stable. Bauto betrayed no reaction to their theft; Florian trembled helplessly at this declaration they weren't alone, at his short-term prospects. He was hardheaded, not made of marble!

"This is how we go forward," Bauto murmured, with a glower that brooked no dissent. "Nod sometimes to show you understand. Don't talk."

Florian nodded.

"Doff the pauper's cloak. You have to look rich. Good, your tunic's a brighter white than anything around us. The purple stripes are fine, they paint the lily. You're getting soaked, but don't worry, soon you'll be so wet you'll get no wetter."

Florian nodded miserably, shivering in lieu of trembling.

"I've maneuvered and fought in forests. You haven't. You hit the road to town, in plain sight. I'll be in the undergrowth where they won't see me, but I'll see you. Maybe they're watching us now. Doesn't matter."

Florian nodded, though he felt his coherence dissolving in the rain.

"To avoid an arrow in the back, you have to look like someone who can raise a ransom, who's worth more alive than dead."

Florian nodded, dearly hankering to ask if Bauto had ever done this before, how it had panned out. He was too stupefied to judge whether the plan were masterful or harebrained.

"When they break cover to waylay you, just stand there and quake in your shoes. They'll kill you otherwise. I'll have surprise on our side. You've seen me at work. You trust me, don't you? Now get started, and mince along like a senator, yes, that's good."

Had Bauto not barred him from speaking, Florian would have alluded to the atrocities in the byre and chapel, to the suspiciously unbovine remains, implying the horse-thieves weren't *sensu stricto* bandits, were quite possibly immune to the enticements of kidnapping. And "mince along"? Florian was walking as anyone would in a downpour!

He frequently had to curb his tempo when tension and resentment prodded him with the riddle, How had a simple errand to retrieve his due unraveled into this ordeal? He also had to concentrate on gazing straight down the muddy road, not toward the roadside lest he expose Bauto or behold the highwaymen too soon, whereas failure to do so the instant they leapt out might result in a severe pummeling. God almighty, he must have trudged a mile! If only he'd noted landmarks riding out, he might be rejoicing to identify urban outskirts. Maybe he would re-enter town without molestation. Maybe mere sneakthieves had poached the horses.

Florian was about to commend himself for grace under fire when an ear-rending shriek spooked him into a headlong dash. His feet slid out from under to land him prostrate in the mud, noble countenance, shiny white tunic and all. After a breathless second he scrambled up and onward, constantly amazed and grateful no iron missile pierced his spine. No telling whether Bauto or his victim had caterwauled; how should he recognize Bauto's scream?

He'd never heard the like but once, and that during tender childhood. Father had fobbed him off one summer with country relations, ostensibly to better appreciate agrarian virtues, more plausibly for father's better appreciation of a new mistress. Florian was roaming the woods with a cousin harvesting mushrooms when Goths as intent on bread as gold raided the homestead. The cousin hid Florian in a hollow log and raced off to join the defenders. He couldn't have gone far when the galloping hooves of the Goths' rearguard preceded a petrifying scream. As a boy he'd been too terrified to move for hours; as a man he was too terrified to govern breakneck panic.

To stagger in one piece through Winchester's west gate, what a miracle! And since Florian was technically a Christian, wasn't he obliged to thank Jesus, consecrate a lamb or something to Him? A guilty pang at his own faith's unfamiliarity stung him. God grant he could expiate his laxity! For now, though, he had to glare at those bumpkins who dared regard him askance, while he affected a seemlier pace and swabbed at mud that flowed in streams of rainwater off his face and clothing. His hauteur was reinstated by the time he marched into the inn.

The damned Britunculus innkeeper was snoozing in plain sight across the courtyard, under the colonnade, against a wood-pile. Florian woke him by digging a mucky foot into his thigh, and demanded a strigil immediately, before the lout had shuddered free of Morpheus. He boggled openmouthed as if at Coptic, but Florian repeated his demand more harshly. Like an earwax pick or a nit comb, it belonged in every hotel's kit of basic courtesies for guests. The lazy pipsqueak bolted as from a riled-up hive, to slouch back shortly with a dented, old-fangled strigil from the inn's grubby depths.

Berating an inferior exerted a tonic effect, restored Florian's composure to dwell on Bauto. He scraped caking clay off his face, his arms, and flicked it into the courtyard. The hygienic routine further mellowed him, tinged his musings with melancholy. Would he ever see Bauto again? Sounder of limb than Florian, he'd have overtaken a "mincing senator" half a league from town, were he still unscathed. Florian was sorry, though gruesome de-mise was a bodyguard's occupational hazard, wasn't it? Manly dispassion was appropriate when reflecting on a soldier-of-fortune's lot.

Florian's flinty stance suffered a setback as he bent to apply the utensil to some spatters under his tunic hem. A laceration the length of the strigil was oozing blood down his calf. A stone in the roadbed must have gashed him when the unseen havoc sent him sprawling; he'd been too overwrought to feel it. His knees went wobbly as he planted a hand upon a column to support himself, and bellowed for the hotelier, who slunk in from parts unknown with a fatalistic pout, apparently aware he'd be worse off for the duration if he didn't snap to it.

Florian fluttered his free hand at the lesion. Was a physician, he carped, too much to hope for around here?

Why, two physicians had attended to a retired lieutenant in a villa within view of the south gate. It went without saying, they all cleared out a decade ago. A Christian priest had also been versed in medicine, but he was dead. A Greek freedman operating as a barber from a tent in the forum was Florian's best bet. The hotelier was fixated on Florian's wound, but with the blankness of grasping unsuccessfully what the fuss was about.

At least the rain was letting up. Amidst the forum's sparsely stocked fruiterers and butchers hawking indeterminate cuts, the barber was manifestly the shaven-pated codger shaving another codger. The customer was courting splinters and pneumonia by sitting on a sodden stump in the resurgent sun, and the barber was attired like Florian, that is, above his station, likely cultivating credibility via his (most probably late) ex-master's castoffs.

Once the oldster hobbled away, Florian requested treatment for his wound "before gangrene set in." The barber fetched a jar from his tent, and a wad of dry linen to encourage his rare patrician client to perch upon the stump "for both their sakes." The jar contained a piney balm, cool and numbing, which the barber slathered liberally atop the wound, promising it would "repel flies and baneful spirits."

Oh, and were baneful spirits an especial problem in Winchester? Florian was himself unsure whether he intended condescension or sarcasm. The barber replied with the tone-deafness of practiced subservience, "What is a baneful spirit?" He, for one, had kept his strigil handy, scooping off the analgesic balm with it. From a leather pouch at his belt he extracted a silver needle and spool of catgut suture. "You'll have to put up with some twinging, but not as you would without the unguent." Ouch, ouch, ouch! The Greek was right, it hurt like hornets, but was marginally bearable.

"You'll have to remain seated. Your leg will be unfit to hold you up awhile." Florian grunted acknowledgment while otherwise riveting his attention on the forum's shabby provincials, its shifty, presumptively outlaw foreigners, and the quality few who trod circumspect, as if through a bog. He guessed the barber babbled on to distract him from the needlework. "The legions, and with them the official faith, our way of dealing with one another, and with the world, are gone, and thus a vacancy among us, and in our souls, has been replenished by much that Rome had ousted. Don't fidget."

Florian carelessly glanced down while the barber flourished a pair of scissors. He redirected his sightline to the sea of strangers. "You scoff at baneful spirits," the barber resumed. "Ah, but are they spirits who return to move among us bodily? Not only do foundering towns and regrouping tribes vie to seize authority; apostate worshippers and what they worship have also come into conflict. The methods of soothsayers from a more regulated age are unreliable in claiming certain spirits or gods can be deflected by walling off certain streets." The barber tapped Florian's intact shin to signal he was done.

"You'll have a scar, but that's not the worst of your troubles, is it?"

Florian sighed in relief, even as he contemplated rebuking up-start barber for insolence, and a heartbeat later was dumbfounded that his painstaking surveillance had missed someone in a gray hooded cloak who loomed beside him now. In the sun, the starker shadow within the hood from Florian's perspective blotted out the newcomer's face, but who in that garment who was not the Belgian would accost him? "Bauto!" enthused Florian. "Thank God! Where have you been?" He entertained a comradely impulse to stand and clasp his hireling's forearm or shoulder, but luckily, he resisted.

"Bauto?" The speaker had the uncouth resonance of a blowfly in a crypt. "Bauto is dead."

Florian had no ear for more. Despite the barber's caveat about limited mobility from the painkiller, Florian lunged up and almost fell flat as his knee buckled, but sheer dint of stricken will goaded him forward, dipping, limping, rocking at full tilt in his besmirched toga, to the amusement of boorish onlookers, in zigzag flight toward the church fronting the forum. Sanctuary! Astonishing how the herald of Bauto's death hadn't collared him, though he wasn't in a state to ponder that, only to focus on consecrated ground, because whatever wore the cloak was foremost unholy. He felt that like the blast from a bathhouse flue.

On the forum's periphery, gawkers no longer obstructed his view of church façade. Loath as he was to criticize the abode of a God about to rescue him twice in one day, the church was drab, unprepossessing, compared with the average temple. Beneath a pitched roof, narrow windows in a brick wall plain as barracks watched indifferently as he stumbled up the semicircular ripple of steps to the bulky door in its horseshoe arch. As a further kindness to him, the door was ajar.

Inside, though, the malodors of dust, mildew, birdshit fostered doubts that God was home. Perhaps He'd left with the legions, as the barber had professed. In fact, nobody answered his halloos, nobody was home, not even pigeons, though their telltales were everywhere. How well could this dark, abandoned building function as sanctuary? The contrasting echoes of his good and then leaden foot, soft, loud, ruined any pretense of stealth as he traversed the nave, mounted the threshold to the chancel, slumped against the massive butcher's block of an altar as if it likeliest qualified as a last island of sanctity. Yet the smell here was much ghastlier.

Florian flattened his palms upon the nicked and pitted altar and peeked over. Behind it lay an almost fleshless skeleton, clerical vestments ravaged by moths and mold, ceremonial sash likewise riddled except for gold-thread outlines of a fish and a chalice. A yard away, the skeleton's mandible was embedded by its incisors in the tile floor. A wave of queasiness made Florian clamp on-

to the edges of the altar, which he unhanded at the jolting realization he'd neglected to shut, much less lock or bar, the church
door. His thudding footfalls must have been audible from outside,
signal drums to lead the enemy, even if Florian had lost him
among the marketgoers.

He swiveled toward the entrance, and there was Bauto's putative impersonator, just beyond the chancel threshold, observing
him serenely. The eyes within the hood palpably transfixed him,
though the shadow masking the face was all the more impenetra-
ble here.

"This church has been unhallowed fifteen years," rumbled the
unholy informant, to whom Florian's mind, or anyway rationale,
was patently no secret. An outwardly normal arm swept up from
under the cloak; an outwardly normal finger pointed at Florian's
stitches. "And no, you couldn't have eluded me, not with your
scent of blood for a trail."

"You killed Bauto," accused Florian, to no good purpose, he
fathomed even as he spoke.

"Did I?" Not a denial so much as a rebuff to Florian's flawed
logic: was this a bit of cat-and-mouse sparring? If he could have
marshaled the wits to riposte, Florian's heart was pounding such
that the strain of vocalizing would absolutely have ruptured it.

"Why do you assume I want to harm you?" Oh God, Florian
quavered, just the question a cat would put to a mouse! "What of
me gainsays I'm a fellow traveler incognito, going native the same
as you?" As if in bombastic counterpoint to his contention, Bauto's loose facsimile winked out an instant like a star, and in his
stead floated Jesus, bearded, swaddled in a loincloth, palms up-
held to exhibit stigmata. No less swiftly, Jesus winked out and the
counterfeit Bauto's feet were on the floor. "Forgive me, I must
have my jest! Do not, in short, draw conclusions oversoon."

Florian deferentially shook his head, though it was like shift-
ing a millstone. The "fellow traveler" had exploded his own argument he was only as he seemed; that alone was clear. Childhood
catechism bobbed up in Florian unbidden, some esoterica where-

in Christ was a man with God inside. Was dredging up that attribute of the divine a desperate bid to assign a benign, intelligible face to this entity, externally a man, albeit once more without a discernible face?

"Aren't you curious why I followed you?" A fed-up snort interrupted the soliloquy. "Damn all, but this hood's confining." With a backward jerk of faux Bauto's head, the cowl fell away, and for a measureless interval Florian seesawed between two insolubles, two more than sanity could harbor: was that a face? Was this what a god was?

"Always better to be comfortable, don't you agree? As I was saying, I sniffed you out to thank you. He who has presided over this town beheld two of you depart the west gate, and then reenter, according to his malleable perceptions, one right after the other. This, while he, through his augurs, bade the people protect the north gate with spells and masonry."

Florian was digesting none of this, for his effort to reconcile the garbled mosaic of skin, bone, hair, teeth, orifices into a face (it tended toward a volatile three) led him only to emit an earsplitting series of shrieks. He hadn't the resources to read the expression on mercurial features as pained. "I'd have solicited you to join us, though now you create a public disturbance, and how to win converts with testimony like yours? Will you shut up?"

With that, Florian became party to the last marvel he'd ever have witnessed, could he but have processed what his eyes absorbed. The hand that protruded from under Bauto's cloak transformed into a crowfoot of flames as it elongated toward Florian's recalcitrant larynx.

In the tranquility that afterward reigned over the church, the barber stole in, candle aloft to establish his was the sole animate presence. Hurrah, the charring of Florian's soiled tunic had spread only as far as the sternum! From the pouch tied to the belt of headless torso, the barber extracted the several coins Florian still owed when he fled. Not the barber's problem if a client never enjoyed the benefits of services rendered! He was no less entitled to the fee he'd earned in good faith.

This, in a nutshell, was why he loved the new Britannia: patrician types couldn't cheat you with impunity, and even gods competed for your allegiance. The Hooded One who'd appointed him divine eyes and ears, who'd beckoned him churchward, promised incalculably more than payment due for needlework once the Shining One was expelled. Despite the vaunted clairvoyance and opulence of Winchester's current god, that Shining One had been shamelessly stingy to adherents, and his priesthood had been easy as the Christians to purge. At least, come what may, those humorless, rood-worshipping, Romish zealots were gone forever.

One Across

As such cells went, it was airy, bright, and it overlooked the flowerbed in the circular turnaround fronting the well-heeled institution. Insofar as Imrie had been certified mostly harmless to himself and others, and emanated a disarming, if snarky, charm, he as much as anyone merited this relatively privileged placement. The windows' iron bars were really a formality, and did not a prison make per se, to paraphrase some dead poet or other.

Sometimes after engaging with Imrie, Dr. Pimm questioned the decision to commit him at all, almost ready to relegate the paperwork's OCD, delusional disorder, and self-defeating personality profile to hasty misdiagnosis. At other times, Imrie would no sooner open his mouth than damning evidence for prolonged confinement babbled out.

Today, pensive Imrie was hunched forward in his velour easy chair, cobalt eyes fixed upon the crosswords magazine on a little, round coffee table. Dr. Pimm leaned over oblivious Imrie's shoulder, thought better of it—too Big Brotherly—and broke into Imrie's reverie with a request to peek at whatever was so absorbing. Imrie slid the magazine across the table as the doctor came around to fetch it.

Only one across had been filled in. "I see under 'Spielberg movie,' four letters, you've written '*1941.*' Are you positive that's the most promising move?" What's more, Imrie was wielding a Bic and not a pencil, a brio the doctor would have admired in a sane gamester.

"No use wrangling about it now," Imrie drawled. "Why not come back in twenty minutes, and we'll see?"

"Okay, you're on." Dr. Pimm attributed his clinical success, mixed as it was (like everybody's, after all), to picking battles wisely. Thus between humoring or gratuitously challenging Imrie, he opted for the course of less resistance.

The orderly readmitted him half an hour later. Imrie was dozing in his comfy chair, his open mouth tilted toward the ceiling, and blue ink in every square of the puzzle on the table. He opened one eye as the door relocked and gestured lazily in his handiwork's general direction.

Dr. Pimm scooped up the magazine, studied the page over his tortoiseshell rims, executed a shameless double-take, and flipped to the answers section at the end. Good God! Every solution of Imrie's worked individually and en bloc, but none matched the puzzlemaster's. Yes, even *1941* made sense in its alternative context.

"I gather you're amazed," Imrie inferred, a tad cockily perhaps. "It's just down to word hoard and imagination. Enough of both and you can dash off three or four versions of any crossword."

"Okay," Dr. Pimm proceeded cautiously, "that still begs the question of why you'd apply your prodigious 'word hoard,' as you put it, to no more creative or rewarding purpose." He was expecting a reply steeped in banality, if not incoherence, citing mental exercise as its own reward, or the value of play in killing time.

Instead, Imrie blindsided him with the starkest justification yet for internment. "Oh, I've devoted my skill set to the most creative purpose. By undertaking a mere crossword in the guiding light of intuition, I finish up changing the world. But unless you're exceptionally discriminating or in my company when it happens, you'd never know the difference."

"Come again?" Already this felt like a different world from the routinely breezy one of a moment ago.

"You've heard of quantum adjustments? No?" Imrie was sitting up straighter, eager to trot out his hobbyhorse. "You have experienced them, I guarantee, as when you swear you've seen a word spelled a certain way a thousand times, but suddenly Google produces zero hits to that effect. Or myriad reliable websites post how one director helmed a certain movie though another is often

mistakenly credited, and then those same sources decree the opposite is true. Were you aware Stanley Kramer didn't direct *Spar-
tacus*? Never mind. If not for the Internet, in fact, most of these
ontological switcheroos would go forever unnoticed."

Imrie, gazing earnestly upon the doctor, sat back in smug contentment. "Well, I have the fortune or genetics or enlightenment,
and I say this with all due modesty, to enact quantum adjustments pretty much on a whim. If you'll humor me further, just
what kind of flower does that traffic circle out the window contain? No, don't go look. I know you've seen them umpteen times;
you must have been cognizant of them on occasion."

Dr. Pimm chafed at the threat of role reversal, of the patient
patronizing him. "They're beebalm," he grudgingly played along.
"They're magenta."

"Check again, please? I'm no good at IDing plants. No green
thumb, not in this life, anyhow."

Disdaining to dig into any deeper implications of Imrie's pat-
ter, he strode to the window and had an alarming, inexplicable
sense he'd been imposed upon. The flower bed was rife with nodding, buttery-yellow rudbeckia. Could the gardener have super-
vised this major an overhaul with the doctor clueless the while?

Imrie cleared his throat. "Assuming you've borne with me, I
needn't explain the grounds crew would have no recollection that
beebalm had ever been out there, as indeed on this world it has
not."

Dr. Pimm, with considerable irritation, reminded himself that
he was in charge here. He recked not how suave and eloquent his
mental patient was; that only made him the more dangerously delusional. And especially irksome for the doctor, a confirmed
morning person, was the onus of having to regain the upper hand
so early, when he was ordinarily on top of things. "But Mr. Imrie,"
he objected, dialing up the autocratic sonority of Boston breeding,
"supposing you do have the power to reshape the world, why do
nothing more impactful with it than switch out the contents of
garden patches?"

Imrie rubbed at a surprisingly squeaky eye as if the proceedings were soporific. "To spell out our key term more clearly, quantum adjustments are what I do, which by definition do not encompass paradigm shifts, bombshell developments, or sea changes. Maybe others can boast abilities on those levels. Maybe I can look forward to that on some future world."

Imrie's expression shifted from jaded to wistful. "Meanwhile, a man's reach should exceed his grasp, right? Though I've no memory of any such existence, I can posit a universe in which I haven't been institutionalized, from which I was jettisoned by taking a woefully wrong tack in figuring out a crossword. Again, for clarity's sake, it were best I spell out that the sine qua non of the personhood seated before you is my wild talent with crosswords in every iteration of the cosmos, come whatever else may. Funny, isn't it, that the unifying theme of all my universes must be the ubiquity of crossword puzzles?"

He surveyed his pleasant cell with a sneaking fondness. "But as long as I'm in the wrong, or less than optimal, universe, I may as well be here as anywhere. Food and shelter aren't an issue, and whoever's paying for my stay will eventually never have doled out a cent, so I'm guilt-free on that score. All I have to do is sit around poring over crosswords."

Actually, Imrie raised a good question. Who was footing the bills for this potential lifer who evinced null interest in getting better, at least along conventional psychiatric lines? "Anyway, when I do access my 'better place,' maybe you'll be there too, maybe you won't," Imrie shrugged. "That's out of my jurisdiction, and if you're not, it won't have been anything personal, okay?"

"No, of course not," the doctor condescended, haltingly excused himself, padded over to the door, and knocked on the wire-mesh window for the orderly to spring him. He consulted Imrie's case notes, and no mention of obsession with crosswords cropped up: maybe he'd been cadging them from the solarium during group exercise and working on them secretly, unbeknownst to Dr. Pimm and colleagues, all along. Researching Imrie's financial arrangements slipped his mind, one task too many on his to-do-list. As for the morphing flowerbed, the doctor may have just taken the renascence of last year's planting for granted. Not that he could even say whether beebalm was an annual or perennial.

Dr. Pimm did try clamping a lid on his own tendency toward intrusive ideations as it chomped on the bait of "quantum adjustments," if those were Imrie's exact words. Child's play at first to dismiss idle second glances at random items, pictures on walls, paperweights on desks, room numbers in corridors, and his concomitant scrupling at whether they were the same yesterday. But in no time, these incidents became more numerous, persistent, clamorous, freighting the ship of his rationality down to the gunwales. The hell of it was, he'd gone into psychiatry purely to wrest control from his inner saboteur.

The obvious remedy, which popped full-blown into his insomniac head at 2 A.M., was mortifying because he hadn't entertained it sooner. To rescue besieged tranquility, he simply had to remove the troubling magazines from the solarium, and when Imrie was in the solarium, from his cell. Staff or inmates who observed the doctor purging printed matter were welcome to brand his behavior arbitrary, quirky, neurotic; he outranked 99% of them, was not accountable to them, didn't care about their good opinion.

Dr. Pimm's sly mission was accomplished the day before his rounds again included Imrie. The white peonies in the traffic circle were making their midsummer comeback, as they had for decades. On nerve-wracking tenterhooks, he made himself attend to patients in the usual order, insist that Imrie wait his turn. Should Imrie lob insinuations about missing magazines, the doctor had rehearsed plausible denials, settling blame on janitorial shoulders.

The instant the orderly locked him in, Dr. Pimm's legs became dead weight and a tingling of panic overspread his body. Imrie, with a flourish of satisfaction, deliberately inscribed the final answer in the puzzle on his lap before raising bland eyes. He remained seated stolidly as if standing would be a waste of energy.

"This is a world on which you didn't check under the mattress." His tone was evenly modulated, not accusing but declaratory. At the same time, was his expression that of a cat with a mouthful of canary, or of a mortician pitying new arrivals?

Dr. Pimm, with no more power of locomotion than a mannequin, felt his heart sink like a lead plumb bob in a quarry pond. Then he felt nothing in a way he never had before, an all-consuming nothing, though he couldn't have said for sure how he'd ever felt because he couldn't remember anything about himself, where he was, who he was. It didn't even feel wrong that the white-coated stranger who might once have been an acquaintance was on his feet, gripping a clipboard instead of a magazine, looking beyond Dr. Pimm as if at thin air.

But then there had only ever been Dr. Imrie alone in the room, certifying it was shipshape for its next occupant. He flipped through the sheets on his clipboard, regarding the bottom one askance, a torn-out page from a puzzle book. As a distraction more than a pastime, crosswords were mostly harmless, but he really ought to swear them off as unbefitting a clinician of stature who always had something better to do. For no apparent reason, that dictum about quitting while ahead sprang to mind.

—*Thank you, Derrick, for putting the quantum bug in my ear.*

Grave Days in Skara Brae

In our snug seaside village, we've always taken pride in our second sight. Maybe we're gifted that way because of all the time we have for looking. It's nurtured our ability to see farther, clear out of the here and now. A mixed blessing sometimes, to be forewarned how illnesses and childbirths will play out, but the fewer surprises, the better, we always say.

Elsewhere, people use up their days growing barley, hunting skittish deer, serving priestly whims at the rings of stones. Not us! Eels teem in the river, fat waterfowl in the marsh, shellfish at the tideline, herds around the lake. Food practically waddles into our strong flagstone roundhouses, half-sunk in earth, sealed in warm midden, heated by the wood and whale bones and seaweed cast upon our beach by weather gods.

Easy to forget we're on an island a day's-walk wide, mostly cold and ocean northward, vast and dangerous lands southward. Strangers are rare and seldom visit outside certain seasons, when they mean to trade or they go astray seeking the priests. In either case, if they behave, we behave. I can't remember our last "sacrifice" of a troublemaker to the god of discord.

We're not, in fine, ordinarily at a loss dealing with foreigners, but at first we approached our holiest man, or "overseer" as we call him, meekly, one on one, about a recent spate of impudent trespassers. Among ourselves we spoke guardedly, dismissively of them, for they were visible to second sight alone, and so may have been figments of unbalance. Always that chance with second sightings!

The overseer would have been a poor fit for his role had he not foreseen our concerns and had a pronouncement ready. He hinted but never said outright he too had beheld the intruders. Still, that was assurance enough we weren't going mad, despite everything harassing our eyes and ears: the outlanders always appear by broad daylight, some days one or two, on others none, and all too often throngs loiter like bossy geese. None have witnessed them approach the village, yet suddenly they're in our midst. They dress in colors, patterns, stuff unknown to us, handily outdoing the most exotic traders and emissaries.

In every instance we're minding our own business at home, and when we see the strangers it's obviously with our second sight because we happen to look up and our roofs have gone missing, and there they are, goggling down from the paths around our semi-underground quarters. They're exchanging jokes and observations in no intelligible words, gesturing at our beds and hearths and display shelves as if they were the owners, absolutely ignoring us.

Do they covet our fur blankets, our chert toolkits, our beads and amulets? Naturally our best valuables are stashed in cubbies behind the bed canopies where thieves cannot lay eyes, gape till they go blind. Some of us perhaps overreacted, boring holes into doorframes to install logs for barring the uninvited, as none have yet traipsed in through doors. By evening, at latest, the last trespasser withdraws, and the harried householders will find they've been in a daze, ogling the whale-rib rafters and smoke-blackened thatch that never actually budged. I, for one, had become reluctant to stay inside much, as if that increased the odds of my roof flitting away.

To intimate we were indeed overreacting, or just to be funny, the overseer had drilled holes and trimmed a hazelwood pole to bar his door from the outside. He told me that showed as much sense as whatever else anyone was doing. His door was dutifully open to the troubled, and as it fronted a paved yard under the sky, the troubled could enjoy sitting cross-legged in sunshine; other houses are conjoined by slab-ceilinged passages to fend off winter squalls. Overseers claim scrutinizing clouds is vital in performing divination.

Privacy is scarce in our cozy flagstone nest, which makes the gawkers' hubris especially galling. Overseers alone are privileged to pursue their work in private, so we detour beyond earshot of their consultations, though this one fairly bellows without a care who overhears. Frankly, every villager's word aloud is common property, on the spot or soon. And what the sage counseled, after my mutterings forced him to lean within a pin's length of my mouth, was for the public good. He may have imparted this same wisdom to others, but embellished it with earnest, searching pauses as if conceiving it now, for me.

"Do not let empty air weigh on you. Be proud instead of how our dwellings were here before the circles of tall stones, before the high-ceilinged tombs in their giant mounds. Our place will remain after we're gone, after we're forgotten, after those who forget us will be forgotten. After them, someday, everyone will depart this place for a different walk of life, and the sand will bury it. The god of fortune has revealed this and more to me." He checked sidewise to confirm onlookers could eavesdrop comfortably from a respectful distance. Maybe he was sick of repeating himself, shrewdly striving to edify everybody in short order.

"Years beyond reckoning will pass, and a mighty storm will bare our village to the sky again. The people of that generation and their children and grandchildren will come in ever greater hosts, from remoter lands than any who come now, to wonder at what we've built. They will even understand our homes were here before everything else. These are the admirers our second sight reveals, unable to do us harm because they haven't been born nor will be for more lifetimes than we have numbers to count."

"We see them now, though. They're very annoying." I was sorry the instant I spoke. Bad form to address an overseer except with deference! I was venting a frustration everyone felt, which didn't entitle me to complain, leastwise in front of a judgmental crowd.

The overseer took my impertinence in forgiving stride. "Were you never curious about the stones shaped like spiky burrs and kernels that our forefathers put on every home's display shelves?

There they collect dust, bereft of meaning and purpose, abiding purely because they always have. But now they serve a use. Go on and throw one at the next trespasser. It will fly right through him, but you'll feel better doing something against something that annoys you. You can really do no more." If, though, the trespassers and open sky were "empty air," mirages of second sight, wouldn't projectiles hit the ceiling and plummet to the floor?

Before I could frame this objection tactfully, the cross-legged overseer turned his hands palms up, lapsed into a stiff-lipped smile. The interview was over; it behooved me to retire once my token of gratitude, a heaping bowl of hulled barley, was in his serene grasp. As I dusted off the seat of my woolly tunic, he generously bent the rule about dismissing clients in silence. "I'll venture you were going to ask when these nuisances will desist. That I cannot say, for I cannot say why they've descended on us."

He'd ventured wrong, and while his was the worthier question, it was no less fruitless. And since the people of that inconceivable time acted as if they didn't know we were here, why assume they, any better than we, knew why they were among us? My wife was caustically unimpressed with the overseer's "winter-night beer jabber." I found it calming, though, to heft the spiky ball on the shelf and picture hurling it at a gawky target. Touching the stone, in fact, made me wish trespassers would appear.

What's more, in my less fraught state ideas came to me. The second sightings, I realized, began afflicting us right after the woeful fire. At my cousin's hearth, a spark had ridden an updraft into the thatch. She should have been more watchful. When burning straws fluttered into her lap, too much of the ceiling was ablaze to save more than the baby. The roof caved in before flames sprang to other houses, but everyone was flustered, on edge for days, and the cousin's household had to crowd into surrounding homes while we rebuilt the roof. A hard pebble in the quern of village routine!

I couldn't swear my cousin's folk had been first to behold the encroachers. They've never admitted to seeing them at all. But no others had actually been without a roof, and second sight often arises during grief and disturbance. Like the fire whose aftermath outlasted the smoking embers, or like disease, maybe an outbreak of second sight at my cousin's spread from house to house. Maybe musing on the encroachment too much brought it back down upon me, along with its riptide of unwelcome revelation.

That morning I should have been out with the family raking up hazelnuts, not lagging indoors to savor the luxury of solitude, contemplating the overseer's pronouncements on the amount of time between now and our village's emergence from its tomb of sand. I could not make room in my head for such a magnitude of anything, and the effort left me staring nowhere, as if I'd fainted and revived while standing. The way the overseer had spoken, time was a thing, like an urn of grain or forest of kelp, leading me to ask, how much time is there? Even more than the gods can hold in mind?

To foresee the world without me in it was difficult enough. And the gods have granted us much longer lives than other creatures, as long as four or five generations of dogs or sheep. But how paltry that was next to the quantities of time the overseer described! How to get more time, to whom could I appeal if time were a thing of which more could be had, like water or flint? We had no god of time. How unjust! Then I discovered my hand weighing the burr stone as if yearning on its own to enact my resentment, waiting for something obnoxious to fling it at.

Had my mood or my musings the power to conjure? The weak, restful light brightened and stung my eyes, and I squinted up toward the sun riding a brilliant white cloud across blue sky. On the rim of the yawning pit my house had become, a fantastically hued woman crouched, shielding her eyes from stark sunshine to peer obliviously straight through me. Her legs were encased in some lurid green stuff; a garment upon her torso and arms was like leather but in patches of red, yellow, brown. She was fat as only a goddess can manage, not a mortal woman at the mercy of lean seasons. But nothing about her inspired reverence.

To her, with all her colors and fleshiness, I was invisible as a ghost, and the notion of being the ghostly one here frightened me. My submission day in, day out to habit and routine, miring me in dullness, had never given me pause before. But was shuffling in more or less of an ongoing daze truly natural, my wits unequal to recounting what chores busied me a week ago, whether I had cheese or broth for breakfast yesterday? I could recollect nothing momentous from the past except the disastrous fire. What if my wits were those of a ghost, tethered to monotony forever?

In the pouting, overfed trespasser I detected the smugness, the superiority, that the living can't help feeling toward the dead. How dare she! Gripping the ball so that its spikes dug into my palm, I used the hurt to sharpen my aim, my resolve, and my arm did the rest, with all its might. My mark none the wiser, the ball shot through bulging, garishly clad midriff, and must have bounced amid the roofs.

I had to ensure I'd done no one else harm, restore the ball to display-shelf enshrinement. It had met nothing where the roof should have been; why would I? Balancing atop the bedstead slab and boosting myself out, I braced to bang into invisible rafters, and when I didn't, was too glad to ponder it overmuch. Instead, the rooflessness of the whole village bewildered me, yet I was more intent on the squatter, slack-mouthed as if a simple domicile surpassed her understanding. I circled behind her warily, as I would a wounded animal, since I had hurled a rock through her. Had she not fidgeted, I'd have blamed witchcraft for ousting her soul.

Once her gaudy back was to me, I attended to retrieving my stone burr, but had to thread a loopy course along the curving strips of turf in which our houses were enclosed. My eyes I fixed upon my feet, to avoid missteps and a bone-cracking tumble, and also because I was loath to look down and learn whether more than roofs were missing from our lodgings. When I raised my eyes to verify I was on the right track, a neighbor was in my way, peering out to sea and unmindful I was behind him. A glance backward affirmed the stone would have felled him a heartbeat after perforating her.

Unless I tapped him on the shoulder or peeked at his profile, he would go unnamed, for most tunics and haircuts are alike from the rear. The nerve to do anything failed me. He must have been as insubstantial as she, or I'd have struck him down, so either his was a familiar face and proof that we were ghosts, or he was not of my kith and time, but, like her, of an unborn generation, my own unborn grandson in his manhood, who's to say?

Nobody, that's who; hopeless mysteries begone, I had an errand to finish! I squeezed by my heedless obstruction, and forward on the path flanked by sheer drops into house pits. Barging in front of him, blocking his view provoked no outcry, reaffirmed his otherworldliness or mine. My earthward sights finally located the ball on greensward fringing the village. As I bent to grab it, a twinge of disquiet shook me. I couldn't have been mistaken about my lifelong domain. It must have contracted by several houses, for me to be shut of it already.

The ball was as solid as I. It was in bluntest sense my talisman, my sole attachment to everything that had been real before. Without its weight in hand I might have gone to pieces when I straightened up and cast my eyes toward the horizon entrancing "my grandson." A moot point whether I'd been a ghost for impossible quantities of time, or a living witness to that unthinkably distant time. Here was a corruption of how the world had always been and rightly would be, a desecration the gods would never tolerate while they drew breath.

Had the gods not negotiated together where to put the ocean, the shore, the land? Madness even to dream of the ocean overstepping its god-given bounds, vagrant storm-tides notwithstanding! Yet grassland that should have stretched farther before me than I could have thrown the ball again ended mere paces beyond my toes. Past the edge was an ugly slope of gashed, furrowed soil and gravel down to a pebbly beach and the choppy waters of the bay. Surf crashed hungrily as if unsatisfied with the ground it had already swallowed. And that ground, I was positive, included several houses of the village.

Second sight must have been deceiving me; bad spirits in their travels weren't above staging tricks and illusions in passing. Thus I could insist forevermore, but couldn't stem the sickness in my heart from fathoming the truth. The gods would die or forsake us. I turned and slunk back, lowering my gaze once more, away from the "unborn" face that may have been shocked like mine at the sea's incursion, and away from the squatting trespasser who seemed as dumbstruck by my home as I by her godless world.

For me to stray into that world came down to my worst luck ever. Or was it luck? The overseer had advised me and, by virtue of eavesdroppers, everybody to lob display-shelf decorations at the invaders, a harmless gesture to placate frayed tempers. Since he always knew what we'd see before we saw it, though, would he not have known what would greet us when we went to fetch our ornaments? Perhaps he deemed it wisest for us each to cope privily with learning our customary rounds are those of the long-ago deceased.

At least my roofless home's interior is as it was when I clambered out. I take that, as I feed the hearth some sticks, for a sign I should carry on as if in ignorance our world is doomed. What else to do? I cannot discount the chance we're alive in the here and now after all, that nothing in our second sight will be real till more years than we can measure have ebbed. And the second sight might not show so remote a time with utmost clarity. Putting out of mind what I've seen today is the only path toward fulfilling my place as a householder, a villager.

In any case, I have to go help my kinfolk rake up hazelnuts. I'm very late and don't want to upset them more than I no doubt have already. I especially don't want to upset them by sharing what I've just gone through. Still, I tend the hearth, telling myself I must stoke the fire lest it gutter in my absence, till I notice the sunlight has winked out and there is a roof over my head again.

Avenging Angela

Something bounced off the back of her head and pinged against the hardwood floor. She whipped around, ready with a choice word or three for the lame-ass joker or jokers. Everyone knew she'd been jumpy, like much of the waitstaff, ever since the Club had reopened after renovations. Lights went on and off, glassware staged suicide dives off counters; Cheryl, too psychically sensitive for her own good, was especially on edge.

And now? Oh, hell no. Either the offending party had set a land-speed record exiting the gallery before she'd turned, or it was no earthly joker. She slid her tray of empty wineglasses next to the gallery assistant's computer, and off the floor scooped up half of a little old-fashioned mother-of-pearl button, from a cuff or lapel maybe. It spooked her out of all proportion to its size and physical impact. Striving to keep a lid on her jangled nerves, she hollered to her coworker, tromping upstairs from the Café, "Hey, Jackie?"

Cheryl's best efforts to tamp down anxiety never fooled anyone. Jackie rushed the rest of the way up, and chalky-faced Cheryl greeted her on the landing by holding out the half button between thumb and forefinger. "What's that?" asked Jackie.

"Someone threw this at me!" After the Art Club hosted a private party, the skeleton crew folding up furniture, washing dinnerware, dousing lights was always leery of the bogeyman, likelier a sex criminal than lurking ectoplasm in the mazy, olden, scary building. Therefore Jackie, an avowed skeptic on the ghostly front, hadn't braced herself for Cheryl's idea of an emergency, and only ticked her off by gaping at the projectile and voicing what instantly sprang to mind. "Where's the other half?"

"Why don't you ask Angela?" Cheryl shot back. And don't tell her Jackie didn't know who that was!

The tremor called time out. No boneshaker, but the glasses on the tray rattled; what reading on the Richter scale wouldn't derail trains of thought? This must have been the fourth around the East Side after the Club's relaunch, and its shockwave had come up through the girls' insteps, as if a fault-line were underfoot. They adjourned to the kitchen and joined the dishwashers on the fire-escape overlooking the parking lot and the massive iron barrier behind it that sealed off an ancient railroad tunnel. No visible damage, but everyone kept staring into the night as if something was wrong and they were missing it.

~~~~~

Harry's wistful gaze wandered among the myriad details of the Cabaret. He wondered idly if, for all his celebrity, he was in a club he'd be welcome to join. Not that he played Providence enough to bother trying. This cozy sanctum to one side of the Café would have qualified as a snug in Merry Old England, and its charms were considerable: the quaint Mitteleuropa chairs and table, the Colonial hearth replete with bread oven, the silhouettes of es-teemed members on the walls, the sooty mural of Mephisto under the low ceiling, leering at dusty, empty Chianti bottles dangling from the rafters.

He'd dined in the Cabaret before as honored guest of Sydney Burleigh and other Art Club bigwigs; Burleigh had requested his company for lunch today. Harry hoped his host wouldn't show till he'd had a minute to get a handle on his pal Cliff Eddy's pal How-ard Lovecraft. Curious name!

Harry's wish came true. A tall, gaunt, diffident fellow, thirtyish but with a callow air, led with his sizable chin as he scuffed in. He fit inside his charcoal suit as if it were the uniform of a Brahmin, worn though it was and far from modish. He carried himself with the certainty of moving through his rightful element, his inaliena-ble home grounds, yet with the guardedness of an infiltrator. He bowed slightly and proffered a deferentially unassertive handshake. "Mr. Houdini? It is an honor." His voice was both boyishly high and weighted with gravitas.

What to make of this rare Yankee bird, this man of conflicting parts? "Call me Harry, will you, so long as it's all right if I call you Howard? After all, we may be working together."

Howard nodded—a bit warily, perhaps? Attempting to put him more at ease, Harry brought up their mutual acquaintances, Cliff and Muriel Eddy, who'd commended Howard's cerebral approach to the supernatural. Without warming particularly, Howard professed meeting them face-to-face only recently, after corresponding a while. Harry curbed his surprise that apparently like-minded folk who lived scant miles apart would send letters instead of arranging a rendezvous or at least phoning.

After several rudderless seconds of silence, Harry rose to the challenge of a tough nut to crack and pressed on, "Your worthy debut in the newest *Weird Tales* aside, your feud with some astrologer in a local paper convinced me you were the man for a peculiar job. I take it you haven't softened your position on astrology."

"Astrology?" Howard huffed. "It's the bunk!" Ah, the tight-wound Yankee was loosening up at last. Just give him something to denounce!

"Yes, Howard, precisely. And as you may know, I've applied myself lately to debunking spiritualism, a much more villainous racket. It's in that capacity I've been retained at the Art Club."

Howard perked up, almost to the point of flippancy. "Someone's saying the old place is haunted?"

"In a word, yes. Are you familiar with this 'old place'?"

Howard gave the Cabaret a townie's overfamiliar once-over. "My Aunt Lillian exhibited some watercolors in the gallery not long ago."

"So creativity runs in your family!" When this bid at personability also sank without a ripple, Harry punted, "I'm here at the invitation of Sydney Burleigh. Quite the accomplished artist in these parts. Maybe you've crossed paths?"

"I know who he is," Howard stated noncommittally.

"A man of wide-ranging repute, wouldn't you agree?" Howard's nod was pure politeness, with nary a trace of conviction. Harry soldiered on, "Besides his success as a painter, he's been a very generous patron of the arts, and he even designed that distinctive Fleur-de-Lys house two doors down." Uh-oh, was the green-eyed monster fussing at Howard's cuffs, glinting behind his wire-rims? Or was something else eating him?

"Oh, that?" Howard intoned at length. "A distinctive eyesore, if you'll pardon my opinion, the silliest, most misguided excuse for revivalism. That Tudor half-timbered freak does not belong in our beautiful Colonial environs, and adding insult to aesthetic injury, it flouts itself directly across the street from the finest Georgian steeple in America!"

"I stand corrected, but please soft-pedal your disapproval when Mr. Burleigh arrives. He's due anytime now."

"Of course." Howard, the old-line gentleman, smiled complaisantly. Harry entertained the possibility he might be a pedant. Conversely, might Howard, on architectural grounds, have branded Harry a philistine?

The seats beneath them and everything on the table trembled; the shrieking whistle, the stupendous chugging and clatter of a train might have erupted from the adjacent room. "Good God, Howard, it sounds like we're on top of a railroad track!"

"Basically, we are," Howard affirmed. "Several trains per day go by behind the Club, to and from Bristol. A tunnel into the hillside out back runs all the way through the East Side. The dishes in here have been rattling since 1908, if I'm not mistaken."

Harry didn't suppose he would be, and then as foretold, Burleigh entered, filling the doorway with expansive presence rather than bodily stature. Everyone was cordial as Harry made the introductions. Burleigh's baggy casual attire and trim, birdlike frame imperfectly offset a patrician bearing; likewise, the sprightliness he projected imperfectly offset his bushy gray Van Dyke and the inroads of frailty. Howard, Harry observed, unfavorably eyed the floppy beret Burleigh wore indoors, even after sitting down, but thankfully let this lapse of decorum pass.

Fixing his glance on Howard and Harry in turn, Burleigh fairly whispered, "Gentlemen, I've been the target of a cruel imposition, of a sort that put me in mind of Mr. Houdini's skill in exposing occult hoaxes. I'll be profoundly in your debt for whatever light you can throw on my situation. And for bringing any culprits to justice." That last clause sounded strangely like an afterthought. Was Burleigh absolutely positive a hoax was involved?

"I shouldn't assume you know this, but going on two years ago a dear, longtime friend of mine cut her life tragically short, in the studio directly above mine." Both Harry and Howard nodded because they knew exactly whom he meant.

"Well, I've entered my studio several evenings this month to discover a divan turned toward the door with a mannequin lounging upon it. It was wearing the same Arabian Nights ensemble my absent friend, Angela O'Leary, had worn on that divan for a series of charcoal sketches I'd dashed off in the weeks before her death. The mannequin was in a different pose each time, mimicking a different sketch, but with the costume in a state of vulgar dishabille. The uncanny part is, I destroyed those studies after she died; the associations they conjured were too painful. Nobody alive has seen them."

Was Burleigh out to recruit debunkers or convert them to goose-pimpled believers? "Furthermore, my studio door and the casement windows in the wall opposite were always locked, and though I lack Mr. Houdini's expertise in these matters, none of the hasps or latches appear to have been forced." Harry nodded thoughtfully, whereas keen interest was writ plain on Howard's features. Perhaps the prospect of a real-life "locked room mystery" excited him.

"Any other spirit activity, so to speak?" Harry asked.

"Why yes, twice now an easel with a blank canvas has been positioned as if for the mannequin's inspection. On the canvases were messages in greasepaint, of a sickly green I've never worked with, and without a wet brush anywhere around."

"And the messages?" Howard chimed in.

Burleigh was unfolding a notepad sheet from his shirt pocket. "I've transcribed them. Gibberish, as best I can make out."

Harry accepted the paper, arched his eyebrows in capitulation, and passed the paper to Howard, who gave it a more searching appraisal. "It's Gaelic. I don't understand it, but perhaps your friend Miss O'Leary, or relatives at her funeral, could have?"

"So can either of you produce a scholar of obscure languages? Or an Irish cop maybe?" Harry and Howard feigned mild amusement at Burleigh's attempted humor.

At the doorway someone cleared his throat as if waiting to be noticed. "Ah! Young John, come to receive our orders!" Harry and Howard traded discreet looks of bemusement. "Young John" was squarely mired in middle age, hairline in retreat, wan indoor complexion, garb like a banker's on seaside holiday, except for the white apron over his incipient paunch. He was, estimating leniently, Burleigh's junior by a decade. The two of them briefly conferred sotto voce with their backs to their guests.

"Gentlemen, we're in luck!" Burleigh announced as John stood by with arms folded. "John's brought some excellent swordfish, caught off Little Compton yesterday."

"Sounds wonderful!" beamed Harry, only to bite his tongue on glimpsing Howard's queasy expression and sudden pallor. "But I'm afraid Mr. Lovecraft is allergic to seafood. I don't suppose you can rustle up anything else?"

"Um, there are some leftover beans and franks," Burleigh ventured.

"Yes, that would be most appreciated, thank you!" Color returned to Howard's cheeks.

Burleigh ill-concealed his amazement at a fellow Rhode Islander spurning such a feast, till the thought of his own more important problem retook center stage. "I don't mind telling you this is preying on my nerves. Why am I being victimized?" Hah! If Burleigh didn't know that in his heart of hearts, Harry reflected, who did he expect to clue him in? "Is there anything you can do?"

"I'll want to confer with my colleague before going out on any limbs, and naturally we'll need to examine your studio. But let me declare categorically, you are the target of an imposition, as you say, and not of the supernatural. If I may ask, has anyone approached you offering to solve your problem?"

"No, no," Burleigh shook his head, overtly unsure of Harry's drift. "I've broached this business with nobody beyond you two and Young John."

"But as the proverb goes, it is no secret if three people know of it," Howard pointed out. "Especially in Providence."

Before the insinuation that 'Young John' was a blabbermouth could sink in, Harry proposed, "And perhaps someone is waiting for word of your 'haunting' to get out, and when it's common knowledge, he or she won't sound as suspicious contacting you."

"You're implying someone is staging these incidents to trade on my bereavement?" Burleigh stammered.

"What a callous fraud!" Howard exclaimed. "Yet people stoop so low as to trade, as Mr. Burleigh puts it, on bereavement?"

Harry was thrilled Howard hadn't blurted "guilt" as opposed to "bereavement." "It's their bread and butter," Harry shrugged.

Burleigh, as if flustered at failing to get Harry's drift sooner, sustained a slight quaver as he said, "Pardon me, I just want to see what's delaying Young John at the stove."

Once Burleigh was out of earshot, Harry speculated, "On the other hand, it may not be extortion. Considering the circumstances of Miss O'Leary's death, friends or relatives mightn't be above some macabre retribution. You're probably aware of rumors she and Burleigh were romantically involved?"

"Burleigh's bohemian tendencies are known to me. Perhaps other jilted paramours are playing tricks on him. Or a cuckolded husband. Or Burleigh's wife?"

"Other paramours, pray tell! And I suppose the suicide spawned no less gossip than the affair?"

Howard drew a voluminous breath. "Since you ask, Burleigh

had broken off their affair a few days earlier, which she deemed unacceptable. That Friday the Art Club threw a Hallowe'en gala, just as it will two days from now. While the party was in full swing, Miss O'Leary locked herself in her studio and 'took the pipe,' as they say. She inhaled enough gas to lose consciousness, but not enough to kill her outright because of a kink in the tube. Perhaps she twisted the tube herself in the expectation she'd be found in time. Sadly, she was not.

"In fact, not until the next morning did someone show up, a friend named Aldrich, and he went away on receiving no answer to his knocks. He thought nothing of it, but grew worried on trying twice more to no effect. He forced his way in, and she was lying on the floor, unresponsive, the tube in her mouth. She lingered a while in hospital, but was too far gone and passed away a day later. I imagine Aldrich might have harbored some guilt for acting no sooner, and some resentment that Burleigh hadn't checked on her when she sat out Friday's party. This Aldrich who discovered her, by the way, is the same Young John grilling your swordfish. And his profile in silhouette is on the wall right above my head."

"My God, this is a small town, isn't it? Still, how are you so well versed? Many of those details weren't in the obituary."

Howard's shrug was as world-weary in its way as Harry's had been. "As I said, this is Providence. And how are you so well informed of our small-town doings?"

"A clipping service, Howard. An investment I've never regretted. You might want to hire one as a research tool in your writing."

"If only!" Howard lamented. "The sole way I could afford that would be as a plotting device in a story."

They dummied up as their extempore waiters trouped in, Burleigh with his own swordfish, John with Harry's plus Howard's beans and franks. John, with nary a peep, turned on his heel and departed. No sooner was Burleigh seated than a succulent pungency overspread the chamber and Howard blanched, clamping a desperate hand over nose and mouth. Harry was about to quiz

Burleigh further about Miss O'Leary, but paused while Howard grabbed his plate and utensils, wheezing, "I'm sorry, the air has become too close in here. I'll be at a table in the next room." He was out before anyone could utter a syllable.

By the time Harry and Burleigh adjourned from the Cabaret, Howard had cleaned his plate like a trencherman and was admiring Latin graffiti on the plaster above the walnut paneling. Nodding feebly at him, Burleigh, ashen and shaky, plodded out. Harry sat opposite Howard and apologized, "I had no idea seafood made you so nauseous."

Howard smiled benignly. "I had a thoroughly delightful repast, thank you, and respite enough to contemplate the dimensions of Miss O'Leary's tragedy. By all reports, she was intelligent, beautiful, vivacious, cultured, well traveled, abundantly talented, poised to achieve international fame. Can you imagine someone of such sophistication and promise acting so rashly under the influence of an emotion, especially one as transient as romantic love?"

"Of course I can, Howard! But the truth may be somewhat less straightforward. Burleigh may have been more of a last straw. She'd become much more 'begrudging' of him, as he put it, after her mother died a few months earlier. An older brother, a doctor, died several years previously, having contracted TB from a patient at the sanatorium where he practiced, and her oldest brother died in 1911 soon after turning forty-four, which was Miss O'Leary's age as of her birthday, which fell on the same Friday as the Art Club party."

"She committed suicide on her birthday, then," Howard clarified, "during a soirée she may have viewed as antipodal to a birthday party."

"Anyhow, she may have seen forty-four as a tipping point: middle age breathing down her neck, her best years squandered on a married man decades her senior, and she very much alone in the world. Losing Burleigh may have triggered her ultimate despair, as he confessed just now through gushing tears, though he may be taking too much credit for that. The wondrous male ego!

It actually craves the guilt, to prove it's tough as nails and can stand it. But I digress. If you have time, would you mind inspecting Burleigh's studio with me?"

The studio, on the Fleur-de-Lys' ground floor, comprised two bright, high-ceilinged rooms, a palatial space where nobody lived and one ego chased glory, Harry noted ruefully, recalling the cramped tinderboxes where his family of nine had sweltered and frozen during his boyhood. In the front room was a balcony of zigzag wooden slats, perfect for staging *Romeo and Juliet*. It overlooked Burleigh's atelier, the walls chock-a-block with framed landscapes and portraits and people in landscapes. Beyond a partition wall punctuated by horseshoe arches was a classroom with easels, cabinets of art supplies, trunks of costumes and props. In one corner leaned a jumble of naked, jointed, sexless plaster mannequins. Too bad Burleigh hadn't preserved the dummy more recently *en déshabillé* for examination.

"Already," Harry proclaimed with a cavalier wave, "I can puncture the argument for a supernatural agency, or even a 'locked room mystery.' With students and associates coming and going, a nimble intruder could easily secrete himself on the balcony or in a hamper while Mr. Burleigh was distracted. Once the intruder was alone, he'd be free to work his mischief. He could let himself out or, if he were locked in, sneak out whenever Mr. Burleigh re-entered and his back was turned. A good hoaxer is supremely gifted at covering his tracks. Nothing more cryptic here than the same principle of misdirection behind most magic and escapes!"

Burleigh heaved a dolorous sigh. "I'm afraid I've withheld something that may forestall dismissing the supernatural." His tone had a hapless ring. "During her final poses for me, Miss O'Leary recounted nightmares she ascribed to her Celtic second sight. They presaged doom, and a rift between us, as symbolized by her futile search for me in a deserted, squalid city of colossal masonry, which she accessed via the train tunnel out back. She'd entertained no self-destructive urges prior to these dreams, which perhaps merely signaled the onset of nervous collapse. But I've been having these same dreams, as if her troubled spirit has invaded mine."

"Mr. Burleigh," Howard essayed, "while I am no alienist, I'd conjecture Freud might be able to explain why both you and Miss O'Leary had those dreams, without invoking the spirit world. Perhaps it would be of consolation, reducing them to mundane subconscious origins."

"I'm no Freud either," Harry leapt in, "but I concur, don't go looking for the occult where it's not thrust upon you." Besides, he was raring to jettison the intangibles of dreams and psychology, get back onto the solid ground of fakery, where he had a firm grip on the reins. "And if ever the occult were to be thrust upon you, let's consider Friday. Your masquerade will occur too near the anniversary of Miss O'Leary's death for your harassers to resist. After taunting you all month, chances are they're plotting some bolder, nastier stunt during the party. Mr. Lovecraft and I, with your permission, will be in attendance. I presume you can lend us disguises."

Harry and Burleigh arranged to reconvene in the studio Friday after nightfall, but before ill-prepared partygoers typically came begging Burleigh for last-minute costumes. Burleigh tendered his two pillars of composure profuse thanks and damp handshakes. Filing out the door, Harry espied Howard critically eyeing Burleigh's beret on a coatrack. The preening old duffer hadn't seen fit to doff the headgear till he was in his own bailiwick. Yes, Burleigh did hone affectations to promote his Boho image, forsaking polite custom in the process.

Out on the herringbone brick sidewalk, Howard beckoned Harry to step uphill and into an alley between the Fleur-de-Lys and a spruce Colonial mansion.

"Howard, I gather our client doesn't strike you as one hundred per cent sympathetic?" They both squinted sidelong on passing by the casement windows, and relaxed on determining Burleigh's attention was elsewhere.

"Is he not a bit of a fop?" Howard countered. "Even for a traditionalist like myself, he represents a stodgy, passé vision of art.

And you may have noticed, he never directly addressed me. Hardly the ploy to win my sympathies!" They were schlepping across a swath of saplings, weeds, and litter beyond the alley.

"No, I'll grant that, but people under pressure are seldom at their best, and he'd be lost without us."

Howard grunted noncommittally and extended his arm to block Harry from tumbling down a graveled slope and onto the tracks. To the right was the ominously gaping mouth of the tunnel. "If you'll permit an intuitive leap, this railroad portal may have a role in our business. Burleigh's tormentors used some outwardly preternatural knowledge of Miss O'Leary's poses in positioning the mannequin, and as we just learned, it's no feat to peek into Burleigh's windows unbeknownst to him. Furthermore, might there be something to Miss O'Leary's apprehensions, at least in her dreams, about the tunnel, based on a glimpse she may have unconsciously absorbed of skulkers within? As a hidey-hole it appears foolhardy, but a mindful scoundrel with a timetable would be relatively safe."

Harry stared into the dark as if seeking a rejoinder. "Even if we establish a clear sightline between the tunnel entrance and Burleigh's windows, aren't you putting the cart in front of the horse? Why would peeping toms have spied on Burleigh before they had the motivation of Miss O'Leary's suicide to avenge?"

"True, true," Howard admitted, "but as the adage goes, 'When you have eliminated the impossible, whatever remains, however improbable, must be the truth.' And haven't we eliminated occult influence as impossible?"

"Ah, the wisdom of Conan Doyle," acknowledged Harry, "before the crooked mediums got to him."

"Exactly," Howard nodded genially, one autodidact highsigning another. "Yet the point remains: Burleigh has evidently been under unfriendly surveillance for two or more years, and he never the wiser. We've come this far. Might as well poke our heads in."

Harry shrugged, and Howard gingerly planted his right foot upon the slope. The vaguest trembling, the faintest of rumbles prompted Harry to grab Howard's sleeve. "Hold on! Must be a train approaching."

Howard nodded, and five minutes later they realized they were straining their ears at nothing, that no train was about to materialize. "What was that? Do you get tremors around here?" Bewilderment was something Harry instilled in others; he seldom had to bear it himself.

"Rarely." Howard scooted back from the brink. "But whatever it was, if anything, it coincided with an attack of weakness and vertigo. Those franks may have lain on the stove too long. I had better hurry home." They beat a retreat through the weeds, trod the alley undetected again.

Howard's stance betrayed a remnant wobble as they paused on the steep incline of Thomas Street. "They must have a phone at the Club. Please, let me call a cab for you. I feel responsible."

Howard waved off Harry's solicitude. "I'm just up the street. Don't worry, I'll be home by shank's mare in twenty minutes. If you don't mind, though, could I borrow that sample of Gaelic? Easy as pie to scare up an Irish cop, or a well-versed equivalent, in my neighborhood." When Howard loped away, it was at the intrepid pace of a career pedestrian. Harry had preferred not to complicate the situation by mentioning how Howard's symptoms had coincided with weak knees of his own and a headache fleeting but like an icepick.

In addition, he hadn't entirely blinked away a mirage like a double-exposure superimposed on the tunnel entrance, of a vast cavern's cylindrical interior, with a ledge that corkscrewed up the wall, and a floor rife with gushing plumes of steam or smoke. What's more, the cavern was apparently submarine, but in what kind of water did stone blocks, slabs, and pillars drift like twigs? This must have been a hodgepodge of images sunburnt onto his retina, transiently visible against the portal's utter blackness. Or had Howard shared Harry's vision and said nothing lest Harry question his levelheadedness?

Come Thursday afternoon, Harry pressed the doorbell on

Howard's side of the prim Angell Street duplex at the corner of Butler. Again, what a luxury of elbow room by New York standards, however disdainfully Howard had described the place. Harry admired the red and yellow foliage of curbside oaks and maples, positively Arcadian compared with Manhattan, till Howard popped out the door like a cuckoo-clock automaton. He sported the charcoal suit once more, a wardrobe choice Harry couldn't envy, heated as he was in shirtsleeves and chinos. "It's such a nice day, Howard. Care to join me on my rounds before we collate notes?" Howard seemed well pleased to pound the pavement.

They headed down Angell and right onto Wayland. "I find walking invaluable in getting the brain to fire on all cylinders, don't you?" Before Harry could frame an answer, Howard resumed, "But if you're gathering information on the QT, aren't you afraid you'll be recognized?"

Harry wedged his clipboard under one arm, put on a pair of spectacles from his shirt pocket, and a tam-o'-shanter from a trouser pocket. "Less is better. Nobody tries seeing through so thin a disguise, whereas beards and the like look more like concealment and command more probing attention. And who would expect the famous Houdini to turn up as a surveyor for the Providence House Directory?"

On Wayland Avenue, Harry counted several Victorian hulks. Mostly, variants on bungalows and Dutch colonials catered to the new century's middle-class tastes. "Be on the lookout for Doane Avenue. Angela's niece and nephew, with their spouses, are renting in adjacent houses there, so to that degree they're a close-knit family. They'll be the last of her relations to canvass around here. Do you know many people in this neck of the woods?"

Howard gravely shook his head and dourly imparted, "When I was a kid, this whole section was woods, and I loved playing in them. A more halcyon era!"

Harry let the topic lapse. Yep, he reckoned, whenever anything used to be how Howard liked it, change was an ample portion of bitter fruit.

Halfway along Doane, the entirety of which ran one short block, Harry stayed their course between two blandly utilitarian new houses divided into two flats each. "Howard, would you please have a seat on those porch steps across the street, yep, that house with the scary vine up one wall? Since we are in your part of town, best to keep your plausibly familiar face at a distance. If anyone asks, I'll say you're my field assistant and wave. You just wave back. At one address they did act a mite suspicious, because these door-to-door guys usually travel in pairs."

A few minutes later, re-attaching a pencil to his clipboard, Harry strolled over to Howard. "Their response was in line with everybody else's. You and I were speculating that an aggrieved relative of Angela's might have it in for Burleigh. I lucked out. Both her niece and nephew were home, but when I inquired if any household members or close kin had died in the past year or two, they each drew a blank and had to be finessed into remembering their dear departed aunt. Maybe the shame and scandal of a suicide in the family encouraged willful amnesia. But in a nutshell, I'd say clan O'Leary is in the clear."

"And I have some results as well," Howard reported as they turned left onto Elmgrove.

"Great! First, though, I have to confess all this sleuthing has put me in need of refreshment. A good soda fountain between here and downtown would do nicely. My treat." Howard led them back to Angell, where he fixed longing, morose eyes upon the faded glory of a Victorian mansion at the corner.

As they proceeded, Howard tore his gaze away and explained, "That house is my birthplace. I spent a wonderful childhood there. A much more halcyon era!"

"But home is wherever you have family, isn't it? Do you still live with the folks?"

"My mother passed away a few months before Angela O'Leary, but you don't catch me blubbering in public like Sydney Burleigh!"

They ambled down Angell in silence a while. To go nonverbal

too long felt, reasonably or not, like defeatism, and at length Harry had to venture, "My word, Howard, I do hope you aren't alone in the world."

"In point of fact," Howard brightened, "I am affianced to a smart, attractive correspondent and authoress, more cosmopolitan and pragmatic than myself. I'll have to pull up stakes for some far-flung clime, though, upon our nuptials. She is a businesswoman of the Hebrew persuasion, and my aunts may never approve of her."

Was Howard even aware Harry was of the same "persuasion"? What to do except forge on, in for a penny, in for a pound? "A nice Jewish girl, eh? Good for you, Howard. May she make you very happy, wherever you settle down. Anti-Semitism is such a blot on humanity. I'm delighted it's not a prejudice you condone!"

Howard nodded circumspectly and said no more, though Harry was suddenly obliged to step up his pace to match Howard's. In a trice they were surrounded by a shopping district, and with a flourish Howard indicated a black door opening onto one corner of a busy intersection. "Here we are. E. P. Anthony's. It's been around almost as long as I have."

Which, Harry deduced, qualified as a virtue in itself. He couldn't help noting the door belonged to yet another pseudo-Tudor building, but Howard was quite unperturbed by this one, perhaps because Burleigh had nothing to do with it, perhaps because Howard hadn't the scratch to indulge a sweet tooth every day. The midafternoon lull afforded them an unrestricted choice of stools at the counter. Howard, Harry readily allowed, hadn't steered him wrong: black marble and ornate brass made for classier decor than, say, Woolworth's. A slow-moving fogy with pince-nez and double-chins got around to them. "Sirs?"

Howard recommended the Rhode Island delicacy of a "coffee cabinet," whatever that was, and for himself, blueberry pie à la mode, "with vanilla of course! And coffee, four sugars, please." The soda clerk laboriously rolled up his white sleeves and shuffled off. Howard already had an old A&P receipt out of his vest pocket; his smudgy scribble filled its backside. "My mother and I, when she was feeling flush, used to hire an Irish kid down the street for odd jobs. I stopped by his house, and begorra, but didn't his grandpa from the Old Sod retain the Erse enough for our purposes."

He also extracted Burleigh's transcription from his jacket, where it had subbed as a pocket square. "For your files, along with my translations. I can tell you, both phrases raised every eyebrow in the parlor, and it was an uphill battle to trivialize them as obscure literary quotations, which indeed they may be." Howard's coffee slid into sight, and he took an eager slurp. "The top line," he expounded, with a finger on *Seo an doras isteach purgadóra,* "means 'Here is the door into purgatory.'" His finger hopped to *Anois a thosaíonn do leorgníomh.* "Even less auspicious is the second: 'Now your atonement begins.' Shuddersome, yes, had only Burleigh been able to understand them."

"Do you understand them? Or rather, what they're getting at?" Howard, Harry decided, wasn't striving for pedantry. It just bodied forth from him as automatically as showmanship from Harry.

"The reference to purgatory does fit a genuine Irish locale that Angela or her avenger could have visited or read about. An islet in a lough of County Donegal was reputed to have a cave frequented by medieval pilgrims from across Europe. The cave owed its popularity to a legend about Jesus showing it to St. Patrick, vouchsafing that anyone who abided within for three days would witness visions of purgatory. These harrowing visions were equated with time spent in actual purgatory, so that the longer one withstood them, the sooner one would attain heaven postmortem." With extraordinary stealth, meanwhile, the decrepit soda clerk delivered their orders, as Howard lectured on, none the wiser.

"The etiology of these visions was never established, be it noxious gases leaking from the earth's bowels, or the toll of too much hunger, thirst, or darkness, or simple power of suggestion, mass hysteria if you will. And the cave was extolled by myriad authors, Marie de France in the 1100s, William Staunton in the 1400s, Thomas Carve's *Lyra Hibernica* in 1666, Edward Ledwich's *Antiquuities of Ireland* in 1790, to cite a few. The cave either collapsed in

1632 or was plugged up by the Church following a scandal over admission fees. A monastery still dominates the island; monks nowadays charge pilgrims for a gander at the plugged-up opening."

"Howard, your pie's getting cold and your ice cream's melting." Furthermore, the "coffee cabinet" came in a sundae glass but had a deceptively bitter quality because the ice cream in it and the milk were alike coffee-flavored, and were those coffee grounds in the foam? Not that the name hadn't been a tipoff! An acquired taste, and one for another day, if ever.

"Oh!" Howard gave a start as if the pie had magically substantialized. "Thank you, Harry. But as I was saying, whatever the source of the Gaelic, it would have been totally apropos above the cave entrance, though no text I've consulted alludes to any epigraph." Howard picked up his fork and zealously tucked in.

"Be that as it may," Harry contended, "harassing Burleigh in terms he didn't even perceive as language could only seem savvy to an outright lunatic, well educated or not." He could choke down no more spoonfuls of "coffee cabinet" and shoved his sundae glass a scritching inch away. The tiny noise alerted Howard as if he had the ears of a bat; his plate was nigh clean. He eyed Harry's leftovers, and with a discreet gesture Harry consigned them to him. Technically, Howard was guilty of scavenging, yet nothing in his deportment ever qualified as graceless.

"Madman or no," Howard conjectured, dragging the cabinet closer, "the culprit is employing phrases that can apply equally to the train tunnel, is he not? I might propose he regards it and St. Patrick's Purgatory as interchangeable, to some purpose nefarious as it is opaque. Poor Burleigh!"

Harry nodded pensively. He was most struck by the correspondence between the Irish cave's nightmare visions and his mirage in the tunnel mouth. Had St. Patrick's Purgatory occurred to Howard in the first place because he'd also experienced that illusion? And if it had beset them both, was it simply illusion? Whoa there! That line of thought led to some murky harum-scarum waters. Still, he couldn't just brush off the possibility Howard had beheld the ghastly marine cavern and dared not speak of it, dwelling instead on some remote counterpart. Talk about Freudian sublimation!

The clink of spoon upon the bottom of the sundae glass distracted Harry from his woolgathering. Howard paused in polishing off Harry's confection. "I wish my commonplace book were handy. Naturally my first concern is Burleigh's welfare, but my imagination keeps spinning aspects of his case into a wilder, more fantastic yarn, wherein I'd assign Miss O'Leary a minor role at best. The drilling, blasting, and quarrying that went into the tunnel's construction, and the ongoing din and disturbance of trains hurtling through it, would make for a much grander threshold onto the weird."

Howard gulped coffee with the gusto of a bon vivant, an enthusiast in his element again, as when he'd knocked the Fleur-de-Lys. "The railway has plumbed subterranean depths that languished in hermetic darkness for eons. These depths, moreover, lay under a hill, the storied abode of nonhuman races and primeval creatures. Which of them would the noise jar awake after dormant ages, ravenous and incensed: an Algonquin manitou, the last survivor of Paleozoic titans, the spectral guardian of a Stygian city under abyssal floodwaters? You must agree there's more promise along these lines than in the bedevilment of an old dandy by a ghost impersonator."

Harry suppressed a double-take. Did allusion to "a Stygian city" imply that Howard too had visualized masonry aswirl in a submerged cavern? If not, though, what would Harry gain by fessing up to barmy hallucinations? Meanwhile, were Howard's "giants in the earth" really more promising story material than the hopeless struggle of human beings—Burleigh in this instance—against their sphinxlike, albeit self-inflicted, fates? Tactfully he bunted, "I leave the literary judgments to you."

"And haven't I been digressing shamelessly!" As if underscoring a job well done, Howard plunked his spoon into thoroughly grubbed-out sundae glass. "But to treat of Miss O'Leary's recurring nightmares, I find it apposite that she resided in her studio, and ipso facto slept and dreamed there. As such, it's plausible that her dreams, and her state of mind overall, had their genesis in a gas leak from her fixtures or a discharge of noxious exhaust that accumulated in the tunnel. Toxic fumes may at least have reinforced her suicidal impulses."

Harry harrumphed soberly. These were natural, measurable causes that hadn't crossed his mind.

"Putting aside Freudian complexes for the nonce," Howard added, "the same alleged dreams on Burleigh's part may indicate a buildup of poison gas in his studio as well. Certainly to warn him of this possibility would be prudent." He filled his lungs, as Harry beckoned over the sluggish clerk, to elaborate. "Were Miss O'Leary and Burleigh to serve me as characters, though, I would posit that their nightmares were psychic emanations from the subterrene malignity, to whose influence artistic temperaments would be especially susceptible."

Harry had divided his attention between Howard's ramblings and paying the tab. "Keep the change," he said as he swung off the stool. Howard followed suit after a dubious blink at Harry shoving off while Howard was still declaiming. Out on the corner they reconfirmed the specifics of Friday's rendezvous and shook hands, at which point a soundless tremor shivered through Harry's soles and up his legs. Howard's eyebrows conveyed he'd felt it too. "Could that have been a train?" Harry grimaced. "Or a quake?"

Howard spread indecisive hands. "The tunnel is pretty much underfoot. But I've never ascertained whether railway vibrations could travel through two hundred-odd feet of rock and earth. Perhaps it's our manitou!" Harry wished Howard had grinned more broadly at that ostensible jest.

For better or worse, Harry had scant time for any jests to get under his skin. After twenty-four hours of catering to Burleigh, he had correspondence to dash off, contracts to pore over, tour dates to iron out. He did, when concentration flagged, lapse into gazing vacantly upon Thomas Street from his suite in the Biltmore; that was the closest he came to mulling Burleigh's predicament. Hence, seasonably mild and fine as Friday evening was, he felt too ill-prepared to enjoy it. Out in front of the Fleur-de-Lys, he surveyed its glut of whimsical bas-reliefs, and maybe his blue mood made them seem annoyingly fey.

Howard and his charcoal suit were, needless to say, punctual. "Why the long face, Harry?"

"Sorry it shows, Howard." Harry tried waving away his blues as if they were mosquitoes, smiled morosely. "I just wish we'd had time for proper legwork. We should have reconnoitered local mediums sizing Burleigh up as fat pickings, or vindictive pals of Angela, or 'Young John' while we're at it, or the tenant currently upstairs in Angela's former studio, though Burleigh insists he's renting to someone unacquainted with her."

"I wouldn't feel bad," Howard opined. "You came here on extremely short notice, despite your hectic schedule. Whatever Burleigh is paying you, I cannot doubt he's getting his money's worth from the 'Great Houdini.'"

Harry had to curb a wince. "Thank you, Howard, but on principle any debunking I perform is pro bono, even for landed gentry like Burleigh." The issue of sordid lucre hadn't previously come up; Howard nodded understandingly, but too hard-set a poker face telegraphed his disappointment. Good heavens, had he expected remuneration, he should have brought that up at the outset.

The Fleur-de-Lys' ponderous, faux-medieval door burst open and Burleigh barreled out, jittery, hands aflutter as if baffled over what to do with them. He lurched to an abrupt, swaying halt and spouted from the rustic portico, "Why are you standing around? It's happened again! Come in, come in!" Harry and Howard traded a put-upon glance. Burleigh had cause to be high-strung, but the bossy, petulant act wasn't helpful, especially outside if he meant to keep his troubles private. Just as well he wasn't wise to Howard's translation of the baleful Gaelic.

"Look!" exclaimed Burleigh, preceding them into his studio, flailing one arm toward something nobody could see from the doorway. "The street door and my door and the windows were locked all day, even when I was here. This happened when I went over to the Art Club for ten minutes an hour ago."

In the middle of the atelier, a mannequin in black Cleopatra wig and diaphanous harem garb sprawled upon a divan. Who could tell if those duds were dishabille or not? Its hands melodramatically shielded its featureless face from the implicitly overwhelming canvas on the easel confronting it. Harry and Howard stepped around tremulous Burleigh to read the superficially banal "Teach Donn." The scribble had apparently been squeezed from a tube of slimy green pigment, more conducive to a shiver than the rest of the tableau. Burleigh betrayed no reaction to its rancid, fishy reek; age must have blunted his sense of smell.

"My nerves are going to snap!" Burleigh quavered. "Whoever or whatever is persecuting me, their timing could not be more excruciating. I cannot attend this masquerade without fearing for my life. An enemy could approach unbeknownst, and then it will be too late. No, I shan't go. I can hardly stir from this spot."

"Or is that how your enemy is hoping you'll behave?" Harry argued. "Remember, Miss O'Leary came to grief alone in her studio. If you stay here or go home by yourself, you may be setting yourself up for a lunatic's fulfillment of poetic justice. Mr. Lovecraft and I will not be with you. We're going to the party, as agreed earlier, to nab your tormentor whenever, and however, he shows his hand." Burleigh sucked on his luxuriant mustache as if about to protest or bark counter-orders, but refrained, perhaps recalling Harry and Howard weren't servants.

"I understand your trepidation," Harry continued, "but you'll be less vulnerable in a crowd, and we won't let you out of our sight. If you want to be rid of these 'impositions' once and for all, tonight's our best opportunity, and you'll have to trust us."

Eyes downcast, Burleigh affected a martyrly submission to the vagaries of fate. Four measured knocks on the studio door tabled further discussion. "Hello? It's locked!" Oak panels muffled the patrician accents of a caller patently unused to obstructed entry.

"Young John," mouthed Burleigh, "borrowing a costume." His guests nodded and stole off to the classroom and makeshift concealment between an armoire and a windowseat. Snatches of back-and-forth over the merits of various steamer trunks' contents wafted to them.

"Young John," whispered Harry. "Speak of the devil." They listened a minute for any nuggets of self-incrimination, till Howard pursed despairing lips and breathed, "Has it dawned on you, given Burleigh's precautions and the narrow time frame available to today's malefactor, that Burleigh himself may have posed the mannequins and inscribed the poison-pen canvases—perhaps in a fugue state or while sleepwalking or immersed in recurrent nightmares—in any case, guilt-ridden over Miss O'Leary's suicide? Farfetched, yes, but preferable to crediting an occult agency, wouldn't you say?"

"As you and Conan Doyle recommend, we have to do every improbability justice. That leaves the riddle, though, of where Burleigh got his Gaelic."

The studio door thumped shut and its key clattered in the lock. Good! Harry preferred nobody from the Art Club barge in before he and Howard were incognito. Burleigh bustled back, temporarily chipper in his traditional role of costumier. He grabbed Howard's wrist and beckoned him along. "Mr. Lovecraft, let's get you gussied up!"

For a lark, Harry eavesdropped till the two hidebound Yankees wrangling over sartorial minutiae reminded him of squabbling yentas. How they'd splutter were he to pronounce them two peas in a provincial pod! He drifted to the classroom's diamond-paned windows, decided to check for Peeping Toms, gauge the quality of sightline between tunnel and studio. From this angle only a thin crescent of the portal showed, but were his nerves more tightly wound than he'd perceived? Though he couldn't peer into the aperture at all, his retinas were treating him to the same head-on mirage as yesterday.

Except today, it was definitely worse. More vents in the submarine floor were gushing more convulsively; fragmentary cornices, columns, lintels spun frantically as in a gigantic eggbeater's mixing bowl. Yet unnaturally, no lesser debris or silt clouded the water. The parallel, diagonal striations of the corkscrew ledge stood out starkly on the wall, and from his brow the question sprang unbidden: of what behemoth pattern was the thing that burrowed so prodigiously into the world? And did the mounting agitation of the whirlpool and the gushers mean that thing was flexing fitfully to burst through constrictive sediments? As for the lay of the seabed, he wouldn't swear on a Bible it had been as convex.

The longer he stared, the more real the vision felt till he was confident Howard would see it too, were he not busy humoring Burleigh. Would Howard also intuit their vision was of no literal space, was rather a breach into a nonphysical realm that would nonetheless impinge catastrophically on mortal existence? Yet none but "creative" types like Howard or Burleigh or, yes, Harry himself would harbor any perception of this impingement via nightmares or their mind's eyes.

Burleigh swept back in, presumably with Howard in reluctant tow, based on balky demeanor. He was also self-consciously jangling and clanking. Harry mightn't have laughed as heartily had he not needed a laugh in the worst way. "Mr. Houdini," Burleigh sighed archly, "your assistant did not warmly embrace the theme of tonight's gala, which is 'Wonders in the Deep.'" Howard framed no rebuttal. "I did finally coax Mr. Lovecraft into donning a souvenir of my travels, by touting its relationship to mythology and classical culture. It came from the Aegean island of Skyros, where it enlivened the pre-Lenten carnival, really a festival of Dionysus under a flimsy veil of Christianity."

Burleigh's motions toward Howard were like an anatomy instructor's. "The hooded smock of black goat hair and the belt of bells hearken to herdsmen and fauns. Mr. Lovecraft should be thankful this exemplar is tailored for the tourist trade, or else the bells would weigh upward of fifty pounds. The white trousers are traditionally Greek. The black mask is the cured skin of a stillborn kid. Those who dance and caper in these ensembles are dubbed Ancient Ones."

Harry fervently hoped Howard had stripped down to BVDs before submitting to such stifling, bulky garb. He further had to credit Howard, doubtless doing a slow burn behind the mask, for mute stoicism in the line of duty. And if Howard had taken umbrage at the evening's unpalatable theme, with its promise of odious seafood hors d'oeuvres, his choice of costume didn't altogether detach him from it: the mask with two round eyeholes was tasseled with the flayings of embryonic goat limbs and the tatters of long wear, which had come to resemble a fringe of tentacles.

Harry couldn't resist teasing, "Good God, Howard, it looks like someone dumped a plate of *pasta salsa nera* over your head. That's 'spaghetti in squid ink' down in Little Italy."

"What a hideous waste of spaghetti!" Howard huffed through his quivering mask.

"The hell of it is," Burleigh interposed, "I distinctly remember packing two outfits from Skyros in the trunk, and I'd have lent Mr. Lovecraft the nicer one, with a white mask, but I must have mislaid it sometime. Another mystery for another day, I guess. Mr. Houdini, come, let's get you dressed."

Burleigh did not make bold to grab Harry's wrist, instead scurrying ahead into the atelier. Harry, sauntering past Howard, became the second person that evening to mouth "Young John." It must have crossed Howard's mind too that Angela's inhibited pal might have filched apparel while Burleigh was rummaging through chests, or weeks beforehand. Howard nodded delphically. If Young John were impersonating an Ancient One, his reasons would emerge soon enough. Howard wasn't, at any rate, pacing around while ruminating, or Harry would have heard him clanging.

Howard's tongue finally loosened at the spectacle of Harry strutting in with pearl-tipped golden crown, luxuriant wig and beard, matching yellow sarong, and garlands of dried kelp and scallop shells. His sandals were studded with little crabs and star-

236 Avenging Angela and Other Uncanny Encounters

fish. "As I live and breathe, King Neptune!" Howard hailed him. "Shiver me timbers!"

Harry goggled and bashed the butt-end of his trident against the floor in mock indignation at Howard's flippancy. Burleigh bounced over and chimed in, "Apropos for Mr. Houdini, is it not, an artiste who has bested the aqueous element everywhere, from inside milk cans to the East River?"

"Just watch how you slam that pitchfork around, Your Majesty," Howard warned. "Neptune was god of earthquakes too, remember."

"Gentlemen, if you'll relax in here for the nonce," Burleigh requested, "it's incumbent on me to throw something on and dole out disguises to any ill-prepared revelers who come knocking." Hah! Burleigh was a fine one advising others to relax.

He hustled off, as Harry called after him, "Mr. Burleigh, please don't let anyone in till you find out who it is!"

Burleigh signed okey-dokey without breaking his stride, and his de facto shamuses retreated to the windowseat. Howard sat with an emphatic dissonance.

"You'll have to lose the bells," Harry insisted in hushed tones. "I've no idea what Burleigh was thinking, but you won't be any good as an eavesdropper or a bushwhacker."

Howard leaned forward for Harry to undo the noisy belt at the back. Harry remarked while he tinkered, "Burleigh's acting relatively composed. We can count our blessings he never pestered us for translations of the Gaelic. He'd be a neurasthenic wreck. But to slake my own curiosity, I do wish we had an Irishman to explain that 'Teach Donn,' not that I see much jeopardy in two words that might be some sort of classroom reminder note."

Harry got the sense Howard was frowning gravely behind the kidskin. "I needed no Officer Clancy this time. If I recall my Padraic Colum correctly, that new message is as inauspicious as the rest, if not more so. It derives from Irish myth, and its two innocuous-seeming syllables can be rendered as 'House of the Dead' or 'House of Death,' or more literally, 'House of the God of Death.'"

It's certainly no improvement over 'gateway to purgatory' in terms of the train tunnel, or if you'd rather keep the railroad out of it, the Fleur-de-Lys or the Art Club."

Harry let the jingling belt clink upon the floor. He subjected Howard's eyeholes to unspoken chagrin at this extra turn of the screw he could have done without. Burleigh, at this juncture, may have been the happiest among them, bumping, clattering, pacing amid his props and garments, oblivious to the palaver about him. On striding back in, he sported seven-league boots, tricorn hat over a bandana, a papier-mâché parrot on his shoulder, and the rest of a pirate's standard accoutrements: frankly, an uninspired letdown. On the bright side, he didn't decry, or else notice, Howard's forsaken belt.

"Gentlemen, in the interests of expediency, I resorted to the convenient fallback of Long John Silver. Should we adjourn to the Club before any tardy guests come demanding I dress them? Into the breach, eh?" His bravado was admirable as it was ersatz.

Harry and Howard rose briskly from the windowseat. "By all means," agreed Harry, unsure if he was calling Burleigh's bluff or stoking moral support. "If it's not betraying a confidence, though, how did you outfit Young John, and, as you say, expeditiously at that?"

They trooped through the atelier, where the exotic mannequin had landed askew in a corner. The cryptic canvas was facedown on butcher paper. Suddenly sheepish, Burleigh muttered, "I did him up as a pirate too. Nothing easier when you're in a hurry."

Harry and Howard nodded without comment. Burleigh locked the studio and the front door, and on the stoop Harry enjoined, "Mr. Burleigh, why don't you go a few steps ahead so people don't necessarily get the impression we're with you, leastwise as body-guards?" Burleigh grunted amenably and set off, joining the uphill trickle of partiers in undersea guises.

Bringing up the rear, Harry said sidelong to Howard, "So it's Young John and Long John, is it?"

"Just so's we can tell them apart. And wonder of wonders,

Long John Silver's amputated leg grew back for the occasion."

"Why, that's right! He did use to have a pegleg. But speaking of wonders, I'm not sold on pirates as 'Wonders in the Deep.'"

"Not that any of this is consonant with our biblical theme."

Nearing the Art Club's green door, they dawdled as a knot of chatty attendees maladroitly tried unraveling into single file to go in. "Biblical?" Harry asked.

"Yes, absolutely, it's a quotation from Psalm 107."

"Howard, I'm amazed a skeptic of your caliber would have the Scriptures at his fingertips."

Howard shrugged a tad coyly. "Why not? I know 'em as well as I do anyone else's primitive mythology."

They briefly lost sight of Burleigh in the gaggle of merrymakers squeezing indoors, but squandered no energy rushing after him. The preceding month's "impositions" had been signposts toward a more dramatic, elaborate outrage than a sneaking assault in the foyer before the party was in full swing. Instead of traipsing into the Café and Cabaret again, Harry and Howard loitered to one side as Burleigh hobnobbed at the foot of commodious oaken stairs with assorted mermaid, fish, and crustacean mimics.

For Harry, a blond wig and beard proved as effective as a tam and cheaters at saving him from being buttonholed as the "Great Houdini." If anything, as part of no clique, theirs was the status of wallflowers, all the better, really, for sleuthing unhindered. Howard's getup probably deserved major credit for deterring small-talk: in an atmosphere of whimsy and effervescence, it was uniquely repulsive. The silly jangle of his belt might have offset the freakishness, made him a little more approachable.

Oops, Burleigh and associates were lollygagging up the steps like water up an Archimedes' screw. Once they'd ascended from view, Harry and Howard moseyed along in their wake; an impartial onlooker, Harry reflected, would tag the two of them, if anybody, for skulking suspiciously. Atop the stairs they rubbernecked in dismay. Drat, they'd lost him again! The gallery-cum-ballroom would have flummoxed them a minute in any event, its capacious dimensions packed with boisterous gabbing and laughter, with shiny scales, lacquered fish heads, rayon tentacles, leatherette chitin in a kaleidoscopic ferment of angles and curves. And ratcheting up the bedlam, a jazz orchestra commenced blaring from a stage at one end.

Halfway across the sea of chaos, a black tricorn bobbed in and out of visibility. Harry glimpsed it first and clutched Howard's shaggy forearm, pointed his trident thataway, and plowed forward like an ice-cutter, clacking his glorified fork just hard enough to split the sea without offending it. Before Harry was within range to poke his objective with the tines, though, he imagined Howard's heart sinking like his, for no parrot bedecked this pirate's shoulder.

Howard hung back as Harry tapped Young John on the pudgy bicep and shook hands as if that had been his aim all along. "Wanted to thank you again for that delectable swordfish!" he ad-libbed at a roar to beat the thunderous band.

Young John went blank a disoriented second, then smiled— for a buccaneer—blandly. "Ah, Mr. Houdini! You're very welcome! Have you seen Sydney?" Harry flinched, furtively checked around, relaxed; nope, it'd take a megaphone for his name to carry in this ruckus.

"When I do, I'll pass along you have a weather eye out for him!" He had a hunch it didn't matter what he said; as the band inched closer to a crazed fortissimo, John would have beamed and nodded at anything. Harry bowed curtly and rejoined Howard.

"At least you've reduced the likelihood Young John nicked that other disguise," Howard shouted over the tumult. Newfangled hot rhythms had inflamed a few couples to dance, fishtails and claws swinging recklessly.

"Could be, but I won't lie to you," Harry volleyed back, "the mystery of Burleigh's whereabouts is making me nervous. Let's find him."

"These raucous so-called musicians aren't doing us any favors!" Howard complained. "Footpads could get away with murder and we'd be the last to know!"

Harry told Howard to stay put and clacked an Olympian path toward the stage. By his return, strident jazz no longer enriched the general pandemonium. "I slipped the maestro a C-note to take ten," Harry explained. "That should give us a chance to locate Burleigh before it's too loud again to think."

As they gazed hither and yon, Howard asked with overtones of awe, "Did you say you shelled out a hundred bucks? I bet the Club didn't pay 'em that much."

"Seems like a princely sum, but the bandleader has to divvy it up with a lot of guys, and as you said, this may be a matter of life and death. Considering the stakes, I shelled out gladly and of my own free will, though it annihilated the stash in my sarong." In the diminished hullabaloo, they were casing the maroon, windowless room more stringently.

"Harry, I'm not criticizing you, but I hate to see that excuse for musicianship receive so much encouragement."

Harry half listened to Howard while studying the decor of curtains and partitions of undulating seagrass and kelp suspended from tracking lights and crown molding, adorned with crabs, seahorses, oysters, starfish, lobsters. "Not a jazz baby, I gather?"

Howard was likewise absorbed in a slow 360° scan of the environs. "Don't get me wrong, I was a drummer in my tender youth, but we played the time-worn chestnuts, 'Bedelia,' 'Sweet Adeline,' and the ilk. I simply cannot condone—Harry, turn around! Not ten feet from us, in that corner with the screen of seaweed across it, are those the toes of seven-league boots peeking out from under?"

They hastened over and each batted away half of the dried seagrass strands, which crackled like glass beads, and there trembled Burleigh like a caged bird in a lion's den. He shuddered more acutely at their encroachment, but otherwise maintained his hundred-yard stare, according them no eye contact, no show of recognition. "Mr. Burleigh!" Harry entreated. "Are you all right?"

Obviously he wasn't, but from Burleigh's mouth to Harry's ear, what kind of shape did he think he was in? "She's here!" Burleigh gasped, with more of an Ancient Mariner's compulsion to vent than a willingness to converse with his mystified allies. "I've seen her!"

Howard blurted "What?" the same instant as Harry's "Where?"

"Pacing back and forth across the room, back and forth in front of me the way she might have done that night, desperate for me to come and be with her. Then she stopped, maybe at the time she gave in to despair. She was looking straight through everyone between her and me. She saw none of them, they didn't see her. She took a step toward me, I couldn't stand it, I broke and ran for cover."

"Where is she now?" Harry demanded.

"On Skyros I told her I loved her," Burleigh related to nobody in particular. "In Ireland I told her that didn't mean I could afford to abandon my wife."

Harry's hapless frown mirrored Howard's. Burleigh was contributing zip toward getting past square one in flushing out the ghostly hoaxer. But then his eyes bulged and he hoisted a shaky arm and feebly wagged his hand from side to side, as if warding off a fiend who, going by the rictus on Burleigh's face, wasn't inclined to cooperate.

Harry and Howard turned precipitately, and Harry assumed Howard had also descried nothing macabre. As one, they implored, "Mr. Burleigh? Mr. Burleigh? Sydney!" Was their borderline paralytic in the grip of trance or trauma? Under the circumstances, the difference amounted to semantics. And was Burleigh unhinged enough to hallucinate, or were they up against an adversary who could hotfoot it like a flea?

In nothing like an answer to their pleas, and in a lilt diametrically unlike himself, Burleigh chanted, *"Anois a thosaíonn do le-orgníomh."*

"What?" Once before had been plenty, but again this Burleigh business was coercing Harry to admit bewilderment.

"'Now your atonement begins.' It's one of those Gaelic phrases. And that's how it's supposed to sound. When did he learn the correct pronunciation of a language he condemned as gibberish?"

In the face of this imponderable, both men obeyed an impulse to survey the ballroom, ascertain whether Burleigh was drawing problematic attention. Some scattered cliques were ogling them, but with curiosity or concern or reproach Harry couldn't tell because of the sea-monster heads, carnival masks, pancake makeup. One further figure, alone in the crowd, was gazing at them. "Harry!" he heard as through a wall of batting. "The purloined costume! Our culprit's hiding in plain sight!" Yes, but where had their culprit been ten seconds ago, when his eyes had raked that same space?

Never mind. What mattered now was keeping their quarry in the crosshairs, and Howard had already elbowed a beeline halfway there. But the piratical Young John had also homed in on the statuesque miscreant, and damn him, he was hallooing, "Angela! Angela!" My God, how many gullible neurotics were on tonight's guest list?

Burleigh, meanwhile, reacted as if the repetition of her name was driving a spike into his ears. A good many more attendees were watching because he was emitting unselfconsciously shrill jabber, unless that too were Gaelic, as he shot forward among the spectators before Harry could budge. Younger, fitter Harry sped after him, but Burleigh was perversely more proficient at snaking breakneck through the crowd. Harry was no longer banging the trident's butt-end and brandishing its prongs with any polite reservation.

Howard, unfortunately, had forfeited momentum in colliding with a waiter as narrowly focused as himself. A tray of canapés that Harry took to be scallops and bacon on toast was adhering all over Howard's hairy outfit. Before the waiter could regain bodily or inner balance, Howard, who'd lost neither, snarled, "Damn you and those rotten skate wings!" As he plowed onward, sights still fixed on his impassive target, he peeled off kidskin mask and besmirched outerwear, quick to exploit the silver lining of an excuse to ditch them like an insect moult. And yes, he'd never doffed his white, starchy shirt.

Harry was far from catching Burleigh, who sprinted babbling

like one possessed toward the service door behind the band, whence the waiter had emerged. Harry, in midflight, stole a look at Howard collaring the costume thief; on his vision was etched a "minute movie" to haunt him forever. Burleigh had been right: this other ensemble from Skyros had been nicer, its mask a pristine white, its tunic a checkerboard of black fur and dappled calfskin. The torso had been stuffed to promote the illusion of breasts.

The heat of the moment must have endowed Howard with an impetuosity as surprising to himself as to Harry, for he tore off the white mask by its fringe of tentacles. He then turned to virtual stone, mask in his outstretched arm, as he boggled at the nothingness beneath the mask, while the remainder of the costume collapsed in a clangor of cowbells to the floor. Harry's last fleeting glimpse in passing was of bystanders with hands on hips or arms folded irksomely. Who was this gate-crasher, pulling silly stunts while people were trying to have fun? And wherever Young John had gone, it was likeliest in deference to the better part of valor.

Harry raced down the backstairs into the Café, where clutches of maskless revelers were lounging on the Mitteleuropa furniture, circulating communal hipflasks, precious pre-Volstead fifths, trays of hors-d'oeuvres commandeered from the caterers in the kitchen. No time to process Howard's uncanny incident till Burleigh was safe! A door through the Café's west wall was clicking shut, and he could picture nobody beyond except Burleigh, since none of the sprawling carousers even rose to the challenge of acknowledging him as he scuttled past them and out.

Nor could he picture Burleigh heading anywhere except the tunnel. Till Harry's pupils adjusted to the weakly starlit darkness, Burleigh would blend seamlessly with the night; but hooray, his grunting incoherence made him a cinch to pinpoint. On top of which, the embankment here was steeper than behind the Fleur-de-Lys, obliging Burleigh to slow down or plunge headlong onto the tracks. Harry's night vision began to discern Burleigh's vague, lurching silhouette, along with a source of light in front of him so dim that his anatomy all but eclipsed it.

Burleigh slipped, went down on his backside, slid to the foot of the slope, shedding tricorn and parrot. His mishap afforded Harry an unobstructed view of that toward which Burleigh had been staggering, and it nearly jolted Harry off his feet too. From upslope he heard Howard exclaim, "What the hell?"

The white ensemble from Skyros was a heap on the ballroom floor, so how could someone balancing on the track's nearer steel rail have it on? And did the outfit stand out in the dark thanks to its snowy whiteness alone, or did a wan radiance generated by the wearer suffuse it? Never mind! Such enigmas, however fascinating, couldn't distract him while Burleigh posed a blatant danger to himself, over and above the danger enemies intended for him.

Howard was scuffing through the gravel right behind Harry, Burleigh was picking himself up, and the masquerader on the rail had a wavering hand uplifted, a gesture that served equally well to ward off or to beckon. To Burleigh, as a man possessed, it was all the same as he shambled on, deaf to Harry bellowing at him to wait. The second Howard skidded to his side, Harry had to dash ahead and risk a potentially deadly plummet, counting on the dubious merits of his three-pronged staff to stabilize him, for Burleigh, arms outspread, was scant paces away from embracing "Angela," who carried on ambiguously gesturing.

And as if Ossa needed Pelion's weight upon it, the din and reverberation of an oncoming train throbbed in Harry's feet, bombarded his ears, convulsed his stomach. He was still inches shy of closing the gap between his frantic reach and Burleigh as the fan of headlamp brilliance preceded the engine. Knowing he'd be blind and useless in a heartbeat when the lamp's full glare burst from the portal, he rashly hooked his trident in the junction of Burleigh's crisscrossed bandoliers and tugged with all his might. Then the headlamp bleached everything a harrowing white, mercifully blotting out the slaughter of Angela's impersonator, or whatever wore the costume, but also nixing any certainty he'd saved Burleigh.

In the thunder of the train's onrush, Harry may have made out

Burleigh fussing, "Where am I? What the deuce is going on?" Or it may have been an acoustic effect of too much noise bouncing around Harry's auditory canal. The trident, he tardily realized, was out of his hands, and in the throes of tinnitus, slow-fading dazzle, and numbing stupor, he sensed Howard's mitt around his arm and pulling on it, with the reproof, "Get back, both of you, you make me anxious!"

Harry recovered the wherewithal to apprehend that Howard had him and Burleigh in tow, and they were ascending the gravel slope. Suddenly feeling more self-conscious than ever in his wig and sarong, Harry observed, "Y'know, Sydney, you've outdone me. That was more of a miraculous escape than I ever managed."

Burleigh was still poking along unresponsive. Harry hazarded a backward squint. The only sign a train had been and gone was its squeal of brakes a quarter mile away at Union Station, and he was surprised no submarine grotto fronted the portal, after all the other eeriness. Instead, he noted a spring in his step, the dispersal of a burden that registered on his consciousness solely in its absence. Whatever had inflicted recurring mirages was quiescent again after failing to claim a victim; surely it wouldn't resume straining against seafloor captivity anytime soon. But egad, how had such tommyrot sullied his mind? He was giddy with relief, nothing more, at overcoming danger.

Of course, the foregoing five minutes of phantasmagoria weren't so easily dismissed. And on reflection, was it natural that his backward glance had shown no blood on the tracks, no shred of carnage or Bacchic disguise? Had a sham Angela been atomized—and if not, he'd careened down one slippery slope tonight, did he really have to navigate another one, albeit figurative, already?

Harry was glad Howard had at some point let him toddle under his own steam, as opposed to Burleigh, whom Howard was piloting by the elbow toward the door into the Café. "Howard, I'm still looking through a layer of gauze on account of that headlamp, unlike you, apparently. What are you, part cat?"

"Very flattering, but no. I shut my eyes before the engine exited the tunnel. Nothing else for me to do, was there?"

They had Burleigh's back as he doddered indoors, his conduct elderly beyond his age, no less so as he fussed, "Bring me upstairs! Bring me upstairs! This is my party and that's where I want to go! I have to see how Young John is doing!"

Howard threw up his hands in resignation. Better to humor the poor duffer; less stress all around. They had, in any event, a grossly more fraught issue to resolve. Harry cleared his throat as they piloted their hatless and disheveled Long John past the tables of roués-for-a-day with their stocking feet half blocking the path. "I saw what happened with you in the ballroom." A logy couple of hail-fellows tossed at Burleigh fell on miles-away ears. Harry took it as a blessing he and Howard were ciphers.

Howard met Harry's dourness with his own. "And there's what happened with you outside."

"You think she was trying to warn him off or destroy him?"

"We'll never know. No use even asking." Nor was Howard dragging in the whole other issue of the lurker within the mirage, if indeed any such issue was in his purview. Another thing Harry would never know, because he wasn't about to broach it.

"Couldn't agree more, Howard, and that goes for everything else the last five minutes have wrought. We'd be damn fools to let five minutes undermine a lifetime of healthy skepticism and critical thinking, wouldn't we?"

"Couldn't agree more, Harry."

"And till we can articulate a rational explanation for what we've been through, and sooner or later we will, I propose we speak of this with nobody."

"It's a deal, Harry."

Harry and Howard were herding Burleigh up the backstairs, a step below him in case he faltered and tipped over. A dull awareness of the orchestra blatting furiously again had nagged at Harry on re-entering the Café. At the head of the stairs, the prospect of reimmersing himself in the racket and congestion so soon after cheating death set his teeth on edge. Howard's tense shoulders hinted he too was girding himself.

Flanking Burleigh, blinkering him in effect, his escorts maneuvered him past the band, off the stage to the main floor, through the gauntlet of partygoers to a wooden folding chair up against the nearest seaweed-screened wall. The clutter of white costume on the floor was gone; out of sight, out of mind, Harry decided, was the best policy. Had Burleigh had the clarity to realize he was being herded, he'd probably have taken umbrage, but the appeal of sitting down was too strong to question. And several rasping breaths later, he'd rebounded sufficiently to fret, "Where is that Young John?"

Harry, for the sake of appearing cooperative, craned his neck to and fro. Annoyingly, despite the solipsism rampant everywhere, the tableau of Howard in sweaty shirtsleeves, a scruffy King Neptune, and a bedraggled Long John was drawing an audience, its sentiments opaque behind fishy disguises. Oh, for his trident whose judicious twirling might secure a perimeter and give Burleigh air!

"You there, in the dirty shirt," Burleigh motioned toward Howard, "go fetch Young John! How hard do I have to beg?"

Exasperated Howard melted into the throng, clearly not sorry to be off and running. Harry, sighing, curbed his own exasperation, strove to be more understanding. Burleigh was old and delicate, however gamely or stubbornly he pretended otherwise, and he'd been through a brutal wringer, both bodily and psychic. Still, as he huddled ornery enough to keep his audience at bay, Harry's vision latched onto that dandified Van Dyke and he couldn't help musing, Was the tragic Angela, in the deepest recess of his heart, ever more than a mannequin to him? Or is that what she'd rightly feared becoming?

Burleigh yelped and put a hand to his nose. With downcast eyes and mumbled imprecations, he fished around the baggy lap of his knee-breeches and enclosed something tiny in his fist. Whatever it was, he wasn't disposed to say, and Harry was in no mood for Twenty Questions.

By the time Howard emerged, nudging Young John before him, the interest of onlookers had strayed from Burleigh and Harry, who'd fed their appetites for drama on nothing but sullen pouting. Howard had plausibly flushed Young John from some remote fastness of the Café: he tottered along at least two sheets to the wind, his condition redounding to piratical glory no more than Burleigh's.

Yet for all Burleigh's nonstop pother about his chum, Howard was the object of his passions. "Young man," he railed, winning back their fickle audience, "that was a mean and petty gesture on your part, the more so in light of my trials this evening!"

Howard stared dumbfounded; nor had Young John insight into recent developments, going by his slackjawed stance.

Burleigh at last held up the upsetting item between thumb and forefinger. "Don't play coy with me, Mr. Lakefront or whoever you are. You deliberately flung this in my face from across the room!" "This" was half of a mother-of-pearl cuff button.

"Why would I do that?" Howard's temper was audibly fraying. "What makes you think I threw anything?"

"Look at your cuff!" Burleigh sputtered. "It's unbuttoned. And the button is missing! Why did you do it? Why does flaming youth do anything? Envy, ignorance, hubris? To tear down and rebuild on the foundations, to steal all the credit and condemn the true builder to oblivion!"

Harry was nearing the end of his rope himself, and thank God nobody in the gawking semicircle recognized him, not positively enough to broadcast his name anyway. Young John was no less groggy than a minute ago. Harry clapped him on the unsteady shoulder. "He's all yours, Young John!" Fed-up Harry blazed a trail into the nonplussed oglers, Howard at his heels, gratitude writ large on his features. None of the smart set could summon the chutzpah to stop them.

Atop the commodious front stairway, Howard remarked, "Harry, thank you! The reek from the hors-d'oeuvres was really getting to me."

Harry nodded, though he'd smelled nothing of a gustatory character. "I'd say we've done everything we could here." They pounded down the stairs with juggernaut willfulness.

"Our duty and then some! I hope this line of work isn't always as thankless."

"Let's say tonight was exceptional in a number of respects." They were out the green door, and Harry pointed downhill with his palm flat out. "I have a key to Burleigh's. Let's reclaim our civvies."

No further occult activity had disturbed the studio. They disrobed in front of each other; why stand on bashful ceremony after the ordeal they'd been through? While tying his brogues, Howard, with a tinge of reticence, declared, "Harry, I don't know what to say about that flying button. I'd never do anything so boorish. And why the devil would I break the button in two first? And where's the other half?"

Harry bit his upper lip philosophically. "On top of everything tonight, what's one more little enigma?"

Wisdom dictated leaving it at that while they finished dressing. Some seconds of awkward silence followed, and then with dispatch, as if he'd been remiss, Harry whipped out his wallet. He extracted a wad of sawbucks, lunged toward Howard, grabbed his wrist with one hand, and pressed the money into his palm with the other before Howard could react. "For your wedding!" Harry announced. "Mazel tov! Sorry it's not more, but it's all I have after bribing the orchestra."

Howard goggled as if at a heaping platter of manna. He was, if nothing else, too thunderstruck to refuse it. Good! Harry felt pretty bad that Howard had misunderstood the pro bono nature of debunking. "Thanks, Harry, thanks a million," Howard intoned as if the cash had mesmerized him, "if you're absolutely sure?"

Harry threw up his hands for Howard to stop, please.

"And frankly," Howard went on, "I've been recompensed already in a less quantifiable way. Since Wednesday—good lord, have we been at this a mere two days?—I've been jotting notes on several aspects of this case: the prophetic nightmares that trigger suicides, the ruinous undersea city Burleigh mentioned, the netherworld monstrosity that awakens once in an eon. These are threads that should be invaluable in tying together some ideas I've had kicking around, so please accept my humble thanks for including me in this inspiring business!"

Harry nodded, choosing not to call him out on his little *lapsus linguae.* Burleigh had described a colossal deserted city, but never had he placed it underwater. That was a detail solely in Harry's mirage, and, as Howard had inadvertently admitted, in his mirage too. But why open that can of worms now, get into a profitless flap over figments that had come and, for the foreseeable future, gone?

Harry locked up as they departed the Fleur-de-Lys. Thank goodness Howard hadn't quizzed him about the provenance of the key. It would as easily have opened another thousand doors in Providence. Just one of his tools of the trade! He also knew better than to offer Howard the committed pedestrian a taxi home. The diehard Yankee would have branded it a profligacy for sure. Only one loose end pestered conscientious Harry.

"By the by, Howard, a mutual acquaintance told me Henneberger at *Weird Tales* wants you to ghost a story for me. When he gets in touch, maybe it's best not to let on we were ever introduced."

"Mum's the word. And would that acquaintance be Cliff Eddy? I thought so. He's off in the hinterlands of East Providence, so he won't hear anything about tonight in the normal course of things. I'll have to tell him all this brouhaha with Burleigh was a false alarm, and swear him to secrecy about the little he knows because the least whiff of gossip would cause grave embarrassment for all concerned."

"True enough, Howard. By the same logic, I won't divulge anything now about the story we're to cook up together: safest if the particulars came as news to you."

Howard nodded reflectively. They shook hands with more

warmth than Harry figured was typical of Howard. Parting words were called for, but brief goodbyes were best, weren't they?

"It'll be a pleasure meeting you in the future, Mr. Lovecraft!"

"Likewise, Mr. Houdini. It'll be a pleasure working with you."

~~~~~

The dishwashers were out on the poor man's balcony of the kitchen fire escape, taking the load off their aching feet, which they dangled in the cool, muggy autumn night. Behind them, Cheryl and the other waitresses rested their arms on the railing or leaned against the wall. The fire escape overlooked the Art Club parking lot, and to one side of that, the sealed-off train tunnel. Granted, they could have picked a wiser surveillance post for aftershocks; nothing else was proceeding along sensible lines, though, Cheryl brooded, fingering the half button of mother-of-pearl that had beaned her a minute ago.

It was common knowledge, whether people believed it or not, that the suicide flapper Angela O'Leary had been psychically active ever since months of major renovations had created disturbances in and around the premises. But really, what was the deal with flinging half a button? Poltergeist mischief or some screwy kind of warning? And where was the other half of the button?

When the aftermath of the tremor happened, it didn't shift anyone an inch. It did startle everyone something awful, though, because it was, rather than an aftershock, a furious banging on the tunnel's corrugated steel plug, like King Kong busting the gate on his dinosaur island. Or was it gas under pressure escaping from underground or chunks of ceiling bouncing around because the cement was bound to crumble someday?

No, one of the dishwashers was pointing at the gate and exclaiming something in Portuguese. The only word Cheryl got was "kazinga," suggesting to her they were good as in the toilet. Scattered cracks were showing in the steel, some yards higher than a man's reach. From hairline zigzags water was seeping, but what kind of water didn't trickle down as gravity commanded, instead fanning out all around as if welling from a fissure in the ground and not a vertical wall? It couldn't be water, could it, whatever it was?

That liquid, on top of everything else, cranked tonight's weirdness up to 11 and jogged her memory of a nightmare, no, a bunch of nightmares she'd had for weeks about wandering squalid streets in some city of giants. And with that, she realized what was pounding to get out, what would crash through very soon and very, very hangry.

By the same token she knew that screaming and running would make no difference. But for lack of other options, she grabbed Jackie by the wrist and did both, towing her full-tilt into the kitchen, ahead of panicky coworkers following her lead and stampeding right behind.

Meanwhile, at 4 A.M. on a bleak little island in Lough Derg, County Donegal, watery plumes spurted from a grassy mound surmounted by a rectangular bell tower, the alleged site of St. Patrick's Cave. The tower sank like a finger into cake as the gushers proliferated around it till the earth disintegrated, and like one massive, translucent clump of tentacles they ravenously strained sky-high. Bats were powerless to echolocate them, stuck to them on impact, and came apart like stew meat.

> *To Paige—I couldn't have done it without you!*

Acknowledgments

"After the Legions" is original to this collection.

"Avenging Angela," first published in *His Own Most Fantastic Creation,* ed. S. T. Joshi (PS Publishing, 2020).

"A Box from Blackstone" is original to this collection.

"A Dip in the Bog" is original to this collection.

"Flouting Pascal: An Episode from the Latest Dark Ages" is original to this collection.

"Grave Days in Skara Brae" is original to this collection.

"Lead On, Vergil" is original to this collection.

"The Muybridge Cocktail," first published in *Penumbra* No. 1 (2020).

"Nos Morituri" is original to this collection.

"The Once and Future Waite," first published in *Black Wings VI,* ed. S. T. Joshi (PS Publishing, 2017).

"One Across" is original to this collection.

"The Shaman's Smile," first published in *Weird Fiction Review* No. 9 (2018).

"The Uncanny Comeback of E" is original to this collection.

"Widow's Walk," first published in *Apostles of the Weird,* ed. S. T. Joshi (PS Publishing, 2020).

CPSIA information can be obtained
at www.ICGtesting.com
Printed in the USA
LVHW051547300122
709757LV00017B/1728